THE JACOBITE'S WIFE

MORAG EDWARDS

FOREWORD

This novel is based upon the life of Winifred, Countess of Nithsdale (1672 – 1749). The story of her husband, William Maxwell, and his escape from the Tower of London is well known but Winifred is by far the more interesting character, her life shaped by the turmoil of late seventeenth century politics and her family torn apart by faith and loyalty. Winifred's motives for attempting to rescue her husband from the Tower remain a puzzle, since she was not a young woman and she stood to lose everything: her home, her children and even her own life if she failed. I have used my knowledge of child development to help me understand Winifred and the forces that drove her to save her husband but there remains much scope for readers to reach their own conclusions. While the most important events happened as written, some names, details and dates have been altered to suit my purpose as the author. The personalities of the characters, their motives, desires, and conversations are entirely fictional and bear no resemblance to how they may have actually thought, acted, or spoken.

BOOK ONE

1688–1690

CHAPTER 1
1688

I can hear a thump, thump, thump like someone is bouncing a ball along an empty corridor then a man's voice, hushed by a woman. I listen and listen until my ears crack and pound to the rhythm of my pulse. There are no more sounds. I reach for my comfort cloth, torn from Mother's petticoat when she was taken to the Tower of London. But it's lost in the folds of my bed and my hands sweep across the counterpane searching for the touch of silk. My fingers find its ruffled edge and I burrow back under the covers.

Now I hear hooves scrape on the cobbles and the jangle of a harness. There are horses in the yard below my window. Through the open hangings at the end of my bed I see that the fire is out. It must be very late.

There's a strip of grey light, where the shutters on the windows don't quite meet, and I feel my way down the bed and slide over the edge, my toes finding the carpet that lies at the foot of the bedstead. It's so cold. Outside the horses snort and whinny and I hear the stable boy slap at their necks to calm them. The sound echoes in the courtyard like the noise the maids make when they shake out sheets to air. I hold my comfort cloth to my cheek and feel my way across the room, recognising familiar pieces of furniture by the smooth turns and ridges in the wood. I think about being blind, like the old man who begs in the street by our square.

I prise open the shutter with my fingers. The glass is frosted on the inside and I use my cloth to rub at the ice. Our carriage is below and boxes and bundles are strapped onto the roof behind the coachman. I recognise him by his hat and I can see by the way he pulls at the reins then lets them go again that he's impatient. A light falls from the door to the kitchen and two servants, dressed for night travel, carry blankets and parcels of food into the carriage. The pane mists with my breath and I smear at it with my fist. Droplets of water trickle down my wrist. I hold my breath. Father stands in the light thrown from the kitchen. Shrouded in steam, a tall woman reaches for his hand and he helps her up the steps into the carriage. It's Mother. There's someone else, another woman, and I recognise my sister Lucy from the hood of her winter cloak. My father embraces her then closes the carriage door, hard. The coachman snaps his whip, the coach jolts forward and disappears beyond the frozen panes.

I hear someone scream. 'Mother!'

I awoke to a full fire, stacked high and glowing. The room was warm and I could see my clothes airing to shake off the damp of the night. I closed my eyes and listened as my maid moved around the room. She wasn't rushed, there was no difference to her routine ... perhaps it all had been a dream and Mother and Lucy were waiting for me downstairs. It was nonsense that they would disappear in the night without me, it was a nightmare, nothing more. I parted my eyelids just enough to see Grace pull the curtains apart, her heavy brows set in their perpetual frown of concentration. Her pretty face with wide-set brown eyes and a scattering of freckles was unmarked by anxiety or fear. Perhaps it was safe. I could rise and face the day ahead.

'Are you awake, Lady Winifred? They're all downstairs having breakfast. Your father has asked that you join them as soon as you can. Your sisters arrived an hour ago.'

I turned on my side, my back to her, and pulled the coverlet over my face. 'Why are they here? What do they want?' I felt the mattress sink as Grace sat down behind me.

'My lady, such a fuss last night. Cook had to get out of bed to prepare a meal for the travellers and then your sisters asking for an early breakfast. Cook's in a foul mood. I'd get up if I were you or there will be no food left. You can't expect anything special today.'

I pulled the sheet down from my face and looked at Grace. Her brows were knitted but in the half light her eyes shone. I felt my throat tighten and something drop inside my stomach. 'Last night ... I thought I saw Mother leave with Lucy. Is it true, have they really gone?'

'Come on, out of bed before your water cools. I'll tell you while you dress.'

Grace had chosen a simple home dress and I turned first one way then the other as she threaded my arms into the sleeves. She tugged at my bodice and I felt the bones of the corset tighten across my ribs and lift my breasts. 'Cook says that the queen has had to flee to France because the king fears for their lives. The Countess and Lady Lucy have gone with the queen and the new baby prince.'

I felt a chill, as if icy fingers had touched the back of my neck. 'But she's my mother.'

'The queen asked for her specially. Cook says the queen wouldn't go without her.'

'Why didn't she take me?'

'You're all grown, Lady Winifred. You don't need a mother now. That little prince is poorly. Cook says he needs your mother because of her special skills.' A pink flush of excitement had spread across Grace's cheeks and neck.

I sat down in front of the mirror so that she could brush my hair. 'What special skills? She's only my mother.'

'Your mother understands things, midwife things, healing things. You know how she makes all her medicines and visits the sick. Cook says she knows about babies and how to keep them well, so the queen couldn't leave her behind. What if the prince fell ill in France? The queen couldn't take the risk.'

'But I might fall ill,' I protested. 'Who will look after me?' I stood up and turned to Grace, who took both of my hands in hers.

'My lady, I will.'

My father sat at one end of the dining table with his back to the window and my older sisters, Anne and Mary, on either side. The table had been cleared but an empty place remained for me; a bowl, a knife and a cup waiting as a rebuke for my lateness. Father wasn't wearing his wig and his round, bald head seemed too small for his neck. In silhouette he looked like a turnip. My curtsy towards him was swift and shallow and I dipped my head towards my sisters who lowered their eyelids in return. I sat in my place, next to Anne, and a servant brought me bread and cold meats from last night's dinner. My throat hurt as I thought about last night's meal with Mother and Lucy and their casual talk. They had lied to me. I pushed the meat away and insisted on currant jelly. Mary rolled her eyes, so I took care to eat my bread and jelly in tiny pieces, chewing each small square until it was liquid in my mouth. When I had finished, the servant poured some quince wine which I swallowed in small sips, dabbing the corner of my mouth with a napkin and fixing my gaze on my plate. I finished at last and my father flapped his hand at the servant clearing my plate, 'Go now. We are not to be disturbed. Close the door behind you.'

He cleared his throat and waited until all our eyes were upon him. 'Winifred, your mother and your sister Lucy had to leave suddenly last night ...'

'They didn't say goodbye to me.'

'Don't interrupt your father,' said Anne, interrupting him.

'There was no time,' Father frowned. 'Our queen and the infant prince have been forced to flee for their lives because of the invasion of our country by the king's ungrateful son-in-law, William of Orange. God willing, they should all now safely be in Calais. Your mother is to be governess for the prince and since she's not a young woman, she has taken Lucy to help.'

'She should have taken me.'

My father sighed and rubbed his eyes. 'You are too young and your other sisters are all married. Your mother had no choice.' His voice rose. 'Do you really think, young lady, that I would allow my dear wife to travel to France without the support of one of her many daughters?'

This wasn't a question that expected an answer. I looked down at my hands.

'What I am going to say next will go no further than this room. You ... Winfred, look at me ... must not gossip about this with that little maid of yours, or you will both go to the Tower of London. I shall also be leaving for France, imminently, with the king. I can't say when but William of Orange's army is already moving towards London and there is a possibility the king may be taken prisoner. A messenger will call for me, probably in the middle of the night. One morning, soon, you will find me gone.'

Mary and Anne both reached for my father's hands and he leaned back in his chair. 'The consequences for those of you left behind may be serious. When it becomes known that the Countess and I have chosen to remain loyal to the king and queen, you may be harassed or worse. Remember what happened after I was released from the Tower of London?' My father paused, measuring the impact of his words. As if we needed to be reminded of men hunting us in the night with torches, the flames licking at the bottom of the stairwell, the smell of our burnt-out home.

He smiled at Mary and Anne, showing his long brown teeth and squeezed their limp hands: 'I want you to live here with Winifred. Your husbands may join you if they wish. Your sister Frances will be safe in Scotland with her family. Your brother William is travelling from Powis and should be here this afternoon. The household must be protected and I want the family to stay together until the political situation is more secure. I believe you will be safer as one unit and your brother can act as head of the family and manage the estates in my absence.'

I spoke quietly. 'It's not fair.'

Father frowned at me. 'Winifred ...' his voice was low but heavy with threat.

I felt a thunder cloud burst in my chest and stood up, my hands clenched tight into fists. 'It's not fair, it's not fair, it's not fair!' I screamed, astonished at my own behaviour. 'I don't want them to live here.' I gestured wildly at my sisters. 'I want my mother back. You should both stay here with us. You don't belong to the king and queen.'

I turned and ran; terrified of my father's anger, terrified I might be guilty of treason. I pushed past the servants hovering behind the door and almost tripped over the maids who were sweeping the staircase. At the top of the stairs I stood between two pillars that rose to the ceiling and grasped the solid wood of the banister. I felt I was on a stage and looked down at the upturned, astonished faces of my audience. I thought of throwing myself over the edge to punish my parents but knew it would make no difference. Self-pity drove me along the hall and under my bed, where I lay in the cold and dust and waited, picking at threads from underneath the mattress. The smell of old dog surrounded me; a rank mixture of damp hair and sweat. I listed the family in order of my hatred. Father was at the top of the list, with Mother a close second. Despite his fears for our safety, he hadn't been able to hide his pride and arrogance at being chosen by the king. In fact, it was Mother that they wanted, not him. My mother had left me so that she could protect a new child that wasn't even hers. My parents were strangers, abandoning me again because of their beliefs.

I waited, aching with cold as the wooden floor bit into my shoulder blades. I listened but there were no sounds; no one was coming to find me. I pulled myself from under the bed, dragging my back along the floor by tugging on the frame.

I knew I must be covered in dust but could only reach far enough to brush my shoulders and the back of my head. Where was Grace? My fingers felt stiff with cold and when I blew on my hands, I saw my breath mist. I needed to find some warmth. The drawing room always had a fire but as I eased open the heavy door, I heard my sisters talking in low murmurs and retreated, allowing the door to close silently. Father's study would have a fire but I wasn't going near him. The remaining option was the kitchen but Grace had already warned me about Cook's mood. I went anyway, tiptoeing down the servants' stair to the long, dark corridor that led to the kitchen. Out of habit I went into Mother's stillroom, wishing that she might be there. The room was empty but her handwriting was on the labels of the jars, listing the ailments the medicines were used to cure. I ran my finger along the shelves, reading aloud: *'cough, cold, swelling, itch, cramp, bloody-flux, worms, gout,*' my words becoming quieter as the empty room swallowed my voice.

The kitchen door was always open because of the heat. Cook sat alone at the scrubbed table, with a mug of ale, and I thought I would risk her temper. She rubbed her hands across her oily, polished face and pulled so hard at her lips it looked as if she might strip the skin from the bones beneath, like a carnival mask. She looked more weary than angry. The fire lay behind her and I crept through the door, keeping my back to the wall. If I stayed very quiet, she might not even notice me. I eased into one of the wooden chairs and felt the cold seep from my bones.

Sleep prickled across my eyelids and I jumped at Cook's voice.

'Lady Winifred,' she turned towards me and nodded. Cook had long given up curtsying to anyone in the family except Father. I moved across to sit next to her, my back now warming against the fire.

'This is a terrible thing, the Countess going off, leaving us all. We'll not see her again, you mark my words.' Cook wiped her eyes on her apron then pulled herself out of her chair, resting her knuckles on the table before waddling across to the range where she lifted some bread wrapped in a cloth from the warming oven. She fetched cold butter from the pantry and another bottle of ale. I darted across to the sideboard and brought two plates and another mug. At last, an adult was on my side. We ate in silence, butter sliding from the warm bread down my chin.

'What about the sick? How will they fare now? Old Mrs Austen is dying, Mr Crouch isn't well and Mary Price's daughter's due in a few weeks.'

I noticed that my loss wasn't mentioned.

'And what about Christmas? Lady Mary says you'll stay here and not go to Powis.'

'Not go to Powis?' I echoed.

Cook nodded. Things were getting worse by the hour. I couldn't remember a Christmas when we hadn't been at Powis, even during the long years of Father's imprisonment.

'I won't be able to go to my sister's.' Cook's eyes were shining, like the glaze of butter around her lips.

I wasn't used to tears from adults, let alone Cook, whose emotions usually swung between rage and a terrifying jollity. A weight settled on my shoulders. Christmas here, in London, without my parents or Lucy and worse, Cook thought that my mother might never come home. I turned away so that she wouldn't see that I was fighting my own tears. Behind me, the table creaked as she pushed herself up. I heard bowls and knives thrown onto the table and could smell onions. Cook bellowed out of the open door to the kitchen maids. If I stayed, I risked being asked to help make lunch.

'Where's Grace?' I asked, biting a fingernail.

'You leave that girl alone, she's got work to do,' Cook snapped. I waited until she went into the pantry for the meat and slipped away.

'Grace, do you still have a mother?' We lay side by side on Grace's narrow bed in her attic bedroom. I liked to come to her because if we stayed in my room, she would sort and tidy and not sit still. 'You never see her. Do you ever go home?'

'I think I must have been about ten when I came here first. I'm the eldest girl and my mother and father thought it was a great chance for me. Of course I go home. What do you think I do when you're at Powis?'

I'd never considered that Grace had a life beyond me, assuming she stayed in our house in Lincoln's Inn whether I was there or not. I felt ashamed and quickly changed the subject.

'I hate my mother,' I announced. 'I hope I'm never a mother.'

Grace screwed up her nose. 'Lots of girls our age are already mothers. My younger sister's a mother.'

'But we're only sixteen,' I protested.

'You can be a mother from when you start to bleed and we've been having those for two years.'

I sat up, horrified. 'I could be a mother?'

'You'd have to do *it* first. You won't catch a baby otherwise.'

Grace and I often talked about *it* but I hadn't fully understood that you needed to bleed and have sex to have a baby. Mother had never talked to me about those things. I'd thought sex was about giggling and boys touching you. Once, we'd watched a gardener's boy take one of the kitchen maids on the compost heap behind the glass house but their clothes had got in the way of a clear view. Grace had to hold onto my arm, so I wouldn't run off and reveal our spying. We'd talked about it for months, making a list of all those in the household who might have had sex. It was our favourite game and the list was regularly updated. I'd reluctantly agreed to include Mother and Father because Grace had explained to me that sex was supposed to happen after you were married. The thought of my sisters and their husbands having sex made me sick but I'd had to concede because, apart from Lucy, they were all married. We felt certain that Cook hadn't, which made her a virgin. We'd fallen from the bed laughing at the idea of Cook as virginal. We were virginal; young and pretty with firm breasts and shining eyes. Not Cook.

'So which of the boys here, in this house, would you want to do it with?' I asked.

Grace shook her head, then touched my arm and put her fingers to her lips. 'Listen ... horses ... in the stable yard. It must be your brother.' She smiled a soft, secret smile. 'If I had my pick, it would be him.'

I leaned over the bed, pretending to vomit. Grace pushed me onto the floor. 'It's time you got ready for dinner. Remember I have to dress your sisters as well.'

We hurried to my room and Grace brought a jug of rose water from Mother's stillroom and hung my favourite dress to air before the fire. It was a deep pink with an embroidered bodice and turned-back sleeves. She said I should wear it in honour of my brother's safe arrival and chivvied me to wash and dress.

Grace hurried away to help my sisters and I sat in front of my own fire trying to read. It was dark and the candles only helped to make the room seem cold and secretive beyond the circle of fire. I thought I might try to find my brother because he often teased me in a way that was fun and not cruel. He could be funny about our parents too, making me laugh by copying their voices and gestures, although afterwards I often felt ashamed.

I heard the raised voices from Father's study when I was still some distance away. There was no need to try and hide my approach as both men were shouting at full pitch. Never had I heard men bellowing as if they were bulls in a field and I listened at the door, ready to flee.

First my brother's angry voice: 'You're nothing but a bloody, selfish old fool.'

'And you are betraying your religion and your monarch,' my father shouted.

William yelled back, 'And you're betraying this family and our inheritance. Your misplaced loyalty will mean the loss of our estates ... everything we've worked for. You'll put our lives at risk ... again.'

'Some things are more important. There are principles that

must be upheld, justice for our monarch, the future of this country for people of our faith!'

My heart pounded and jumped in my breast and the tight bodice threatened to make me faint.

'How can you do this to us? Have you gone mad? Did six years in the Tower teach you nothing?' William demanded.

Outside the door, I cheered him.

'I have no choice.' My father sounded weary, as if he had lost the will to fight. 'He is my king, chosen by God. It's my duty as a member of the Privy Council. Can you imagine how the king feels, to be betrayed by his daughters?' Father's voice drifted for a moment, as if he had turned away.

I would betray you, I thought.

I guessed they had moved away from the fire towards the tapestry hangings on the opposite wall. Anxious to miss nothing, I leaned closer to the door but their voices had become indistinct. I ran back to my room and waited, crouching by the fire until the gong echoed in the empty hall.

At dinner we ate in silence. William smiled at me when I entered but kept his eyes focused on the carvings around the fireplace, as if they were of unusually great interest. I was glad to see that father was wearing his wig. It helped him look more authoritative, as if there was a chance he might still be a man we could rely on. But he sat in his place at the end of the table and chewed his food as if we weren't there. His eyes were in a far-off place and occasionally he muttered aloud, conversing with someone who wasn't present. He was already in France.

CHAPTER 2

Without Mother in the house, my sisters were determined to keep me occupied by teaching me how to run a household. Mary, the eldest, spent much time with our father. I'm sure, like me, he would have preferred to be left alone but I imagined she kept him busy with lists and plans about how we would manage once he was gone. When he wasn't with Mary, Father spent time at Whitehall with the king, no doubt also with lists and plans.

Anne had decided that she would be in charge of Christmas and had ambitions to have a turkey, since it was the new thing and she spent hours trying to track down a supplier, with me trailing along behind her. We always had goose at Christmas and I resented her changing things, as if she had already replaced our mother. My brother William disappeared every day on business but Grace said that she saw him go into Jonathan's Coffee House in Change Alley.

One morning, Father called us to his study after breakfast with news from Mother and Lucy. They were safe but the royal party were being treated as hostages by the king of France. I couldn't understand why our king would send his wife and baby

15

son to somewhere they weren't welcome and risk the lives of my mother and sister as well.

'Weren't the French expecting them?' I asked, looking between the adults. 'Shouldn't the king have checked first before sending my mother and sister off to be taken hostage?'

My father sighed and shook his head.

I turned to William but he stared out at the garden beyond the study window. My sisters exchanged a glance beneath their lowered lids.

Angered by the adults' refusal to acknowledge me, I ran outside and stumbled along the paths of the parterre until I found my favourite bench in the rose garden. It was a still, damp morning and mist drifted around the statues, so that they formed and disappeared like apparitions from the next world. The garden was drained of colour but birds searching for insects amongst leaf litter sounded like gravediggers. I missed Lucy. Together, we would have talked about what all this meant. Lucy listened to me and thought about her answers, as if my questions mattered. She never said things just to sound as if she knew, when she didn't.

I heard my brother's footsteps long before I saw him. The pattern of his footfall sounded like searching; he was looking for me and I wanted to be found. 'Hello,' I called out like a bell. William shouted back and I saw his shape form and vanish in the fog until he appeared distinct and solid. His head was bent inside the hood of his hunting cloak and his hands were wrapped in its folds. He sat down beside me and nudged me with his elbow, so that I would look at him.

'I thought you might want some company?'

I kicked hard at a stone. It arced towards a robin, who flew only a few paces and studied me with one eye.

'Why is the French king treating Mother and Lucy as

hostages?' I hoped William would notice that I was indifferent to the fate of the queen and her brat.

'Some people say James is very wise. Some say he's very stupid.' William shrugged. 'In trying to please everyone he has managed to make enemies of all, including the French king. The gossip in the coffee shops is that Louis doesn't know where he stands with our king, he doesn't trust him.'

'Why wouldn't he trust him? They're both Catholic kings. They're cousins.' My only teacher, our priest, had a simple view of political matters.

'Win, I'll try to explain. You know that the king's son-in-law marches on London. Louis has been warning James for months that William of Orange was arming his fleet but our king's answer was to throw the French envoy into the Tower of London. Our Catholic king has managed to anger the very monarch who should have been his closest friend. Not well done. Also, why on earth did he allow his daughter to marry William, a declared enemy of France?'

Such talk was treason and I glanced behind me, horrified that we might have been overheard. Father had been imprisoned during my childhood for less than this. 'Don't say such things ... we can't talk like this.'

'We're safe here, no one is listening.' William gripped my upper arm. 'Try to understand. There is much you have to know or whatever happens next will make no sense. You will have to make decisions too, starting with where your loyalty lies.'

I hesitated. 'So why does Father admire James?'

William leaned back and stared into the fog. His lids drooped and his eyes were emptied of colour, like the mist around us. 'Because our father is a fool, like James II. Fools attract other fools.'

It felt as if William was addressing some other audience, not me. These were words he had rehearsed.

'Catholic families like ours should live quietly and not attract attention. We'll lose everything, absolutely everything.' William slammed a fist into a cupped hand. 'When news of our family's involvement in the king's desertion gets out, the mob will come again, like last time. You remember when Father was released from the Tower? I'll never forget seeing our house burn, Winifred, never.' William leaned forward and pressed his brow into his fists.

I was frightened. I wanted to be reassured, not treated like an equal. I didn't want an older brother who reminded me of the terror of that night, fleeing through flames and choking smoke. I shifted along the bench to be closer to him but felt no warmth as he linked his arm through mine. I pulled my cloak tightly around me and shivered. The fog was heavier and the robin's busy presence could only be guessed at by the sound of leaves turning.

My movement roused William and he lifted his head. His eyes widened as he turned to me. 'Don't worry about Mother and Lucy. It's just posturing. As soon as the king arrives in France they'll all be freed. I'm quite sure they're being treated well. Louis XIV is a gentleman and I'm told he likes pretty women, so he's not likely to treat the queen badly, or even our mother.' William winked at me but there was a bitter edge to his words.

This sounded worse. How could Lucy and Mother be safe if their security relied on a powerful man finding them attractive? 'I thought Mother had been chosen by the queen to look after the prince; not because she's beautiful, but because of her healing skills. I hate hearing you talk about her like that.'

'I'm sorry, Win,' William moved his hand and squeezed my elbow. 'I was trying to make you smile but it wasn't funny.'

I had another worry. 'What if the king is captured by

William of Orange and kept prisoner? Or he might even be beheaded. What will happen then?'

'He'll be allowed to escape. William and Mary don't want to imprison him, he'd just attract rescue attempts and they won't behead him either. Mary would never kill her own father.' He shook his head, 'Once he's gone, the story will be that he abdicated. That means he gave up the crown willingly.'

William was trying to make me feel better but anger threaded through his words and there was something else.

'Are you frightened?' I dared ask. William stared into the depths of the fog, struggling with his answer. I saw his shoulders drop. 'I'll be imprisoned, Win. I don't know what will happen to the rest of you. And it's all because of our mother's interference.'

'How can you blame Mother?'

'She saved the life of the baby. Think about it, Win, a Catholic prince, James Francis Edward Stuart.' William's voice rose and cracked with emotion, as it had when he was fifteen. 'Parliament wanted the child to die. If our mother had let nature take its course, if she hadn't meddled, we would still have James II on the throne. Yes, a Catholic king but one who would have passed on the throne to a Protestant daughter. William would never have invaded. Our family might have lived in peace for generations.'

I had a memory of a mewling child down in the bowels of the house. The maids had rushed around with hot water and towels, everyone had frowned and whispered and meals were late.

'The baby prince was here, wasn't he? She brought him to our home to cure him. What was wrong with him?'

'He wouldn't take the nurse's milk. The country's most learned physicians couldn't help him. He was dying. But our mother saved him. There's even a rumour that she swapped him for another child.'

I jumped from the seat to face him. 'Mother wouldn't do that. She wasn't trying to save a prince, she was trying to save a baby. Grace says that she's learned how to do it, to help dying babies and heal other things as well.'

'So Grace knows everything ... it must be fact then.' William's voice was heavy with sarcasm.

'Cook told her.'

William stood and tossed the folds of his cloak across his shoulder, his eyes dark and blank. 'Well that settles it, Win. Perhaps the king should take Cook to France, not our father.' He turned from me and disappeared into the hoary mist.

Alone again on the cold bench I removed my glove to feel the warmth vanish from where my brother had been. I knew he spoke the truth. My mother's loyalty lay not with us but with her faith and her monarch. I understood, finally, why people would hate us in the months to come. We were finished.

On Christmas morning, our father was gone. Nothing was said. Father's place was empty at breakfast but at dinner, my brother took his seat at the head of the table.

For once, the house was warm and scented with the sap of fresh-cut logs. Mary had instructed that there should be fires in every room. In the dining room and drawing room, the fireplaces trailed with foliage from the garden. Anne hadn't been successful in finding a turkey so we had goose as usual and Christmas pottage and later, some sugarplums in the drawing room. We tried to laugh and pretend that everything was the same but our efforts flickered and then died away, like the ash in the grate. William sat slouched in his chair, his wig at an awkward angle, from the effects of too much wine. My brothers-in-law smoked pipes and murmured over a game of cards and my sisters were at either side of the fire, working a tapestry.

By late afternoon, I felt restless and walked the long, silent corridors of the house. Anne had decided that after dinner was served, servants who had family in London would be free to visit them, so the lamps were unlit and fires now smouldered untended in empty rooms. My father would never have allowed the house to be left in darkness. The familiar corridors seemed full of shadows and I hurried to Mother's room. Some remnant of late, grey afternoon light filtered through the small window panes and I pulled from her closet the gowns, petticoats and stays she had left behind. I piled them onto her bed and burrowed deep into the scented mound of cloth.

I woke, stiff and chilled, to hear muffled sounds from the street. At first it was just a murmur, as if two men were passing the time of day. I sat up and listened, pushing the clothes from me and allowing my eyes to adjust to the moonlight slicing through the un-shuttered windows.

A soft whistle rose from the street, like a man calling a dog. The uneven glass of the window panes sparkled and lights flickered from below. I tiptoed across and knelt on the box under the window to look down. It was men with torches. I ran back across the room, tripping on the edge of a rug and falling hard against the fender around the dead fireplace. I stumbled out of the door, nursing my bruised elbow and ran down the empty corridor, my voice echoing ahead of me. 'They've come! They've come!'

Candles guttered in the galleried landing. I lifted my petticoats and ran down the stairs, calling to my brother, 'William! They're here.'

William opened the door of the drawing room, staggering backwards as I pushed past him. 'For heaven's sake, Win, what on earth's the matter?' His voice was slurred and he had to prop himself upright against the doorframe. My sisters and their husbands froze like a tableau as I fell into the folds of their tapestries, wiping the soot and tears from my hands and face.

'Men are outside,' I wailed. 'I saw them from Mother's room. They've got torches and sticks.'

My sisters' husbands, neither of them fit men, rose in alarm from their game of cards and looked first at their wives and then across to my brother, now slumped forward in a chair, rocking and moaning. In that instant we all understood. We had no idea how many manservants remained. Apart from the men in the room, we were undefended.

William rose, holding himself steady against the back of his chair. 'We have to fight them. Let's fight them. Come on, Carrington! Are you scared, Molyneux? Are you both cowards?'

Viscount Carrington pushed my brother back into his chair. 'Sit down.' He steered Lord Molyneux towards the door by his elbow. 'All of you remain where you are. We'll judge the situation, determine what to do.'

But I knew that our situation was beyond any judgement. I'd already seen it all. At least twenty men in the street and more to come, here to destroy us just like before. But we waited, silent, listening to small cracks and shifts from the dying fire. Anne rolled up the tapestry and William cradled his head beneath his folded arms.

The two men returned, their ruddy complexions glistening with exertion and fear. 'It looks like we're outnumbered,' wheezed Viscount Carrington. 'Are there any records of which servants remain or those who might have returned?' Mary exchanged a glance with Anne who frowned and pursed her lips. 'But what shall we do?' Anne asked her husband and both sisters looked towards their husbands for help. In turn, Carrington and Molyneux glowered at my sobbing brother.

Someone had to act. I stood up and caught my reflection in the mirror, as tall as any of the men. We must flee and I knew how to lead us to safety. 'We need to check the servants' quarters and rouse any who are here. Carrington and Molyneux should go to the men's quarters and Anne and I will do the women.'

Everyone turned towards me, even William lifted his head to listen. 'Tell them to gather in the hall. Mary, you count heads. We'll escape through the garden. There's a gate at the back that only the gardeners use. Be quick,' I clapped my hands. 'There isn't much time.'

I ran to Grace's room and burst in without knocking. She jumped from the bed, her hand over her mouth.

'Quickly, Grace. We have to leave. There's a gang of men in the street who look as if they're going to attack the house. We'll have to show everyone our secret way out through the garden. We're the only ones who can do it. Hurry, go to Mary in the hall.'

I ran to my room and pushed my nightshirt and Mother's old, torn petticoat into the embroidered purse that Anne had given me for Christmas. Instead of joining the others as I should have done, I ran towards Mother's room at the front of the house. I had to see the men again. Keeping my head away from the window, in case my shadow attracted attention, I now counted about fifty. Some carried torches, others sticks or swords. A group at the front had their heads bent together in low talk and the rest were waiting. Last time they had shouted. This silence felt worse.

Down in the hall my brother-in-law took charge by counting heads but Grace beckoned from the front that the group should follow her down the servants' stairs and along the narrow corridor that led to the kitchen. I kept to the rear of a ragged line of servants; those who were orphaned children or not quick-witted enough to create a fictitious family. As the line paused at the exit to the garden, I stole into Mother's stillroom to slip a bottle of rosewater into my purse.

Grace called over the line of waiting heads that we must walk through the garden in absolute silence and carry no lamps. While they shuffled behind her in single file, I remained for a few seconds at the outside door until I was sure that no one was left behind. We crept through the stable yard, fearful that the horses might whinny in fear or pleasure and give us away. There was no moon and with each step through the formal garden, I expected the dark shapes of the statues to jump out and grab me by the neck. I imagined a sword through my heart, or worse, to be stolen from the end of the line by a group of men. The paths narrowed and I feared that the women's petticoats made too much noise against the foliage. Someone stumbled and called out and we stood still, our breath frosting in the darkness, hearts bumping in our chests, waiting to hear the mob bray with delight that we'd revealed ourselves.

I followed the group into the kitchen garden, past the rows of turned earth ready for planting in the spring. We squeezed through a gap between the glasshouses and staggered over the stinking heap of rotten vegetables and fallen apples that the gardeners thought useful. At last, my family and our servants gathered, silent and expectant, waiting at the solid garden gate. A sound of glass breaking carried across the garden from the house.

Although I knew where the key was kept, our urgent need to escape seemed less important than hiding from my older sisters that I had used this gate before.

'Come on, girl!' Viscount Carrington growled at me through clenched teeth. 'I thought you knew of a way out.'

While Grace fumbled with the heavy key, Carrington spoke over our heads too loudly, as if addressing troops. 'Once we're on the street, we head for my residence.' I glanced over my shoulder, terrified we'd been heard. 'Keep together and don't attract attention to yourselves,' he intoned. 'If any servants have family nearby, make your way there. It's best if we're not too big a group.'

I allowed my brother-in-law the dignity of being the leader. I bowed my head to him, the senior man in the family, a role that ought to belong to William, who swayed between two gardener's boys. I watched my family push ahead of the servants to be first through and waited with Grace to lock the gate. The refugees shuffled ahead of us down the narrow gardener's passage, their small bundles held close. Grace and I pulled our capes over our heads, our faces hidden. She looked up at me from under her hood and I took her hand. 'Don't go home to your mother. Stay with me, please,' I whispered.

I was used to the smell of fire from fireplaces and garden bonfires but this odour was so different from the smell of ash or charcoal. It was damp and sour and grew stronger as we pushed deeper into the ruins of our home. I searched the broken rooms with my sisters, picking our way amongst the shattered glass and sodden rugs. A mouldering, acrid, rotten stench caught in the back of my throat and I covered my face with my cloak. Anne, Mary and I entered each room, the skeleton chairs, broken glass and twisted metal a choking reminder of the power of fire. Inexplicably, recognisable objects remained exactly where they had been dropped and isolated corners of rooms remained untouched, framed by blackened walls. Doors had been left ajar for us by the servants who had been first to check on the house but the door to Father's study had been left shut. Anne pushed through the door, only to close it sharply behind her and bar my way from entering.

'There's no need to see what's in there. There's things

written on the walls ... vile words ... I don't want you to read them.'

'What is it?' Mary joined us from the drawing room.

'There's words on the walls ... written in excrement, I think, describing what they want do to the women. I don't think Winifred should see it.'

'Quite right, Anne, and I don't think I want to either. How much worse this might have been – at least no lives were lost. I'm glad we decided to let the servants have the evening at home. It was better for us to escape rather than try to fight back.'

I didn't agree. Had our able men been with us like last time, they might have helped to defend the house. If the mob had met some resistance, perhaps there would have been less damage and I wouldn't have been left without a home.

'Perhaps they knew that we were practically alone. That's why they chose Christmas Day,' I murmured.

Mary turned to me. 'Winifred, you can't mean that one of our household betrayed us?'

'That's exactly what I mean. I'm glad no-one was hurt but perhaps we wouldn't have been attacked at all if they'd thought we were defended. It wasn't a good decision. We've lost our home and all the servants have lost their positions.'

Anne's face reddened and I was afraid I'd said too much but it was Mary who spoke, her calm words more terrifying than any anger. 'I don't recall that you expressed a view at the time, Winifred, although the decision about the servants was known to you, as it was to everyone else. The only people who are worthy of blame are the men who were hell bent on destruction. You are lucky to have a home with Anne and not be sent to Frances in Edinburgh.'

'I'm sorry, Mary,' I felt my skin flush and lowered my gaze.

'Remember Father's words,' Mary continued. 'We must stick together and think of others, not just ourselves. Now wait here and reflect on what I've said while Anne and I make a quick inventory of any furniture that can be salvaged. Don't use the staircase, it might not be safe.'

Of course, I disobeyed her. The upstairs rooms were strangely unaffected, although everything was covered in a fine, greasy layer of soot. From my room I took my hairbrush and comb, from Mother's a perfume bottle and from Lucy's her old doll, left behind in her rush to France. I tucked these treasures under my cloak and by the time my sisters returned I stood exactly where I had been left.

CHAPTER 3

My sister's carriage dropped us at the Middle Tower. It was a warm day but Grace and I pulled the hoods of our cloaks over our faces to walk up Water Lane. The path was uneven and the walls high, one side in full sun the other in deep shade. We kept close to the dark wall and turned left through an archway, past the Bloody Tower on our right-hand side and climbed the steep incline to Tower Green. I heard footsteps and the high voices of women and children, but kept my eyes down. They might, like us, be prison visitors and therefore deserving of a warm smile but, more likely, they were the wives and children of the wardens, disparaging of treasonable families like ours.

I stopped at the royal chapel on the green and pulled back my hood. The stone shimmered like rich butter toffee. I looked down at the small crosses that marked the executions of Anne Boleyn, Catherine Howard and Lady Jane Grey and frowned. A soft wind lifted strands of my hair, which drifted across my cheeks like cobwebs. It was too peaceful here for violent death.

'Grace, my mother might have been executed right here. Yet I had to pass this place every time I came to see her. I'd been told the stories of the executions and at night I used to imagine my mother's head rolling on the ground.'

Grace pulled me away. 'Don't think about it, Winifred, you'll start your nightmares again. I've never understood why the Countess was accused of treason. I was only a scullery maid at the time and not allowed to ask questions.'

We joined arms and walked slowly down to the Lieutenants' Lodging, where my brother William was imprisoned along with other male prisoners of rank. The sun shone in my face and I threw back my head to feel its warmth in my hair.

Grace sat on a mounting block with her back to the wall. 'I'll wait here for you. It's so dark inside that place.'

I sat down next to her, delaying my visit to my brother's unwelcoming rooms. 'Do you remember a woman called Elizabeth Cellier? She often visited my mother at our Lincoln's Inn house.'

Grace shaded her eyes and frowned. 'I didn't like her. She always made Cook annoyed because she used the kitchen to boil herbs.'

'I didn't like her either. She and Mother were always out, trying to heal the sick. Anyway, they started visiting Catholic prisoners and met a man called Thomas Dangerfield, who accused them of plotting to kill the king.'

'That's ridiculous,' Grace interrupted.

'It is ridiculous,' I continued, thinking of my elegant mother and the hatchet-faced Mrs Cellier conspiring to commit murder. 'But he had planted some evidence which was taken seriously and they were both arrested. I wasn't told much about the trial but I remember my father saying that Mrs Cellier was very convincing in court.'

'I remember her arguments with Cook. She usually won and that didn't happen often.'

'Mother didn't see much of her once they were both released. I don't think my father wanted it. Mother never spoke of the matter again. I've often thought about how things would have turned out if she'd been found guilty. I was only eight and my father was in the Tower too.'

Grace frowned and rested her hand on my arm. 'It would have been awful for a little girl to lose her mother like that but it didn't happen. You had her with you until you were sixteen. It's best not to dwell on what might have been.'

'I also wonder how things would be right now if Mother had never met Mrs Cellier. My mother's chance friendship with that woman has brought so much harm. If the baby had died, the people might have been happy to keep James as king and we wouldn't be having all these terrible battles. It frightens me that so much can depend upon such a small thing. Maybe it would have been better for everyone if my mother had been executed.'

'Winifred, please, I don't like to hear you speak about the Countess like that.' Grace looked around her. 'I can understand why you must hate this place but what has Mrs Cellier got to do with your mother saving the baby prince?'

'She taught my mother everything. She was a midwife. She knew about babies.' I felt sullen and angry with Grace for taking my mother's side. I heard myself speak to her as if she were stupid. 'Don't you see? This is all Mrs Cellier's fault,' I sulked, 'every bit as much as my mother's.'

Grace leaned forward and her shadow shielded my eyes from a sun dropping low in the sky. 'We can't predict the future, Win. When we learn something, we can't be sure how we'll use it. We'll be with your mother soon enough and you'll have the chance to ask her about these matters and try to understand what happened. Hurry or you'll be late for William and this food is spoiling.'

She handed me the basket from my sister's kitchen and I walked on to the Lieutenant's Lodging. I wanted a row but it wasn't going to be with Grace. I followed the guard upstairs and waited while he searched through the keys on a heavy ring, worn on a belt around his waist. I had been visiting William for months, always on the same day of the week and always at this time, but every week the guard studied each key as if it was fresh from the blacksmith until I slipped him a coin of enough weight to allow him to find the correct one. I knew I should give him the bribe immediately but I felt we would both miss the pretence.

The guard bowed low as he held open William's door, announcing 'Lady Herbert' as if William might have had a steady stream of visitors through the day. William looked up from his book in surprise. I knew he would have heard the guard's measured tread and heavy breath as he climbed the stairs and listened to the rattle of the key but this was our ritual; William would act as if he wasn't expecting me and I would pretend I was pleased to see him. I pulled my cloak from my shoulders and handed over the basket of simple food and ale from Anne's kitchen. It was a meagre offering and William didn't bother to look inside. Since we had lost Powis Castle and all our houses and estates there was no money. William often complained that his rooms received no natural light apart from early in the morning and had asked to be moved but we couldn't pay what was asked. This room was furnished with a few pieces from the Lincoln's Inn house that hadn't been destroyed the night it was ransacked and retained a slight smell of soot, alongside damp and mice.

My brother's cheekbones stood out, chiselled from his face, the last of the light catching their sharp angles in deep shadows. He hadn't shaved, nor was he wearing a wig. He gestured that I sit down on the other side of the empty grate.

He cleared his throat before speaking, as if his voice had not been used that day.

'Any money from our esteemed parents?'

'They send what they can. Mother says life is very frugal at St Germain. The French king has been generous to fund so many émigrés but she says that more arrive every day. But she's well and Lucy too, although she's worried about Lucy's decision to enter a convent, as you might expect ...'

'I'm sure it's a hard life at the court of Louis XIV.' William interrupted me, trying out a Welsh accent which only made him sound bitter rather than funny. I stood at the window and looked out at the chapel, still glowing with late autumn sunshine, then turned back into the pall of the room.

'They're not part of the French court. It's the English court in France. There are many mouths to feed and everyone has lost their estates, just like us.'

He snorted and folded his arms across his chest but he didn't argue. I was glad because I needed to tell him something difficult.

'I want to be in France with our mother and Lucy. I've asked her to send for me.'

'So my little sister will abandon the family as well? I thought you hated her.'

I felt my chest tighten. 'So what if I do? Why shouldn't I go to France?' I grasped the back of his chair. 'You'll be out of here soon. Everyone's being released. Then you'll be free to live again. You're still young, you can find a wife, a position. But look at me. I'm seventeen and I never meet anyone my own age. Our sister's house is filled with boring old Jacobites and I'm not welcome at court. I have no dowry. I'm as much a prisoner as you. I'm so dowdy. Look at this gown.' I held up its pitiful folds then let them drop, as if my fingers were soiled.

'Have you considered living with Frances in Scotland? I've heard the young Scots lords are a wild and handsome bunch.'

'The Scots are savages, everyone knows that! Anyway, there's no future for anyone of the Catholic faith in Scotland. The clans have retreated and Presbyterianism is the established church. Not even the Episcopalians are safe.'

'So my little sister is a Jacobite after all. You've been taught well by Anne.'

I sat down in the empty chair and rested my hands in my lap, trying to ignore his taunts. 'Lucy's letters show her devotion to our faith and her vocation is clear. She's determined to join a convent, so Mother will need my help with the prince. When it comes, I want to take my chance.'

'With the hope of balls and parties and young men to dance with?' William's tone was conciliatory.

I smiled at him, putting my anger aside. 'You've no idea what life is like with the esteemed Viscount and Lady Carrington. He chews his food like this.' I rolled my eyes and ground my jaw. William gave a yelp of laughter.

'I've been made to study French and Latin and needlework and dancing, but for what? At St Germain, I can use my learning. I have to get away from here ... and you will likely be freed before I go.'

William's expression closed, 'Neither Anne nor Mary has been to visit me. Only you come, every week.'

'They're so busy,' I lied. 'I'm sure they'll visit soon. You know that we can't afford the price of your bail,' I said, rehearsing familiar arguments, but I had little confidence that either of my brothers-in-law had tried particularly hard to have him released. William must know that our sisters believed he had let us down on that dreadful night we'd escaped from the mob. We'd never spoken of it but I had overheard from their whispered conversations that they thought he was a drunk. My own role on that night had been forgotten and I'd had to sit through many accounts, each more vivid than the last, of Carrington's quick-witted bravery in leading the household to safety through the garden.

'And your young maid, Grace,' William broke into my thoughts. 'Will she accompany you?'

'She's not my maid, she's my companion. I have no other. It was Anne's decision and it has made me very happy. I would have gone mad without her.'

William stood to light his lamps and I watched his careful use of the ends of candles that Anne's servants would have thrown away. I thought I saw loneliness in his sloping shoulders and rounded back and resolved to try to be more kind and to bring whatever the kitchens could spare, until I was called to France. I said farewell and as he pressed my head into his chest, I smelt mildew from his clothes.

Grace and I walked down the hill to wait for Lord Carrington's carriage at the Middle Tower. From dark corners, soldiers wounded in James' war in Ireland, where he fought against his daughter's husband, called out for alms and waved their fetid stumps. I had nothing to give. We wrapped our cloaks tightly around our worn petticoats, glad of the night, as carriages full of beautiful young men and women passed by on their way to parties and dinners. I was tired of hiding from society. I couldn't wait to be gone.

I sat in the middle of the long oak table with Anne at one end and Francis Carrington at the other. They had not been blessed with children and as I looked from one to the other it was easy to see why. Both were rotund with overindulgence and I imagined that, even if both were willing, which I doubted knowing my sister, the mechanics of the act of procreation were probably an impossibility. We ate in silence, the noise of Francis' few teeth occasionally colliding in his cavernous mouth. I refused the orange cream and stewed pears, leaving more for them. They licked their lips and spooned down the nursery food like naughty children.

Anne wiped her chin with a napkin and looked at me. 'How was our brother?'

'He looks thin and pale but then he never gets out and probably doesn't get enough to eat.'

'Did he send any word of thanks for the bread and jugged hare?'

'Yes, of course, he thanked you both for your kindness and asked after your health.'

Carrington gave a slight tilt of his head in acknowledgement.

'My lord, he's looking forward to you visiting him and awaits with anticipation your petition to the House of Lords for his release.'

Anne sniffed and put down her napkin. 'I don't know where he thinks we'll find the money.'

I ignored her and took the chance to raise my own situation. 'He suggested I go to Scotland to live with Frances, instead of going to France.'

She rose and bowed to her husband, signalling that she was leaving. 'I think you'll find that Frances and her children are hoping to join our mother in France. Her husband, the Earl of Seaforth, is fighting in Ireland. You will be invited to travel only when you are needed. In the meantime, you must learn patience, as must our brother.'

CHAPTER 4

Two frustrating years followed. I lost contact with William after his release from the Tower, since he was not welcome to live with either of my sisters and there were rumours that if found, he was to be arrested again. Day followed dreary day of morning lessons and afternoons filled with the quacking of Jacobite wives. I lived for Lucy's rare letters from France but there was little of the news I wanted to hear, of young men, dancing and new dresses. I wasn't interested in her role as assistant governess or the rituals of life in the exiled court, nor did I have much sympathy for her complaints that I wasn't there to release her.

One evening, Anne asked me to remain behind after our evening meal to hear news from her husband. Carrington wiped his mouth, as uncomfortable with our proximity as I was. He stared into the distance before speaking, rearranging the position of his bowl and glass as if their precise location was essential to what would follow.

'Lady Herbert,' Carrington enjoyed formality, 'a courier came to the house this morning. He brought three passes from the French government, one for you and two for accompanying servants. Your father has sent money for your passage. I assume you will want Grace Evans to accompany you and I suggest you take that new man, the one who's just started in the stables.'

I knew the boy he meant and was certain he was of simple mind. My mind swung between hope and fear. It might all be for nothing if Grace and I weren't safe on this journey.

I fixed his shifting eyes with a stare. 'Thank you Francis, but Grace and I would be safer on our own. We will dress as boys and will not be troubled.'

Carrington sighed. He liked a quiet life above all else and I'd guessed he would back down. 'If the stable boy is not to your liking then by all means travel with John, the gardener's assistant, but he must come home immediately. Instruct your father to pay for his return passage.'

I almost hugged him but the flicker of recoil in his small eyes stopped me. Instead I curtsied and ran towards the door, keen to tell Grace the news.

'Winifred,' he called. I paused and turned back. 'You will leave the day after tomorrow.'

The household went into turmoil as Anne set everyone confusing and contradictory tasks and made lists which she left all over the house. The head gardener, infuriated by my brother-in-law's decision, confronted him loudly in the hall but although the gardener won the shouting match, to my relief Carrington's decision prevailed. My clothes, such as they were, were packed and unpacked. Anne wailed at their dowdiness and tried to make me take two of her gowns, despite the fact that both Grace and I would fit inside each one. She fussed in the kitchen over what she should send to Mother, then sobbed at the table, certain that Mother would have everything she needed at St Germain.

The night before we left, Anne insisted we have baths. This involved the whole household in boiling water and searching for enough clean drying cloths and required a team of maids to mop the wooden floor of my bedroom. Grace and I sat together, drying our hair in front of the fire. The scent of my mother's rosewater mingled with the smell of fresh sap from the apple tree logs. Alone at last, a single word hung between us, unspoken. *Freedom.*

At Dover, I leaned over the rail of the small packet boat and breathed in the odour of tar and rotten fish from the quayside, watching as ropes and barrels were loaded aboard. I looked along the deck to my two companions. Young John, a dark-haired boy with round cheeks pink with excitement, and Grace, leaning back and laughing, her clean hair loose and tossed by the salt spray. Behind them the sky was almost black, crying seagulls caught like silver arrows in the last of the sunlight. Men scrambled onto the rigging and our crumpled sails became taut, straining to hold the force of the gusting wind. The boat began to creak and shift its way out of the dock towards the harbour entrance. We turned our backs on England and breathed deeply, filling our lungs with joy.

John wanted to go below and play cards with other travellers, so Grace and I linked arms and strolled along the deck, talking about the other passengers until the rain fell in heavy, round drops and thunder grumbled around us. We retreated to our cabin and for the next two days we were trapped, as the boat heaved and bucked against the storm. We took turns to weave along the dark galley to empty our slop bucket, barely able to contain its contents as the ship lifted and dipped. The floor was wet and the air sour with vomit, spilt where other travellers had tried to navigate the corridor. We brought back ale to sip and damp cloths to wipe our hands and faces. Day and night merged. We hardly spoke except to check that each was still alive and sleep was only possible in snatches. Finally, the storm ended and we gingerly climbed on deck to join other whey-faced passengers. The clouds broke from the horizon and a torn strip of blue sky framed a slash of dark coastline that must be France. I waved to John who stood with the other male servants and he hurried over. 'Yes, my lady?'

'Stay with us, John. We shall stand together as we sail into Calais.'

I had imagined running across an empty quay and into Lucy's arms, with Father possibly hovering in the background. Of course, Mother wouldn't be there. Instead we had to wait while the boat inched towards the quay and men with ropes secured her tossing hulk to the dock. Next, the crew tumbled the cargo and baggage onto the quayside. The servants disembarked first and stood guard around their employer's trunks and boxes. At last, a whistle blew and we were allowed to inch down the gangway. The quay was crowded and I had no idea where to look for the carriage we had been promised. I felt suffocated by the crush of bodies that smelt and sounded utterly unfamiliar. French and Irish voices mingled and I understood neither. I wanted to run back to the safety of the ship.

Carrying our trunk on his shoulders, John used his height and weight to force a way through the crowds. I clung to his waist, and Grace held on to mine. As the passengers and crew thinned, John put down the trunk and we scanned wooden sheds, barrels, coils of rope and stragglers making their way to the town. To our left, a path which was little more than a farm track had waiting carriages along its verge, their drivers idly flicking at passing flies while the horses pulled at their bridles to crop the thin grass. By the first carriage, a tall woman stood alone, shading her eyes and watching the groups of travellers mingle and separate. She could have been my mother and my heart leaped, but it was Lucy. I called and she turned towards us, searching for my voice. Grace and I waved and John did that two-fingered whistle that only boys can manage. Between us, we picked up the trunk and staggered towards her. Facing Lucy after all these years, without a farewell between us, I felt immediately awkward and curtsied, as if she were royalty. In the same moment, Grace and John became servants and fell back, busy with our baggage.

Lucy lifted my hand and turned it over, then stepped forward and touched my cheek. 'Winifred,' she said softly. 'You've grown up.'

In the carriage, I found I wanted to look at Lucy without her seeing. Her gown was plain, cut higher across her breasts than was fashionable and she wore her hair pulled back tightly across her crown, without ornament or headdress. At her throat she wore a simple crucifix. She saw me looking and smiled.

'I'm entering a convent in Bruges and the queen is expecting a baby. Now that you've arrived, I'm free to go. Thank you for coming, Win, Mother would never have allowed me to leave if you hadn't agreed.'

'The queen is having another baby?' This was amazing, a miracle in fact. No wonder Mother had asked me to come.

'It's due next spring. I'll stay for a few months to help you find your feet.'

There was so much else I wanted to ask but I felt self-conscious in front of Grace, my closest friend for three years but who was a stranger and a servant to my sister. I nodded and said nothing more, ashamed that my stare had made Lucy apologise for the plainness of her dress, which was nonetheless cleaner and newer than anything worn by me. I looked out of the carriage at the darkening French countryside, which was much like England except that the cottages were white with red tiles and there were more trees. Lights began to glow from windows and I felt an unexpected loneliness for Anne's chaotic household in London.

Lucy pulled curtains across the carriage windows and I buried my cheek into upholstery that smelled of hair oil and sweat. We had lost the contents of our stomachs several times while crossing the channel and I felt hunger fight with nausea as I tried to doze. I thought it would be childish, like the Winifred that Lucy had left behind, to ask if we were there yet or if we would ever stop to eat. I shut my eyes and allowed my head to roll back and forth with the uneven rhythm of the carriage, and in that strange place between wakefulness and sleep I remembered playing with Lucy at Powis Castle, whinnying and tossing our heads as we cantered imaginary horses down the long gallery until our nurse shouted at us to stop. The shouting became a man's voice. There was a man in the gallery, chasing us. The movement stopped and I was shaken awake.

The carriage door stood open and Lucy was gone. Grace cradled my head against her shoulder. 'It's only me, Win, don't worry.'

I pulled back and tried to focus on her face. 'I must have fallen asleep. Where's Lucy?'

'We've stopped here to eat and wash. Lady Lucy has gone inside with the men to find a room.'

I sank back against the cushions and waited, holding Grace's hand, feeling the splintered comfort that rises when a bad dream fades. Lights flickered as the door of the inn opened then closed and men called to each other in French. The voices seemed to roll back and forth across the courtyard and although my teachers said I was fluent, I couldn't understand anything that was said. The horses stamped and blew and I guessed they were being rubbed down and watered. John's face appeared in the door and he gestured that we follow him. He helped us down from the carriage and led us across the courtyard and into the inn. Through the open door to the bar I saw a crowd of men, their voices roaring in a senseless babble and loud laughter that cut through the thick smoke. I lifted my petticoats and quickly followed John to the top of the stairs. He held open a door and we ducked our heads to enter a warm, low-ceilinged room, where food was laid out on a rough-hewn table. Lucy gestured to a bowl and towels where I could wash. She touched Grace on the arm and pointed her back through the door, to an adjoining room, using an authoritative voice I didn't recognise.

'Evans, you will wash and eat in there. You may join us in the carriage for the rest of the journey. We must be quick as the Duchess is waiting to see Lady Winifred.' Lucy startled as she found me standing close behind her. 'For goodness' sake, Winifred, go and get washed.'

'You don't understand,' I hissed. 'Grace is my companion. She must eat with me.'

Lucy steered me back to our room, where she closed the door. All her movements were calm and measured as if she had already entered the convent. 'These are Mother's instructions. Grace can't be your companion. It's best she understands that now. She will be your lady's maid and will assist our mother, who is now the Principal Lady of the Bedchamber. That's the best we can do. Money is very scarce at St Germain.'

'But Anne arranged it all,' I pleaded, hoping that our older sister's authority would carry some influence.

'I know. But there is no place for a companion. You will be part of the queen's court and will support Mother. Please get washed. I will go and explain to Evans. And Winifred,' Lucy hesitated, 'please wash thoroughly, you're both a little ...' She screwed up her nose and left.

. . .

We rode hard through the dark for at least another hour until Lucy pulled back the carriage curtains. In the distance a building rose like a crouching cat, dotted with lights that grew brighter as we approached. There was nothing gentle or gracious about St Germain-en-Laye. It grew out of the landscape like a cliff face.

Once the horses caught sight of home, their canter became a gallop, throwing us from side to side as the coachman negotiated the bends in the road. The lights grew brighter and the chateau filled the carriage window then disappeared as we raced under an archway and clattered to a halt in a central courtyard. The coachman opened the door and pulled down the steps. Grace was out first and helped me down. Men and women appeared from dark corners and, in the confusion and noise, Grace and John disappeared. I looked above me at row upon row of lights as the chateau rose into the night sky.

Lucy gripped my arm and led me to a staircase. We climbed at least three flights of stairs, each turn only dimly lit and stopped in front of a door, already open. Somehow, my trunk was in the room, next to a wide bed. A very young maid curtsied and left. I started to cry and Lucy pulled me to sit next to her on our bed.

'It's strange at first but you will be happy here with our mother and father. The queen is lovely and the prince is ...' Lucy hesitated and her eyes searched for the right word, '... the prince is a lively little boy. Come now and change into this dress. We're pretty much the same size. Mother is waiting.' I was exhausted and nervous and wished this meeting with Mother could wait until morning, when I would be cleaner and more awake.

Back down the same staircase and across the courtyard we entered a wide, better lit set of stairs and climbed to the first floor to reach our parents' suite. A servant led us into an elegant, mirrored drawing room and I tried to balance on the edge of a chair which was not designed for comfort. Lucy sat to my left and folded her hands elegantly in her lap, as if she had spent the day on embroidery. I saw myself reflected from different angles and was pleased at the sight of my fine, slightly pointed nose and quizzical, arched brows.

A rustle of petticoats and Mother hurried into the room, her expression preoccupied, as if she had put something down only a moment before and now couldn't find it. Lucy and I rose up together and curtsied. Mother saw me and held out both hands to take mine.

'It's like seeing myself in a looking glass! My darling Winifred, you are so beautiful, the loveliest of all my daughters.'

I turned to see Lucy's reaction to this unkind comparison but she smiled without envy and I thought that her mind must now be occupied by higher things than earthly beauty. Mother sat down on a third chair and sent a servant for chocolate. We talked of the journey and she asked for news of Anne and Mary. I learned that our oldest sister Frances had remained in Scotland as her husband had returned from Ireland. Without being asked, I told her about William, incarcerated for too long in the Tower and now disappeared. She frowned at me with what might have been grave concern or grave displeasure and turned to Lucy to speak about things that meant nothing to anyone ignorant of life in the exiled court.

Free to study her, I saw that Mother was thinner than I remembered and the light from the candles cast deep shadows under her eyes. She had been right to send for me. She was too old, I thought, to be looking after young children. As she enquired more about our family, the servants, England, I tried to remember loving her. She seemed nothing like the mother who had left me, the mother of my memories. That mother had been scented, soft to touch. This mother was aged, with stiff hair piled high in the new, unflattering fashion and skin that was heavy with powder. She smelt like a stranger.

Lucy took a long time to come to bed; her prayers seemed to go on for ever and I wondered how anyone could be so religious when they were also so tired. I had almost fallen asleep when I felt a cool draught on my shoulder and the mattress dip, as Lucy pulled back the covers and climbed in beside me. We lay side by side in the shared bed. I had not slept beside another human being in my entire life, at least not that I could remember, and I was aware of her body and the importance of not touching. We lay in silence and I tried to match my breathing to Lucy's to help me sleep. Then she spoke.

'What did you think of Mother?'

What could I say? That she seemed old, that I had felt nothing? I hesitated. 'It was wonderful to see her again. I thought she looked tired.'

There was another silence, we both held our breath, then Lucy spoke again. 'I wondered if you'd notice. I thought it might just be me, imagining things. She's looking more and more tired. I'll speak to Father Innes tomorrow. I think she should see a physician.'

I nodded, even though it was dark. 'Who's Father Innes?'

I felt Lucy shift onto her elbow. 'He's Lewis Innes, the most wonderful man. He's principal of the Scots College in Paris but he spends a lot of time here because the king trusts him. He has a room on this floor and has stayed with us since the king returned from the war. I talk to him about my faith and it's through his help that I'm going to Bruges. Mother adores him too so she'll listen to him.'

I could feel a change in the warmth of Lucy's body as she spoke of her friend Lewis Innes and wondered whether she should be going into a convent. Perhaps that was why she had to go, she loved someone who would never love her in return. I turned over and sighed, enjoying the sadness.

'Another really important person here is John Drummond, the Earl of Melfort. He's just back from Rome. The queen likes him but no one else does. Keep out of his way. I'll point him out tomorrow.'

'Do you know everyone here?'

'It's a very small place and we can't go anywhere else except Rome. So yes, you do get to know everyone, at least by sight. It's harder now that so many Irish are here but they'll move on soon.'

'Why are there so many Irish? They thronged the quayside at Calais.'

'I'm sure you heard that James was defeated at the Battle of the Boyne by your king?' I felt there was an accusation in this, a suggestion that I had some personal responsibility for the actions of William of Orange but I also knew from the Jacobite meetings at Anne's that her king, James, had fled the battlefield after only a few hours and run back to France.

'Well,' Lucy continued as if this were a history lesson, 'William of Orange and the king of France have just signed a treaty ending the Irish campaign and all the Irish officers who fought for us have been allowed to leave Ireland. Of course, they've all come here but I've heard that Louis is creating a new regiment for them. He's calling them the Wild Geese. Don't you think that's lovely?'

I didn't answer. My mind had already drifted to a sunset-red sky behind Powis Castle, veined with the dark symmetry of wild geese in flight. The lonely sound of their leaving filled my head and I turned away from Lucy, pulling my bolster over my ears.

BOOK TWO

1691–1699

CHAPTER 5

1691

Despite my exhaustion, any sleep was broken by the unfamiliarity of another person moving beside me and restless, wakeful dreams of searching for something I had lost. Just after dawn, Grace moved quietly around the room, picking up underclothes from the floor and hanging our dresses in the closet. She threw more wood on the fire and noticing I was awake, hurried across to my bedside.

'I'm sorry, I'm sorry,' I whispered in case I woke Lucy.

'I'm fine, Lady Winifred,' Grace pushed the hair back from my face. 'This is an adventure for me. There isn't room here, so I'm billeted with the other servants in the town. I'm sharing with two girls from Wales. John has gone home already. Everyone is impressed by my French but they say I've an odd accent.'

I wiped my mouth with the back of my hand. 'I saw my mother last night. She looks very old and Lucy says she's ill.'

'I met her this morning,' Grace frowned. 'She does look tired. She said I was to be a lady's maid to you and Lucy and run errands for her to the town. Don't worry about me, my lady.

This is easy work. From what I hear, I think you've drawn the short straw having to help with the prince.'

I sat up and pulled my knees towards my chin, guessing at what words might have passed between Grace and my mother. 'Tell me about the prince, is he that bad?'

'The other servants tell me he brings new meaning to the word brat.'

Lucy turned over and sighed so Grace put her fingers to her lips and walked over to the closet. 'Your mother,' she whispered, 'says I've to dress you in something of Lucy's when you meet her later. All your old dresses are to be mine. You're going to be fitted for some new gowns.' She clenched her fists in excitement then waved farewell.

I waited for Mother in her private rooms, which were luxurious apartments with walls of duck-egg blue, panelled with frames of embossed gold plaster, like the crimped edges on Cook's pies. Within these panels were paintings of decorative bunches of grapes and sheaves of corn, covered in gold leaf. Faded silk curtains were bunched and draped at the windows, with gold and blue shutters behind to match the interior of the room.

I sat on a chair covered in matching silk and shifted uncomfortably to stop from sliding off. A servant brought coffee and I shuddered at its intense sweetness and bitter taste. From the window, I watched the endless scurrying activity in the courtyard below until footsteps told me that my mother was on her way. I lifted my petticoats and hurried back to my seat.

Mother was still in her night clothes, a white embroidered shift with a grey, silk robe draped across her shoulders. She gave a slight bow of her head and sat at her dressing table, a frothy affair covered in white silk, with frills that fell right to the floor and a mirror veiled in matching drapes. Mother observed me in her reflection while her maid brushed her hair. She must have seen my eyes dart around the room.

'I know what you're thinking, Winifred, but we haven't spent a thing since we arrived. This suite of rooms was used by the French king before he generously gave St Germain to our king. I'm told he'd only just finished this apartment before he left. It's not to my taste but we're lucky, others have had to wait for their apartments to be decorated and the king and queen have had terrible disruption with theirs. The queen keeps changing her mind on where she wants to live and with another baby expected, I'm sure she'll be on the move again. She might even want these apartments.'

I nodded, uncertain whether I was expected to comment. It seemed that Mother found it easier to speak with her back towards me. I couldn't imagine this mother humming amongst the terraces at Powis, filling a basket of figs and peaches for the kitchen and lifting me to reach the fruit. I remembered her kissing me as she put me down and telling me that my cheeks were as soft as the peaches.

I watched the maid arrange my mother's long grey hair, weaving the strands precariously on top of her head and fastening it with ribbons and feathers. I was so fascinated by the intricacies of her hairstyle that I only half listened to Mother's description of my duties but I did grasp that I was to spend my time with the young prince, perhaps help him to practice his French and once the infant was born I was to help with the baby.

Mother stood to be dressed and I turned my head while the maid removed her robe, but in the mirror I caught sight of her sagging breasts and the bones standing out from her back like angel's wings.

'So can you dance, Winifred?' She was seated back at her dressing table, applying layers of powder and rouge to her skin.

51

'I have been taught some English and Scottish country dances but have had no opportunity to dance outside my lessons.'

'Why is that?'

'Our family isn't welcome at court. Other Catholic families made their peace with the king but we were never invited to do so.' I saw my mother frown. 'Sorry, I meant William of Orange.'

'We are not just a Catholic family, Winifred,' my mother explained. 'We're a Jacobite family, dedicated to the restoration of James II to the crown of England. You should have had plenty of opportunity to mix with other good Jacobite families.'

How could I tell her that too many of the Jacobite families of England had given up on James II and were pinning all their hopes on the brat; that they sat around in stuffy rooms and drank too much and bored each other with past glories?

I looked around at the glittering façade of St Germain. 'Yes Mother,' I replied, 'but we didn't have any dances.'

'What musical instruments do you play? Do you write any Latin?'

'I can read and write some Latin and play the harpsichord. I think I'm a fair singer. Anne has taught me embroidery and I'm fine with simple sewing but I'm too clumsy to make my own clothes, or so I'm told.' Mother seemed satisfied but she didn't tell me what use this knowledge might be to her.

Finished with her toilet, Mother stood and brushed her hands across the folds of her gown, adjusting the creases. She dismissed the maid with a stream of French too fast for me to follow. 'One more thing, Winifred. You may not be aware but your father is now the Duke of Powis and I am the Duchess, just in case you accidentally refer to me as the Countess.' She saw me smile and frowned, snapping her fan. 'Did I say something amusing, Winifred?'

'Mother, our estates have been taken by the government of

England. How can you have forgotten? You are a Duchess only in this building. At home you aren't even a Countess.'

Mother stood quite still, as if I had slapped her and her face coloured in patches beneath the thick powder. I felt ashamed, this was my mother and she was ill. Why had I said those words?

I watched as red blotches crawled up her décolletage and spread across her neck. 'I'm sorry, Mother.'

'I'm sorry too, Winifred. We left you too long in England. You have been ruined.'

I lay on my bed crying and raging between self-pity, anger and shame. I wanted Lucy or Grace to find me but no one came and I had no idea how to look for them. I was hungry and didn't know how to get food. This miserable place was a prison, nothing more than a prison. I hated it. I hated Mother and I wanted to go home.

There was a tap on the door. I sat up, wiping my nose on my sleeve. 'Go away!' I shouted.

There was another tap, louder this time. 'Please, my lady, I have to measure you for a gown. It's an order from the Duchess. I have to make you something to wear for dinner tonight.'

I opened the door and a small woman in a white cap pushed her way in, trailing fabric samples and ribbon. She looked up at me with small, screwed up eyes then quickly looked away.

'Are you alright, my lady?' The seamstress spoke English, with a Welsh accent, and to my shame, I started to cry again. She kept her back to me, laying her bundle of fabrics on the bed and pulling pins and measures from her apron pocket.

'Where is everybody?' I pleaded. 'I haven't had anything to eat.' I heard the whining petulance in my voice.

'Now, now,' she fussed, still not looking at me but surveying the room with her hands on her hips. 'I'll need to find a boy to light the lamps, it's too dim to work in here now the light's gone. You come with me and I'll show you where to get your meals. You'll still be able to get something. They never stop cooking down there. Everyone eats together, you see. Servants in one hall, gentry in another. It saves money in the long run. Except if there's a special dinner, like the one the Duke and Duchess are having tonight. You're to be there at eight. You and Lady Lucy.'

She bustled out of the room and I followed close behind, trying to memorise the way. We went down to the ground floor and crossed the courtyard, entering the chateau again through an arched doorway. The smell of food – baked bread, roasting onions, frying meat – caught in my throat, growing stronger as we turned down a spiral staircase into the basement. Here was a long, wood-panelled room, lined with tables and benches. The seamstress told me to sit down and she disappeared. I waited, watching boys light candles and men lay a fire in the great fireplace in readiness for dinner. The seamstress appeared again, only her white apron visible, making her seem like a headless apparition, followed by a girl carrying a tureen of soup and a platter of bread.

'You eat that, my lady, and I'll make sure the room is lit and warm for your return. You can find your own way back?' She patted my arm.

I nodded and began shovelling huge spoonfuls of fragrant meat broth into my mouth, dipping the heavy bread into the liquid and allowing the juices to run down my chin. I was glad no one could see me. I had never felt so hungry.

In the bedroom, Lucy arrived as my new friend, her lips tight around a row of pins, fastened swathes of embroidered silk around me. I could see that Lucy was angry but neither of us spoke until the seamstress was satisfied and left us alone. I pulled a robe over my petticoats and sat on one side of the fireplace. Lucy moved another chair to the fireside and sat opposite me, staring at the burning logs.

'Where have you been today?' I asked her.

'With our mother, helping with her work. It's what I do every day. Mother says you are to join us tomorrow.'

'She told you what I said?'

'She did. I can't imagine why you said that. Mother was so upset. You should have spent the day with us and met the women of the queen's household but she didn't want you near her.'

'I didn't know where anybody was. I didn't know how to get any food.'

'Mother would have explained all that if you hadn't been so stupid. The dinner tonight is in your honour, so please don't let the family down. The Earl of Melfort and his wife will be there and Lewis Innes. Mother and Father are very important people here. Don't forget it.'

I felt my cheeks redden but I needed her to understand that the people here were living a fantasy.

'Lucy,' I explained, hoping she would listen if I spoke like an adult, 'at home you're not Lady Lucy Herbert you're just Lucy Herbert. Our titles have been taken from us.' I paused to gauge her reaction. 'And you know that our brother was imprisoned in the Tower of London.'

'Winifred, I'm warning you, let it drop or ask Father to send you home.' Lucy's eyes were bright and round in the light from the fire. 'Our mother is ill. I've spoken to Lewis and he will try to persuade her to see a surgeon.'

'Lucy, you can't ignore me. Why did Mother and Father make no attempt to have William released?'

She stared at the fire for several more minutes and with too much care, placed a fresh log onto the already generous flames. 'Because of what you say. There are no estates left for him to manage so what could he do? I overheard Father say to Mother that William was better off where he was. What was the alternative, to get drunk in London with his disinherited friends?'

'That's dreadful, Lucy. Couldn't he have come here?'

'There's no role for him and I've heard he's not to be trusted. But I've already said too much. Please, Winifred, we must never speak of this again.'

The formal dining room in my parents' apartment was grander even than the dining room at Powis. Tall, arched windows draped with heavy curtains and plaster columns rose to the cornice. The ceiling was decorated with a lively fresco of cherubs trailing garlands and the walls covered with cameos of even more cherubs playing with wild animals. Triple candelabra blazed from every wall, making the room as bright as daylight.

My new dress was gathered tightly across my chest and round my back. The bodice ended in a bow just above my bottom from which the fabric fell in generous waves. The sleeves were gathered three times, ending in lace just above my elbow. Underneath the gown, which parted at my waist in the French style, I showed layers of petticoats trimmed with the same fabric as the dress. Grace had woven my hair high on top of my head and pinned it with ribbons to match.

I felt beautiful and elegant and turned my head to catch my reflection in the many mirrors that circled the room. I had plenty of time to admire myself because, after I had been introduced, no one spoke to me.

The table was set with a confusing collection of glasses and cutlery that danced with the flickering light from the candles. I knew I would have to watch Lucy closely to make sure I made no mistakes. Mother sat at one end of the table and was her usual gracious hostess. Father sat at the other end, next to me. He took my hand and patted it but on the one occasion he tried to speak to me, he struggled to remember my name, running through Mary, Anne, Frances and Lucy before abandoning the attempt altogether. One daughter too many, I thought.

Everyone listened when Lewis Innes entertained us with stories and reflections in his soft Scots accent. I could see why Lucy loved him. Although almost forty, he was a handsome man with warm brown eyes that crinkled at the corners when he laughed, which he did a great deal. She kept her eyes downcast but every so often, she raised her head and smiled at him, colouring as she did so. Poor Lucy. I could see that her feelings were not returned. Lewis Innes was generous and entirely without prejudice in his distribution of affection. He made everyone feel special. Even the tiny, bird-like wife of John Drummond, the Earl of Melfort, flushed in the glow of his attention. It was the high-coloured, silent Melfort that I watched. Although he rarely spoke, he missed nothing, settling steel grey eyes on whoever was talking. He answered whenever Mother asked him a question but his accent was so thick, I found him impossible to understand. There were others at the table whose names I forgot as soon as I had been introduced.

The huge bow at my backside made it impossible to lean back in my chair and my neck and shoulders ached with the strain of sitting on the edge of my seat. I ate little, constricted by my corset, and my head throbbed with the unfamiliar wine and the effort to hear over the clatter of glasses and porcelain. The servants demanded attention with an ever-changing menu of food, so I didn't notice immediately that the Earl of Melfort had addressed me until Father touched my arm.

'My dear, the Earl is asking you a question.'

The conversation around the table had stopped, and everyone waited as I strained to understand him.

'Lady Winifred,' he said in his broad accent, 'what support is there at home for the return of the king to his throne? I'm told that he will only have to step on to English soil and the people will rise up to support him.'

I looked at Mother, whose eyes narrowed. Lucy gave a tiny shake of her head. All eyes, even Father's, were turned towards me, bright with hope.

'I didn't involve myself with politics at home. I was too busy helping my sister in her charitable work with less fortunate Jacobite families. Nonetheless, I am sure your information is correct.' I bowed my head.

'Well spoken, lassie,' the Earl seemed pleased with my response, 'there's nae place in politics for girls.'

'However,' I went on, ignoring my mother's threatening frown, 'my brother was imprisoned in the Tower of London on account of my parents' actions. I used to visit him every week. He had no support from any quarter,' I looked at Father, 'for his release. He's been freed but he's a young man whose life is slipping away. I wondered if there was a role for him here?'

'That's enough, Winifred,' Mother snapped. 'No one wants to hear our private business. I'm sorry Melfort,' her tone became languid and apologetic, 'my daughter has been allowed rather too much freedom at home.'

The Earl held me with his hooded eyes and spoke slowly, enunciating every syllable. 'We are troubled here with spies and people we cannot trust. Watch out for them, young lady, and be careful what you say. Follow your mother's example and do your duty to your family and your king.'

It was a warning. I lowered my eyes and looked down at my hands. The conversation climbed with a roar of relief and laughter thundered around me. I dared to look up. Lewis Innes turned from his conversation and saw me watching him. It was imperceptible but it was there. He had winked at me.

CHAPTER 6

I had no experience of children, so was of little help with the prince. I struggled to change his soiled clothes as he fought with me, I gave in to his every whim to stop the screaming and I slipped him sweetmeats when he refused the bland nursery food he was expected to eat. Despite the criticism and disapproving looks of the other women, I was proud to be my mother's daughter. Every day I followed her around, listened to what she said and in the evenings, by candlelight, I wrote down everything I could remember.

At night, when Grace brushed my hair, I looked at her reflection in the mirror and told her everything I had seen.

'My mother manages a staff of eleven as well as servants and footmen ... eleven staff, Grace ... all for one little boy they call the Prince of Wales.'

'The Duchess managed a much larger staff at home, both in London and at Powis,' Grace reminded me. 'You're seeing her at work now, that's what's different.'

'All the other women talk about their babies that have died and their sickly children, as if it's to be expected, but my mother has six living children, all of us healthy.'

'Whatever anyone says,' Grace replied, frowning as the hairbrush caught in a tangle of hair, 'her skills aren't miracles or magic but learned and you should go on listening.'

'And when she's with the prince he eats his food, does what he's told and is a happy child. It does seem like a bit of a miracle.'

'I've heard rumours amongst the servants that even the queen struggles to manage his temper.'

'He's tiny, Grace, but already so clever. He knows the weakness of every person who cares for him, including me, but my mother never raises her voice to him or punishes him. She expects him to behave and he does.'

'Perhaps that's it,' Grace smoothed a recalcitrant strand of hair into my night-time ribbon. 'She doesn't stand for any nonsense. It's a pity he doesn't have many other children to play with. It doesn't seem right that he's surrounded by all these adults.'

'The new baby might help, or perhaps not given how jealous he's likely to be. There are so few children here and we've been told to be careful who he plays with. My mother said that the queen is worried that people might seek favours if their child becomes his companion.'

'My lady, this is not a place for children,' Grace mumbled through the hairpins between her lips.

'And not likely to become so in future,' I laughed, 'because apart from the queen, and us of course, everyone is so old!'

Mother died just before Christmas, taken from us one ordinary afternoon. I had been playing with the little prince, helping him build a tower of wooden blocks, when a servant interrupted our game and whispered that my father needed to see me urgently in his apartments. Excusing myself to my mother's staff, I heard the little boy wail at being abandoned. I lifted my skirts to run across the courtyard, fearing news from William or one of my sisters. When I saw Lucy entering the staircase to our parents' rooms, I knew that it was indeed a serious family matter. We waited together in the anteroom, seeing the surgeon leave and women from the queen's household hurry past. I felt a low growl of fear from my stomach. Servants arrived with cloths and bowls of water. I noticed Grace, her eyes and lips raw with pain and when she saw me, she stopped and shook her head before being chivvied away by the Countess of Errol.

'Dear girls,' said the Countess, taking one of each of our hands in hers as we rose, 'your father is waiting for you in your mother's room.'

Father knelt by mother's bed, his forehead resting on his clasped hands. The shutters were drawn, making the light poor, and there was a smell of dust and lavender. As my eyes adjusted, I saw her lying on the bed, pale and still with a rosary twisted between her fingers. This body looked the same as my mother's but her eyes were closed, although she was not asleep. She was an absence, an emptiness where my living mother should have been.

'Father, what has happened?' Lucy spoke first.

'She has left us, my dearest children. She's gone.'

Lucy rested a hand on his shoulder. 'Poor Mother. She's at peace now, her work is done. We should be glad she didn't suffer.'

I felt rage rip through my chest and into my throat, so that when I spoke my voice growled, hoarse and low. 'She worked too hard. This shouldn't have been expected of her. You have killed her.'

'Winifred, please,' Lucy begged, 'not now.'

'But she hadn't finished being my mother,' I cried. 'I haven't had enough time with her.'

'She didn't choose to leave you,' Lucy's voice was firm. 'Go back to our room. I'll stay with Father, he needs me.'

'She did choose to leave me,' I shouted. 'She chose all of this, instead of me.' I waved my arm in a futile gesture that included my father, Lucy, these artificial rooms and the vast, cold space of St Germain-en-Laye.,

Lucy pushed me through the door but as we parted, she held me close and I could feel her breath in my ear. 'It's God's will,' she whispered, 'you will learn to accept this in time. Go and find Grace and weep.'

After Mother's death, I heard people talk about her in the crowded stairwells and meeting places of St Germain. The gossips said she should have cured herself, if she knew so much about healing, but her close companions, the women she worked with every day caring for the young prince, wept bitterly and blamed themselves for not urging her to see the physician. But I think Mother knew that her heart was going to let her down and that is why she told no one. Being my mother, she would have understood that nothing more could be done.

In the long nights before the funeral I clung to Lucy and begged her not to leave me. I went with her to stand by our mother's body in her resting place, a freezing basement barely lit by candles. In our room, we wept and talked until dawn, reminding each other of tiny details from our shared childhood at Powis Castle before Mother was imprisoned. During the day, when Lucy worked for our mother's replacement, the Countess of Errol, I was excused duties and Grace stayed with me. We walked the miles of garden and forest that surrounded the chateau, the sterile formality of the gardens and dank, decaying, winter forest echoing my emptiness. I felt no sadness, only anger. I had been cheated of the mother I thought would stand by me and help me bear and raise my own children. I had expected to have years of her wisdom and now there was nothing except my memories and a few scribbled notes.

At the entrance to the chapel were two paintings I had passed many times, barely glancing at them but on the day of Mother's funeral, an ochre light fell across Goliath's head hanging by the hair from David's hand. Flooded by memories of my childish nightmares of Mother's execution, I gasped and wanted to run but Lucy, sensing my anguish, gripped my hand in hers and led me to my seat.

Despite storms in the channel, my sister Mary had managed to reach St Germain in time for the funeral and she stood beside my father at the high altar, supporting him by his elbow. I hadn't seen him since the day he told us our mother had died. He looked now as then, grey and shrunken. As ever, the chapel was dark since it was winter and little natural light filtered down from the high windows. Above Mother's coffin was a painting of the Last Supper, with Jesus leaning towards St. Peter as if they were sharing a secret. I stared at the painting, trying to focus on the detail but I couldn't still my thoughts and sweat and fear ripped through me. As the mass mumbled around me and sacred music from the choir roared and faded, I could think only of Mother's head rolling from the executioner's platform on Tower Green.

Following my family back down the aisle, I looked up to the gilded balustrade of the tribune and saw the queen, Mary Beatrice, leaning against the Duchess of Tyrconnel. Without my mother, how would she keep her baby safe from harm?

After the funeral, I ran from the demons in my dreams and through the day I walked for miles with Grace, my head down, my pace fierce, to keep the panic from twisting my heart, my breathing, my hands. It felt as if there was a hole in my chest where the cold winds of January and February had free passage.

Lucy and I ate with Father, in private, once a week. He chewed his food in silence, staring at Mother's empty place, his bald head seeming too small now for his shoulders. Yet, when I stared down into the busy courtyard during the day, waiting for Grace, I saw him cross and re-cross on the king's business, urgent, erect and still powerful. He had his work and that would save him. Lucy had her faith. What would save me?

Before she died, Mother had remarked on my superficial grasp of our religion and arranged for me to have weekly lessons with Lewis Innes. I enjoyed these as he made no attempt to teach me but allowed me to talk freely, respecting my views as if they were worth serious consideration. He allowed me to be critical of the exiled court and sometimes laughed when I made fun of the ladies who worked with my mother. After Mother died, I found it hard to say any words to Lewis, obsessed as I was with the horrors of death but I went every week and he allowed me to sit in silence and sometimes I was able to cry. It was Lewis who noticed that I wasn't attending chapel.

'Winifred, has your faith entirely abandoned you?'

I shook my head and tried to swallow. What could I say to him about severed heads?

'Do you know there is another chapel in the chateau?'

I shook my head again.

'Would you like me to ask if you can use it?'

I wasn't sure. Faith had not helped me in the past and I saw little use for it in the future. Religion had destroyed my family. But I nodded because a refusal might make him suspect that my faith had indeed gone and I didn't know what would happen if my father was told. I might be sent to the convent with Lucy.

The following week, Lewis took me to part of the chateau I had never visited. Across the staircase from the queen's apartments, he showed me into a small room, almost like a convent cell, but washed in sunlight. It was the queen's private chapel. As long as I avoided certain times of day I could worship there, Lewis said. Queen Mary Beatrice liked to pray alone.

I went out of duty, in case Lewis thought I was ungrateful but then I found some peace in the gentle light and I liked to look at the painting of the Virgin Mary and Jesus that hung over the simple altar. I didn't pray but allowed any terrors that needed to escape to come freely and because I wasn't trying to hold them down, they slowly lost their power. I had been visiting the little chapel for a month when, one day, I stood up to leave and saw the queen at the entrance. The queen's ladies frowned at me and I remembered to curtsy.

'I'm sorry, your majesty, I didn't know you were expected. I will leave at once.'

The queen was heavy with child, and she sat down on a gilt chair that Lewis had warned me was for her personal use.

'Wait, Lady Winifred. We have never spoken but I miss your mother every single day and my son has been so distressed.'

'Thank you,' I replied, unsure how to address her. 'I miss her every day too. My family has suffered a great loss.'

The queen nodded as if I had said something important. 'We have all suffered a great loss. You must come and see me. Speak to the Countess of Almond and arrange it. Come soon, this week if you can.'

It troubled me, the prospect of being in the company of the queen. She might expect me to have my mother's skills and would be disappointed. However, I soon learned that she was looking for companionship. Although she was fourteen years older than me, she was still young and beautiful and the women of her household were matrons and well past child-bearing age. The queen's invitation to become one of her household gave me work and I started to heal. The other women feared favouritism and I found myself allocated the most menial of tasks such as writing letters but Mary Beatrice sought me out every day to walk with her in the formal gardens. We would sit by the fountains and trail our fingers in the water and I would listen and laugh while Mary Beatrice talked. It would have been ill advised to raise topics or talk about myself.

'I'm not worried about having this baby, Winifred. Your mother taught me so much.' Her eyes were clear and untroubled.

'What did you learn, your majesty?'

'Your mother said all that was needed was milk from a woman's breast and everything being clean. That's all. If this baby suffers like poor little James, I won't listen to learned men. Your mother said to keep feeding the baby, no matter how often it might vomit and the sickness will pass. I've arranged to have many wet nurses, so even if this baby is sickly too, we will save him.'

Since Mary Beatrice had the same body as other women, I wondered why she didn't consider that she could feed the baby herself but I would not have dared express such an opinion.

'You are lucky,' the queen continued, 'when you have a baby, you will deliver it in peace and privacy with only a woman present. Do you know that I must give birth in the presence of the court so the legitimacy of the baby is not in doubt?'

The shock of imagining her being exposed during such an intimate act must have shown on my face. Mary Beatrice smiled. 'I can see you are horrified and you haven't yet borne a child. When you have, think of me and your sympathy will be all the greater.' She laughed, her head thrown back, and stood so that we might continue down the central boulevard to the large fountain at the end of the garden.

'Enough of babies,' she linked her arm with mine, 'I have some exciting news. The French court is to visit here in two weeks, so you must help me plan the entertainments. You have been in mourning long enough. It's time to have some fun.' It was characteristic of Mary Beatrice to promise too much and I knew that jealousies would not allow me to be involved in any planning, but we walked on, talking about the music and dancing, both of us pretending that it would be otherwise.

I only had a brief glimpse of the Sun King and his wife Madame de Maintenon at the moment of their dramatic arrival through the arched gateway. Like the other ordinary residents of St Germain, Lucy and I had been told to stay in our room since the courtyard was narrow and this was a private visit between the two royal families. We stood at either side of the window and, looking down, saw only the gold top of the Sun King's coach below us in the courtyard. It was smaller than I had expected with one coachman and two white horses. Louis' face was hidden beneath his wide-brimmed hat, which was fringed with feathers, and he wore a long wig that curled over his shoulders. He strode across the courtyard towards our queen and took both her hands in his. Madame de Maintenon was helped from the carriage by one of her ladies and for a moment she steadied herself, looking up at our watching faces. A black hood fell from her hair and draped across shoulders covered by a deep blue cloak, lined with white fur. I almost waved.

'He's never admitted openly that they're married,' Lucy told me, as we saw her pale face scan the ranks of windows. 'That's why she's not the queen.'

'But that's awful. If she's his wife, she should be recognised.'

Lucy hesitated. 'It's something to do with the difference in rank. I think she understands and has to accept it. Everyone says he adores her.'

We watched James hurry across to bow to Madame de Maintenon and kiss her ring. I wouldn't accept it, I thought, regardless of how much I was adored. Our royal household lined the path towards the staircase for the king's apartments and as the two royal couples passed, the group sank low in greeting like a wave. I saw our father amongst them, standing a little too close to an elegant woman I hadn't met. Now other coaches swung into the courtyard and one by one deposited the household of the French royal family, their servants and luggage.

'Have you noticed all the young men, Lucy? Things are going to be very different here, just for a few days.'

Lucy smiled. 'For some, perhaps.'

I was of too low rank to participate in any of the activities shared by the two royal families but every night there were dances to which I was invited and beautiful young Frenchmen jostled each other to dance with me. Their manners were exquisite, yet their conversation was peppered with sexual innuendo and each night I ran up our stairway to Lucy, my cheeks flushed with more than the exertion of the dance. Lucy no longer had any interest in dancing, being in the process of withdrawing from society to prepare for her entrance to holy orders but in the day she joined me for more respectable and sedate entertainments.

Mary Beatrice's master of music, Mr Fede, had composed new works in the Italian style and the theatre company presented a ballet by Lully. I sat through these in the pretence of improving my education but really I was hoping to catch the eye of one of the young courtiers, so that we might walk in the gardens and flirt before the evening entertainment.

The departure of the French court made our daily lives even more mundane, especially as we had to make savings to compensate for the money we'd spent on hosting the royal family. Meals were sparse and entertainment was of the most basic, home-grown kind, all too familiar from the tedious

Jacobite gatherings held in my sister's home. Mary Beatrice withdrew into her confinement and didn't ask me to stay with her, preferring those who had experience of childbirth.

Something else was happening. Our king had disappeared along with the French court and I heard muttering in corners and men stopped talking and stroked their chins if I came too close. My father walked so fast across the courtyard, his legs seemed to be clockwork, but other important men were rarely to be seen, apart from the Earl of Melfort. Soon we learned that there had been a failed attempt to invade England, resulting in the destruction of the French fleet. Nothing was announced or openly discussed, since maintaining a belief that James would be restored to the crown of England was the whole purpose of our existence. But my father, in a careless moment at dinner, revealed that Louis XIV felt he had been misled by false information from St Germain. This was the whispered shame of the exiled court.

One morning, a servant knocked on my door, summoning me to the Earl of Melfort and my stomach felt as if it had turned to liquid. I was escorted to the Earl's quarters and the manservant waited, clearly under instructions to guard me. The door to Melfort's room was opened from within by yet another servant and inside was dark and hung with tapestries of Old Testament stories. It smelled of that particular animal odour of sweat and food that hangs around men who are not particular about their grooming. Melfort sat at a table, reading a letter. He did not look up or indicate that I should sit. I stood before him, studying his small mouth, pursed as if he had eaten something sour.

'This letter is for you.' He tossed it across the table as if it were soiled. 'You may read it.'

It was my brother's handwriting. William began by

expressing his sorrow and regret at the death of our mother but I read on with dismay.

'Your king is about to invade England. He has deluded himself into believing that many will rise to support him but being the fool he is, he has announced his intentions in advance and has issued a proclamation to the people of this country which has only served to rally support around William of Orange. If the invasion goes ahead it will fail. Be warned, my little sister. Your loving brother.'

I felt my skin flush. William's words rang with the disgrace of having been read first by the man in front of me. These words, which would be regarded here as treason, had come from my brother and I would be included in his treachery.

'I am sorry,' I whispered. 'I knew nothing of an invasion. My brother has views that my sister and I do not share. I am loyal to King James II and the Jacobite cause.' I looked down at my hands, hoping that Melfort had forgotten my outburst from the previous year.

The Earl's words were measured. 'Everything that is received here and sent from here is scrutinised by me. I know every movement, every thought, every single breath that you people make. There are spies here from the English government, the French government, the Spanish government and Rome. Sometimes I think that every fucking soul within this chateau is a spy.' He spat the word at me. 'Are you a spy, Lady Winifred Herbert, because if you are, not even your father will be able to save you. People disappear from this chateau with puzzling frequency. They are no loss. A girl like you would not be missed. Do I make myself clear?'

Tears coursed down my face. 'I am not a spy. You can trust me,' I whispered, my voice hoarse, my throat tight.

'Do you have any idea,' Melfort's voice rose, 'what might happen if letters like this got into the hands of a French spy and thence to the French government? We must maintain French support. I saw you dancing with those young fools from the French court. What would you not have done to gain their favour? Would you have passed this letter to one of them if he had asked you for it?' Melfort stared at me with contempt. 'Is your brother in the pay of the French?'

I shook my head. 'He was a prisoner in the Tower of London and he's lost his title and our estates. He's bitter but means no harm. He is an angry man, nothing more.'

Melfort placed his hands together into a steeple and rested them against his lips. He looked at me from under his brows. 'It is lucky for you,' he said, 'that you have become something of a favourite of the queen. I question her judgement. Don't forget, I am watching you. Always.'

A different servant escorted me to my staircase. My limbs were weak and carried me with difficulty up the three flights of stairs. Alone in my room I lifted my gown and stripped away my petticoats. Like a child, I had wet myself.

After my terrifying meeting with Melfort, I hurried to see my father.

'Elizabeth, you must write to William,' he advised, 'and ask him never to contact you again.'

'Father, I'm Winifred not Elizabeth. Mother's name was Elizabeth.'

He peered at me. 'Ah yes, you're so alike. Nevertheless, write the letter and I'll show it to Melfort. It will be proof of your loyalty.'

I imagined William's reaction to reading such cruel words

and said, 'I don't wish to write to him like that. I came to you to seek your protection.'

'I can't protect you,' my father touched some papers on his desk and I saw his eyes glance eagerly over what was written there. 'I'm often away with the king or caught up in his affairs. If you write to William as I've said and stay in favour with the queen, you'll be safe.'

CHAPTER 7

Lucy now spent every day in silent prayer in the queen's private chapel, a privilege arranged for her by Lewis Innes, and ate her meals alone in our room. On the nights leading to Lucy's departure, Grace began to pack her things and I often found a dress or piece of jewellery left in my closet, of no further use to her. At night, in our shared bed, I argued and pleaded with Lucy not to leave us. France was at war with practically everyone and, apart from my own need to cling to her, I worried for her safety.

'I'll miss you, Winifred, of course I will,' Lucy whispered into the icy dark, 'but you have to understand that my life at St Germain is empty of purpose. I must leave soon, under cover of winter darkness.'

'But you are my only family here. Father doesn't care about me or he would have intervened with the Earl of Melfort.'

Lucy turned towards me and I felt her warm breath. 'Thank goodness he's disappeared. I would have worried about leaving you if he was still here.'

'What do you think happened to him?' I asked.

'Lewis hinted that Melfort treated powerful people just like he treated us. While he watched over St Germain, others were watching him and in the end his enemies outnumbered his friends.'

When the evening of our parting came, I shivered alongside Lucy's carriage, my cloak wrapped tightly against a wind that whipped around the corners of the courtyard. There was nothing more to be said and I was keen to get the farewell over and return to the warmth of my room. Father gave no indication of wishing to linger either and I guessed that he wanted to return to his wine and court accounts.

As Lucy climbed into her seat and turned to wave farewell, I thought of the night she left for France with our mother and remembered that I had something belonging to her in my room...something special. I called up to the coachman and the horses startled, tossing their heads and shaking their harnesses. He calmed them with some soothing words before giving me his attention. 'Yes, my lady?'

'Please wait, I've left something in my room that I need to give Lady Lucy.' He gave a grunt of assent but I heard Father 'tut' as I hurried past him towards our staircase. Searching at the back of my closet I found Lucy's doll, hidden there because I had been too ashamed to admit that I'd brought her from England.

Lucy looked surprised but took the doll from me, turning over the threadbare toy in her hands.

'Goodness, it's Elizabeth. Where on earth did you find this?'

'I took her from your room at home, after the fire. I've had her with me all this time.'

Lucy kissed the doll and passed her back to me. 'Keep her with you, my dearest sister, and remember how much I love you. I have no use for toys but one day you might have a child who will play with her and you can talk about me and the games we played.'

My father left as soon as the carriage door closed but I remained standing until the back of the coach disappeared through the archway, pressing Lucy's singed doll against my cheek to catch the tears.

Within a week, we heard from the coachman that Lucy had arrived safely but I knew that war would make further contact between us difficult. With Lucy gone, I had no further meetings with my father. Apart from Grace, I was alone.

As soon as Princess Louise-Marie was born in June and was seen to be healthy and thriving, the queen sent for me and I was allowed to hold the exquisite, sweetly perfumed baby girl. I had never before held a baby. I cradled her in the crook of my arm and she instinctively turned to my breast. I touched her cheek with my finger and her skin felt like the smooth surface of a field mushroom on a summer's day. I knew for certain that I wanted one of my own but I was only twenty and there was plenty of time. I wrote to Lucy to tell her of the birth and months later received a reply. Her description of the convent's ordered routine of contemplation meant little to me and I saw that Lucy and I, so close as children, now travelled paths that very soon neither of us could share.

When the queen recovered from the birth, I was formally appointed as one of the Ladies of the Bedchamber. This caused some resentment amongst the older women, those who hoped their daughters, left behind in England or Scotland might join them in the queen's household. I found Mary Beatrice's court to be a world within a world, one quite unlike the rest of St Germain. The queen was intelligent and politically astute. Her opinion was valued by powerful men and she smoothed the path between her husband and those who despaired of him. Best of all, she shared some of this with us, relying on our discretion or perhaps our indiscretion, ensuring that husbands heard only what she chose. She was skilled at making other people love her, while remaining the centre of attention. She flirted with men yet remained friends with their wives. She was deeply religious but moved with a grace charged with sexual energy.

The queen took me with her to Marly, Versailles and Fontainebleau when she visited the French royal family. More often now she went without her husband, as it was rumoured that relations were strained between James and Louis, but Mary Beatrice's influence with Louis kept us securely in France. She enjoyed the strict French protocol which gave her precedence even above Louis' wife, as there was no French queen and, without James, she was able to command all of his attention.

CHAPTER 8

I t is hot for early summer and I am tired of standing. Ladies of higher rank are allowed to sit on stools while Mary Beatrice, the French king and Madame de Maintenon have chairs. Our fans, so often used to beckon or tease are frantically worked for their original purpose but they only rearrange the stifling smell of powder and sweat. Mary Beatrice and Louis are flirting and I wonder when the interminable game being played out in front of us will end, so that we can go outside and play some real games. I rock on my toes, as I have been taught, to ease the pain in my back.

Mary Beatrice has brought us here to Marly to build bridges with Louis as yet another attempt to invade England has failed and James is in disgrace again. I have never spoken to her about her relationship with Louis or with James. To raise such a personal matter would cost me my position. But I have eyes and ears and I know there are times when Mary Beatrice and Louis are alone together. I watch Madame de Maintenon but she shows nothing beyond her perfectly mannered façade. The sunlight etches the lines around her eyes and the fine down on her cheeks and I wonder what she must feel watching her husband court a younger woman. I hope this never happens to me.

I shift again from foot to foot. My bodice is itching. Tonight there is to be a ball and Grace is laying out my gown and petticoats. She will be placing my combs and ribbons on my dressing table and choosing a scent for my bath. There will be wine and candied fruits on the table by my bed. I will let Grace peel my damp clothes from me and I will lie down, quite naked and feel the cool breeze drift across my skin from the open window.

I lower my fan so that I can wipe away the moisture from between my breasts. My eyes scan the room in case this breach of etiquette is noticed. It has been, but not by one of the Ladies of the Bedchamber. A young man from the French court, like me not expected to move or take his gaze away from the royals, has glanced at me and his lips twitch at the corners. I lower my eyes and flick my fan at him. In the language of courtship, this means I have seen him and the answer is, '*I am willing to meet you alone.*'

As we prepared for the ball, I asked Grace to lace my bodice tightly so that my breasts were pushed high. Without being asked, she left my hair in its natural state and pinned it so that strands fell across my shoulders. During dinner I was gracious and attentive to those who sat near me, asking them about their lives and interests even if these were few. He sat at the end of my table, his role to entertain an elderly duchess, and he never failed in his dazzling attention to her charms. His mannered flirtation made her flush and giggle, like a young girl. But when she shifted to speak to the man on her left he looked for me and I had to turn away in case the anticipation in my smile confused the men around me.

When we danced the Rigaudon, our backs brushed against each other as we spun around our partners and once, his hand stroked mine. Like most of the younger French men, he no longer wore a wig but his long hair was swept back and tied with a loose, velvet bow. His legs were solid in their breeches and the cut of his coat, longer than was the fashion at St Germain, showed off his firm stomach.

It is almost dark but the air is warm and still. The garden is lit with flares that create secret corners and draw long shadows across the grass. The evening's entertainment continues with fire eaters who juggle blazing batons and fireworks crackle into the sky. Servants row couples around the lake in boats that are decorated like the French fleet. The lamps on the prows could be fireflies from this distance, darting and crossing in front of my eyes. We had eaten dinner outdoors, in an arbour draped with ropes strung with spring flowers, but the tables are abandoned now apart from those guests too drunk to stand and those who sleep where they sat. The white tablecloths shine in the moonlight but I can see the stains of spilt food and wine from where I wait. The ground around the tables is littered with linen napkins and broken glass. Cats snake amongst the folds of the tablecloths searching for scraps and are chased away by servants who flit amongst the shadows. The royal party has now disappeared inside to watch the fireworks from a balcony and I am alone. I wait for him, leaning against one of the posts of the arbour.

Couples drift across the grass and into the shadows. I lift one of the loose tendrils from my hair and stroke it across my lips, my eyes straining through the dusk to see my lover. At last, I watch him cross the grass, my pleasure growing as he hurries through the mingling guests, talking briefly to those he knows, while his eyes continue to search for me.

Finally we meet and he lifts my hand to a brief touch of his lips. We link arms and stroll down to the lake, watching the colours explode above us, then slip into the woods under cover of heavy darkness. We stop at a wide tree just off the path and I lean into its rough bark as he kisses my lips, my hair, my earlobes. His skin smells of almonds. We breath into each other's necks, panting like dogs and my pleasure rises with his until he pauses and shudders. He bends his head into my shoulder and swears in French. We kiss again, listening to the applause of the crowd as the fireworks reach their finale, then fumble with our clothes. As the crowds ebb away from the lakeside, we leave the shadows and cross the grass with other couples, our arms linked in acceptable informality. We reach the entrance to the chateau where we have to part and he takes my hand again, kisses it and bows low before he turns away. I don't know his name and he hasn't asked for mine.

The royal party left Marly the next day. Mary Beatrice asked me to ride with her in her carriage and, sitting opposite her, I knew that although her unfocused gaze travelled across the villages and farms, she was not watching the scenery. Like me, she was reliving a private moment. She watched me too and must have seen the same secret smile flicker across my lips.

'He was handsome was he not, Lady Winifred?'

'He was indeed your majesty.'

'And you were careful?'

I had learned everything I knew about sex and how to avoid babies from the queen. She had delighted in my lack of experience and enjoyed playing at being an older sister, whispering amazing secrets to me, some of which she had learned from my mother.

I tilted my head in deference to her concern. 'I was careful, just as you advised, your majesty.'

Mary Beatrice was pleased with this. 'You must enjoy yourself, Winifred. This time will never come again. Too soon you will be like me, with a husband and babies. I take you with me so that you can be free, away from the busybodies of St Germain.'

This was true. My mother's friends took too great an interest in me, inviting me to evenings in their apartments and worrying about my lack of a husband. Even if a suitable man could be found, I wouldn't risk an informal liaison at St Germain, but on these trips with the queen, as long as I was discreet, I was free to do as I pleased.

I bowed my head. 'I am grateful, your majesty.' I looked at her for longer than was perhaps acceptable, wishing to ask her the same question she had asked me.

Mary Beatrice returned my stare with her cool grey eyes, her fine brows arched in amusement. 'If a king wants to have a woman, the woman must respond. The king is directed by God. She is simply following God's will.'

'And if the woman is married?'

'Her husband must agree, since he too must follow God's will. Wise husbands know that they will benefit from such a liaison.'

We smiled at each other. We had reached an understanding. It was never spoken of again.

My father was injured in a riding accident in June and it was rumoured that, at seventy, he had been trying to impress an unknown woman with his horsemanship. But during his final weeks, no woman came forward to offer comfort or regrets. Dutifully, I sat by his bed whenever I could be spared by Mary Beatrice but was always glad to hurry back to her warm apartments, scented by fresh flowers, rather than delay in the rank odour of a broken old man. In his few wakeful moments, my father seemed to recognise me and although much of what he muttered made little sense, there was a moment when he clutched my hand and begged my forgiveness, whispering that he must change his will to leave me some money.

Since it seemed without any doubt that my father was dying, I had already spoken with Grace about our precarious situation at St Germain after his death. If we had to leave and were given some choice about our future, I hoped we might be welcome to live with my brother, since he was settled and had a wife and young children. But I knew that he would not look kindly on me if it seemed that in my father's last moments, I had persuaded him to change his will. Father had always been clear that my brother would inherit everything after his death and, as head of the family, would be responsible for his sisters. So I spoke to the priest who visited my father and instructed him that Lord Powis must not be allowed to change his will, no matter how much he pleaded.

Father's funeral was a more formal state occasion than my mother's and the king, along with many of the more important men at St Germain, were present. Crushed between my sisters Mary and Anne, in my hot, tight mourning dress, I listened to the eulogy for this man I hardly knew and struggled to find some feelings of loss. My greatest concern was for myself and my status at St Germain. I knew there were women in the queen's household who would question whether I should be allowed to remain and that they would waste no chance to remind Mary and Anne about my unorthodox position, without income or family.

My sisters were housed in my parents' apartment and in the days following the funeral, I helped them clear away all trace of our father. I listened to them reminisce, reminding each other of summer days at Powis when he taught them to ride and how he had terrified them at bedtime by pretending to be a bear. I watched their grief and helped wipe away their tears but the father they spoke of had not been mine. If I had hoped that we might be reconciled, any prospect was shattered when my father's will was read. He had left nothing to his daughters except me, and I had been given the last piece of my mother's jewellery. My sisters could not hide their disappointment at this unexpected favouritism and I guessed that my future at St Germain was lost. My sisters would expect the queen to release me and I would return to Anne's household.

Before their departure my sisters were invited to meet the queen to discuss my future but when Mary Beatrice insisted that I be present, I dared to hope that my fears might not be true.

'Your majesty,' my eldest sister Mary said, 'we have agreed that Winifred should return to the household of Lord and Lady Carrington in London, where we might find her a husband.'

Mary Beatrice shook her head and spoke with her usual candour. 'Not at all. Winifred must stay here. I need her to look after my children and it is essential that she supports me in my meetings with the French. You taught her well, Lady Carrington,' Mary Beatrice acknowledged Anne with a tilt of her head. 'Winifred is a fluent French speaker.'

Anne flushed with pleasure and my sisters glanced at each other in unspoken agreement. 'If that is the situation, your majesty, then of course she will remain here.'

'And as for a husband,' the queen continued, 'leave that to me.'

I felt my cheeks burn with relief and gratitude; I could remain at St Germain-en-Laye, under the protection of the queen. I would be entirely dependent upon her favour and generosity and I knew how unreliable she could be, but for now my position was secure.

That night in my room, now empty of any remnant of Lucy, Grace helped me out of my robes and into my shift and we sat on the edge of my wide bed. I slipped my arm around her and told her that for now, we could stay at St Germain.

Grace rested her head on my shoulder. 'I'm pleased for you, Win. Your sisters are considerate but I remember how unhappy you were living with Anne and perhaps there wouldn't have been a place for me.'

'I think they were relieved. My father's last act, thoughtless as ever, only deepened the rift between us and perhaps neither of us would have been welcome. Mary and Anne were seventeen and eighteen when he was imprisoned but I was only six. He barely knew me. Listening to them talk reminded me of what I lost when he was taken to the Tower.'

'Win, you're the youngest of six and I'm the eldest of four. We had a different childhood from our brothers and sisters. When I went home, I didn't recognise the life they had after I'd gone. A life I helped to pay for.'

'What do you mean?'

'A condition of your mother taking me into service was that there would be no more children.'

This shocked me. 'That was too much of her to ask, surely.'

Grace laughed. 'She gave my mother advice on how to prevent more children and your father passed mine work. I think my family were one of your mother's projects.'

'I knew nothing about this. It feels like my mother took charge of your lives. What right did she have?'

'But it worked. My mother and father were only fifteen and sixteen when I was born and without your parents what did the future hold for them? Instead they grew in prosperity and earned enough to build their own house and send my sisters and brother to school. Now they can do the same for my sister's child.'

'But you learned to read and write, Grace, how did that happen?'

'Cook taught me and you left your books lying around, so I read those while I was supposed to be tidying your room.'

'I didn't know Cook was able read and write.'

Grace pulled away from me and looked into my eyes. 'Win! How could she have run the kitchens and dealt with tradesmen without being able to write and do accounts?'

I felt ashamed that I had cared so little about people who had once filled every day of my life. 'So what was it like when you went home?'

'It was hard. I remembered the poverty we'd lived through but my parents didn't like me to talk about it and I envied the younger ones. I never felt that I belonged.'

'That's it, Grace. That's exactly how I've always felt. I didn't belong. There was a family once but different from the one I knew, a family that I had been tacked onto. But I was lucky to have my sister Lucy and you, of course.'

'We had each other, Win, that's what matters.'

CHAPTER 9

G race watched the courtyard below as I finished dressing my hair. Her voice was listless. 'A carriage has just pulled in. It must be the young earl from Scotland. I can't quite remember his name.'

I studied my face in the glass, wiping powder from the corners of my mouth with the tip of my finger and turning my head from side to side to examine my profile. I smoothed the skin under my chin. 'Grace, do you think I'm getting thick around the neck?'

'I remember now,' Grace continued. 'It's William Maxwell, Earl of Nithsdale. He's from a very old Scottish family, or so the gossip goes. He's here to pay his respects to our king.' The news that Louis XIV had recognised William of Orange as the King of England and Scotland had shocked our isolated community and visitors loyal to our cause had become rare.

I joined Grace at the window and we looked down on the head of a young man, supervising his servants as they lifted boxes from the carriage. He wiped his face with a handkerchief and sensing that he was being watched, looked up at my window. We jerked back, covering our faces with the drapes and laughing until we fell on the bed hiccupping and choking like schoolgirls.

In the afternoon, I joined the queen for her walk around the grounds. The other members of her household maintained a discreet distance, knowing Mary Beatrice liked to talk to me in private. Princess Louise Marie skipped ahead of us, followed by at least six of her servants who hovered in case she fell over, drowned in the fountains or suffered any other unimaginable accident.

'The young man, Nithsdale, who joined us today, he is yours.'

I was used to the queen's assumptions but this was more blunt than usual. 'What do you mean, your majesty?'

'He isn't married and he's looking for a Catholic wife. I believe he has a good estate in Scotland. If you want him, he's yours.'

'I appreciate your majesty's concern but how do you know he isn't betrothed to an heiress at home?'

Mary Beatrice's eyes narrowed. 'I have made enquiries on your behalf. You are almost twenty-seven. When I was your age I had been married for twelve years.'

My age and unmarried state seemed to have become a general topic of conversation amongst the women and not always well meant. I didn't welcome their prying but the pleasures of being a single, unchaperoned woman were fading and I worried in private that I might never have the chance to be married. It might be a relief to no longer rely on the arbitrary favours of the queen or the support of my mother's few remaining elderly friends.

The queen interrupted my thoughts. 'Tonight at the ball, I will introduce you to William Maxwell. You have had much practice with young men, so you know how to capture his heart.

But, Winifred,' she stared at me with her cool grey eyes, 'remember that this one is for marriage.'

The moment I saw William, I knew she was right. He was mine. The queen escorted him across the room, his hand held high in hers and when she reached me she took my hand and joined it to his, saying, 'And now you two will dance.' She turned from us, cutting a swathe through the guests. He lifted my hand and kissed it. I noticed amused, brown eyes and a full face like a spaniel puppy. Best of all, he was taller than me.

He held out his arm to lead me into the dancing, 'Lady Winifred Herbert, I am honoured to make your acquaintance.' His generous smile contradicted the formality of his tone. I caught his irony and took his arm, covering my grinning mouth with my fan and inclined my head in a small bow. 'The pleasure is mine, Lord Nithsdale.'

The queen's advice had been clear and she was right. This felt different. As we turned and spun in giddying spirals, the dance reached its climax. There will be no fumbling in stairwells or lying on my back in the grass under the stars, I thought. Here is the man I will marry.

We sought no other partners, reluctantly releasing hands as etiquette demanded. When we grew breathless, we walked onto the terrace. It was early spring and still cold. I leaned against him for warmth and he placed his coat across my shoulders. We stood side by side, facing the gardens, our elbows resting on the stone balustrade and talked as if there was no end to words.

'I am told you are on your own, Lady Winifred.'

'My parents were here but my father died trying to impress some ladies of the court who hunt. He took a jump that was too difficult for him. My mother died just after I arrived, so he'd been alone for five years. I think he must have been planning to take another wife, despite his age. I hardly knew him as a child and we did not meet a great deal here, so my grief was short-lived I'm afraid.'

'I hardly knew my father either, since he died when I was a small child. You must be lonely here, without your family.'

'I have Grace Evans, my companion and lady's maid. She's been with my family for as long as I can remember. We're the same age. I'm also lucky to have special attention from the queen.'

'I heard you were a favourite. What about the rest of your family?'

'We lost our title and estates after my parents fled to France with the king and queen. My brother, who shares your name, married four years ago. I was estranged from him as people here feared he was a traitor but we have tried to be reconciled since my father died.'

'Has the reconciliation been successful?'

'In part – we do communicate but it's hard to stay close to family when the whole world seems to be at war and we are so isolated here. I have a sister, Lucy, who is in a convent in Bruges and two older sisters in London. My eldest sister Frances lives in Scotland. We write to each other, more so now our parents are dead, but still not often.'

He looked at me and frowned. 'So you wouldn't want to leave?'

I appeared to give the question thoughtful consideration, rather than betray that I had already decided to leave St Germain and with him. 'I'm ready to go. Eight years is a long time and the queen needs me less. Tell me about your family and your home?'

I just wanted to hear him talk. His accent was different from the other Scots at St Germain; gentler, yet more precise. He had a way of moving his hands to make a point, turning his palms out then bringing his fingers together at the tips. His hands had never seen physical work, yet they were large and the fingers blunt. William told me that he had inherited the title from his father and he and his sister had been brought up by their widowed mother at Terregles House in Dumfries. His mother still lived there but his sister had married Charles Stewart, the 4th Earl of Traquair. How exotic these names sounded. My imagination was already spinning a Scotland of sophistication, beauty and wealth, quite different from the tales recounted by my sisters of painted clansmen, no better than savages but useful in a fight.

William saw me watching him and stopped talking. He looked at me for longer than was comfortable, then leaned forward and kissed me lightly on the lips. 'I think we'd better go inside or people might notice how long we've been gone. But there is one thing I need to tell you. You are very beautiful.'

When William was not with the young men at court, hunting or fencing, he was with me. The queen excused me from most of my duties provided I attended her evening toilette so that she could hear every detail of the courtship. I resented this because my bond with William felt private but I depended on her to protect me from the gossip at court and I had to trust that she would release me when the time came. So I fed her little bits of information, some true, some exaggerated and others total fabrication. Her eyes glistened with excitement and she would stop her servant's hand and turn from the mirror to face me, so I might repeat a detail that fascinated her.

Every morning I woke to the joy and amazement that William was part of my life and that he seemed not to tire of me. Despite our freedom from family, our courtship continued to be chaste and decorous, although we were able to exchange small kisses and hold hands when we walked, without a chaperone, through the forests around the chateau. Just as the trees were beginning to flower, we walked down to the River Seine through the terraces of the hanging gardens. It had been raining and the earth smelled of fungus and decay. Rain dripped from the bare branches_of the trees and I trembled as a remnant of old fears touched the back of my neck. What if I lost William too?

William stopped walking and turned to face me. 'Are you unwell, Winifred? Do you want to go back?'

I felt the heat and prickle of tears at the corner of my eyes. 'These terraces remind me of the garden at Powis Castle. I miss my mother sometimes. Grace and I used to walk here after she died. It was just a bad memory, that's all.' But I began to shiver and William pulled my cloak tight around me and bent to kiss me with the unmistakable passion of a lover. I heard the song of birds through the long, searching kiss and felt a familiar ache. It was time.

I had never taken a man to my room at St Germain and my brief conquests at Marly or Fontainebleau had been furtive and secretive. It was believed that Jacobite support in England could be undermined if our court gained a reputation for failing to uphold Catholic teaching on moral behaviour. I was closely watched by the women of the exiled community; my mother's friends too interested in my well-being alongside resentment and jealousy from those who had not known my parents and envied my position.

We parted in the woods, planning that William would follow me half an hour later. If anyone saw him using my staircase, there were respectable reasons why he might be visiting a resident on the third floor. As I crossed the courtyard, Lady Strickland waved to me and I hurried over to speak to her. She peered at me with small grey eyes, made more piercing by a generous use of face powder.

'My dear, how are you? It must be so difficult for you without your mother and father.' She clutched my arm.

I glanced towards the entrance to my staircase. 'I'm well, thank you.'

'Ah well, they miss you in the nursery – and your mother of course.'

I made myself look straight into her eyes. 'I'm lucky to have the love of William Maxwell and the companionship of Grace Evans.'

Lady Strickland leaned towards me, as if to share a confidence. 'There has been some talk about you walking out with him without a chaperone,' she whispered. 'I can arrange someone for you.'

'Oh, I'm sure Grace can do that, but thank you for warning me.' I tried to release my arm from her grip.

'No, no my dear, she's too close to the situation.' Lady Strickland patted my arm and let me go. 'I'll arrange it for you. Come to my rooms tomorrow, I can see you're in a hurry.'

'Yes indeed, some business for the queen!'

I felt her eyes on my back as I crossed the courtyard and was relieved to reach the staircase without William having made an incriminating appearance. There was already a fire in the hearth, so my room was warm and I lit one candle, placing it on the table by the bed. In a fumbling panic I stripped to my stays, checking myself for unpleasant smells and cursed Grace, for there was no scented water. I put my dress back on, as well as I could without help, changed my mind, pulled it off and unpinned my hair. I slipped into the bed, shivering between the ice-cold sheets and spread my hair across the pillow. I couldn't find a place to arrange my arms and got out of the bed to put more logs on the fire. I checked myself again for odours and waited for him on the edge of the bed. I felt too naked, so took my chemise from the cupboard and wrapped it around me, then moved the candle to a table under the window. I had chosen to sit by the fire when William tapped at the door.

I closed the door behind him and we kissed again. William slid his hands inside my chemise and pulled me close. My skin tingled as he ran his hands across my back. He pulled away and looked at my body, lifting the chemise away from my shoulders and letting it fall to the floor. Without taking his eyes from mine, he removed all of his clothes. I felt the full length of his warm body against me as we kissed again. Without a break in the kiss, we were on the bed and I was lost inside our love.

When I woke, the candle had burned low, the flame spitting and guttering. Wax had flowed and spread across the table. It was dark and I could see a single star through my small window. William was still beside me, making noises in his sleep like whistling sighs. My eyes adjusted to the dim light and I lay down again, my face next to his, so that I could trace his full lips with my finger. I stroked his cropped hair and round head with my hands. He stirred and rolled onto his back as slowly, gently, I woke him with my touch.

Two weeks later, when my bleeding failed to come, I spoke to the queen.

'Your majesty, I think I am with child. I beg for your leave to marry the Earl of Nithsdale as soon as possible.'

The queen's eyes narrowed and her skin flushed but she spoke with a measured formality that was more worrying than her anger. 'You have let me down, Lady Winifred. We had plans for a wedding, one that would have included the French royal family. It would not have gone unnoticed in Jacobite circles in both England and Scotland.'

I knew that relations with Louis remained cool and it was rumoured that our presence in France was becoming an embarrassment but I hadn't realised that she had hoped I would play a small part in changing our fortunes. Mary Beatrice must be desperate if she believed that a wedding would allow her to regain something of her old relationship with Fontainebleau.

'You should have been more careful,' she snapped. 'I showed you how.' My disregard of her advice seemed to annoy her as much as her disappointed plans.

'I am sorry, your majesty. I didn't choose to be careful. I wanted to be with child.'

'So you've trapped him? That might not lead to a successful marriage, Lady Winifred, although I am sure he will do his duty by you.'

'I am sure of him in every respect. It's true that he did not expect a child but he is pleased. We would have married regardless but perhaps not so soon. It suits me that it has happened now. Your majesty, I am in love with the Earl of Nithsdale and he loves me in return. We want to be in Scotland, together.'

Something dark flickered across Mary Beatrice's face. James was ill, probably dying, and she had not seen Louis for some months. She was used to being loved, not just adored in the abstract as she was by many, but loved physically by men. She was jealous.

'Is he aware that you are four years older than him?'

'Of course he is.' I did not lower my gaze. 'It makes no difference to him or to me. I am my mother's daughter, young and healthy, and likely to remain so for many years.'

Mary Beatrice knew there was nothing more she could do. We both understood that I had to be married within days, so that the birth of the child would be credible within marriage. I spent three days in a convent, where I was expected to repent my sins. Instead I lay in bed until late, already nauseous and listened to the singing of the nuns. I walked in the gardens, excusing myself from any tasks on the grounds of my poor health. The nuns, who had not been told why I was there, saw my pale face and left me alone. At night, in my dark cell, I tossed on my hard straw mattress in a fever of desire for William.

We were married at night in the queen's private chapel, the ceremony attended only by the Duke and Duchess of Perth who knew both our families. Although we were in disgrace, in the flickering candlelight, with William by my side and the familiar words of the nuptial mass spoken by the priest, I felt only joy and a peace that promised to hold me in his love for ever.

CHAPTER 10

W illiam was as excited by the royal court as much as I had tired of it. Without him, I might have been brought down by the uncertainty that clouded those tied to St Germain but being in love made every familiar corner seem fresh and expecting a child renewed my hope for the future, despite my daily sickness. Marriage into a respected Jacobite family, and more importantly a Scottish family, changed the way I was treated and I never tired of the low curtsies to the new Countess of Nithsdale, a title that meant something beyond the closed world of the exiled court.

It felt as if France were as new to me as it was to William and as a married woman I was able to explore Paris, where William ordered several new coats and I some gowns and together we accompanied the royal household to a summer party at Versailles. As my beautiful new clothes began to tighten, I told the household of the forthcoming child and apart from the occasional raised eyebrow, the pregnancy was accepted as a child conceived within marriage.

A letter arrived from my sister Frances:

Dearest Winifred,

I am delighted, as are your other sisters, to learn of your marriage and the expected child. We were naturally disappointed to miss the ceremony and were puzzled by the urgency but whatever your situation, it is not unusual and will be quickly forgotten by those who choose to gossip. I am glad your life at St Germain will now end, as you have been too long without family around you. My husband and I welcome you to a future in Scotland and hope that we will be able to become friends as well as sisters once you have settled at Terregles House.

Your loving sister,

Frances

I had been released from the queen's Bedchamber on my marriage and she remained distant from me but this did not diminish my happiness. Mary Beatrice was preoccupied with James' failing health and there was open talk that Louis XIV might not recognise the young James as king after his father's imminent death but I knew that the queen had the love and companionship of Princess Louise-Marie who, unlike her brother, had grown into a delightful child.

Since I no longer had any royal duties and William was free from responsibility for as long as his family could spare him, the days grew long and warm and we walked and slept and ate and loved, lying together at any hour of the day in our large bed, exploring our perfect young bodies. I had no fears for the baby as the queen had once whispered to me that sex could not harm a child in the womb. William would rest his head on the growing mound of my belly and we would talk about our lives before we met, as if there could ever have been such a time. I wanted to hear every detail of the family I was to join, his mother Lucy and his beloved sister Mary. I understood why William so enjoyed St Germain once I learned of their isolation in the Covenanting stronghold of south west Scotland, where a Catholic family must live quietly and with discretion. An accomplished and fashionable young man like William, generous with money, must have been starved of society. If he thought of going back to Scotland, we never spoke of it.

Early one morning, chilled under the crumpled sheets, I shivered and swung my legs over the edge of the high bed. William lay on his stomach, his face turned away from me and I leant over on my elbow and brushed his back with my lips. Pulling my robe over my naked body, I walked barefoot to the open window and saw a cobweb shimmering with early morning dew. I took a deep breath and smelt the vanilla scent of autumn. We had to leave.

'William!' I shook him but he turned over and rested an arm across his eyes to keep out the light. His breathing returned to the measured tread of sleep. I smoothed the sheets, brushing away crumbs from last night's meal and climbed back in. I was already making lists, my arms folded across my belly. Grace knocked on the door and pushed her way in, carrying a bowl of warm water.

'Oh ...' she startled. 'You're already awake.'

'Grace, we have to leave,' I whispered. 'We'll need to start packing today.' I didn't question that she would want to come too.

'Of course, but why today?'

'It's autumn. I can smell it in the air. We must travel while the weather is fine and be settled in Scotland before the baby's born.'

'But what will the Earl of Nithsdale say? Is he ready to leave?'

'He will see the sense of it.'

William did see the sense of it and we were gone within days. The pall of sadness that hung over the court because of the king's poor health meant that we left without ceremony but we ate with the queen in private on our last night and at the moment of our parting, she traced my cheekbones with one finger. I knew I was forgiven.

We left through the high arch of the courtyard, a train of two carriages and five carts. William had doubled the size of his wardrobe and in Paris had bought books, furniture and other fine goods for the castle at Terregles. I had all my gowns, in the hope that French fashions would not be out of place in Scotland, and all the infant clothes from the royal household, pressed on me by the princess' governess who couldn't bear to see waste. Then there was Grace and her possessions gathered over nine years and William's servants who appeared to share his passion for fine things. While William's enthusiasm for St Germain had exceeded mine, he had no sadness in leaving, but I needed a few moments with Grace to stand together and look up at the high walls and empty windows and remember our arrival and the years that had seen us become women.

Our progress was slow, as I found the jolting and rocking movement of the carriage uncomfortable and we stopped frequently to feed and water the horses. Although I had insisted it was autumn, it was still late August and the heat in the carriage was stifling. I found that I couldn't look out of the windows as focusing my eyes on the bright, shaking landscape made me nauseous. At Calais, we boarded in cramped, dirty inns close to the port as we waited two weeks for a packet with enough space. I became lethargic and quarrelsome, desperate to rest in a place I could call home. We had our first row about money and I blamed William for not finding better accommodation. He insisted he had done his best. We called each other unforgivable names and then he walked out on me and was gone for two days. When William returned we forgave each other but the memory of the words we used and his absence made Calais a hateful place.

The journey to London from Kent was equally torturous

and worse, being recognised as émigrés from St Germain brought silence or even sneering asides from those we met on the way. My health became a concern for William and Grace and, as we approached London, William ordered Grace and most of his servants to make haste to Scotland with all our goods. We travelled on alone into London, to the safety of a trusted household, where I might rest.

A young friend of William's mother, Mrs Mills, was welcoming and kind but I didn't disclose even to her that I had spilled some blood, in case a physician was called and I was kept in London until the birth. I knew enough from my mother and the talk of the women at St Germain that I must lie on my back and take total rest for several days. If that didn't help then the baby was lost. By November I wanted to be in my new home and that meant we should be on our way within two weeks.

At night I lay with William but worried about the discomfort of his weight on my belly and for the first time since our marriage, discouraged his intimacy. During the day I rested on my bed and watched the maids lay fires, change the flowers and empty my pisspot, while listening to their chatter in an accent now unfamiliar to me. When they left me alone, I heard noise drift up from the street, the roll of carriages on the uneven ground, the yelps of children smacked by their mothers and snatches of conversation from the street below the window.

Once I was sure the pregnancy was secure I dressed and sewed baby clothes by the fire in the drawing room. William went out almost every day, saying that he was conducting estate business but I heard that he also met friends in the coffee houses and inns. I missed him but I had married a young man, barely out of his youth, and I wanted him to stay in love with me. I could not put strictures around my husband when I had indulged all my senses in France with complete freedom.

When Mrs Mills considered I was strong enough to venture

outside, we visited both of my elder sisters. I clung to her arm as she pushed her way through traders, beggars and groups of dirty, unsupervised children that plucked at my robes. Everyone seemed to shout above the clatter of horses' hooves and I had to turn away in shock as children as young as three narrowly escaped the churning wheels of coaches. After nine years, London was as unfamiliar to me as Paris and I felt dizzy with the noise and smells and clamour. I felt homesick for the quiet order of St Germain and I missed Mary Beatrice's peaceful household where women sewed and talked in low voices.

My sisters were polite and enquired about William and his family but I saw that our tenuous family bonds were now strained beyond repair. Mary had married again and she was now the wife of Viscount Montague. Neither of her marriages had produced an heir. Anne was also childless. To my older sisters it must have seemed that the least deserving child had somehow grasped everything that ought to have been theirs; time with our parents, the luxury of life at St Germain and worse, I was now pink and round with the joy of a young husband and a baby to come. There was so much I wanted to tell them about Mother and Father's last years. They could have shared with me some news of my brother and his family, now living in a house in Great Ormond Street, but in the end we left each household after little more than an hour.

The baby was due, by my reckoning, sometime between December and January. William would have been happy to extend our stay in London but I felt desperate to reach Scotland, to be with Grace and meet his mother. We chose to continue the journey on horseback, accompanied by two manservants. Horses were better able to pick their way across the rutted surface of the highways and their gentle, rolling movement suited my heavy belly. The weather stayed warm and dry and early morning mists that required cloaks and hats could be discarded by midday. The forests glowed with the colours of an ancient tapestry and at times formed an arch above us that shone with a light more pure than the finest coloured glass. The roadside bushes were heavy with berries and whenever we found a bush that had not been stripped clean by the forest dwellers, William ordered his servants to stop and pick sloes for his mother. Occasionally we stopped and spoke to these local men, charcoal burners or farmers running their pigs through the trees. I found that William had an easy way with men who worked the land and they were comfortable with him despite his fine clothes and Scottish accent. The forest would thin as we reached pockets of cultivated land. Women and men tilling their strips ready for autumn planting stood still and watched us pass, raising their hats in greeting. Farmed land meant that soon we would reach a village or town where we could seek some rest and shelter. We attracted little attention beyond the deference given to people of rank travelling with two burly servants.

Gradually, the forest gave way to open heath and hills and the settlements became less prosperous. Our final night before Scotland was spent in Carlisle where we sat by the fire in an inn empty of customers. The landlord's dislike of both Catholics and the Kirk was equalled only by his passionate hatred of Scots in general. The women, he said, were all prostitutes and the men thieves, although he did concede a grudging respect for the fighting skills of the clans. William was careful to reveal nothing. We spoke to each other only in French and claimed to be a French couple on our way to Edinburgh to conduct some business and while his wife cast a sceptical glance at my belly, the landlord accepted this. He told us that the people of Scotland were starving and that dead bodies lay at the side of the road, their mouths filled with grass to keep them from crying out in their final moments. Gangs of border raiders stole sheep and cattle from the English farmers and their women, too, if they weren't careful. The landlord's wife rolled her eyes at this but that night, in our small, cold room, kept awake by the rustling of rats in the thatch, I clung to William, fearful of the strange land I was about to enter.

I woke early. *This is our last day alone,* I thought and rolled over towards William, resting my head on his chest. He opened his eyes and brushed the hair from my face.

'Winifred,' he spoke my name as if he had heard it for the first time.

'I'm afraid,' I admitted. 'What if your mother doesn't like me? What if I hate Scotland?'

'Is this my brave girl, who travelled alone to France and became the friend of royalty?' William teased. 'Is she afraid of my little old mother?'

'But there seems to be so much hatred.'

'So far we have been safe at Terregles. The Covenanters are zealous in their Protestant principles but we keep the priest well-hidden when he visits. If we live quietly, as we do, we'll come to no harm. My mother has good relations with our neighbours. She will love you and our child. She works hard to sustain the estate but it's been a lonely place for her without children to care for.'

These words brought little reassurance. I imagined battles ahead with my mother-in-law over the care of the child, as my mother's ideas on raising children might well clash with hers. I said nothing but searched around in my discomfort for other fears. 'I've been very happy with you on this journey. It's as if we're back at St Germain, spending our days alone together. When we get to Terregles, I'll have to share you.'

'I'll have to share you when the child is born.' William looked closely at the straw ceiling. 'And don't forget that Grace is waiting for you. I have to share my mother and my home with a spoiled girl from the royal court at St Germain and her lady's maid. What if you find Terregles too plain and too poor? What if you never get to wear your fine gowns and you splash your silk shoes with mud? My poor mother and I will become little more than servants.'

I sat up, shamed by William's words, and saw his serious, downcast expression. Then his eyes crinkled at the corners and his explosion of laughter filled the room. I began to cry and William wrapped me in his arms, kissing my eyes and face, begging my forgiveness until I laughed too. Lying above me, William's eyes looked into mine and we fell silent.

'You're right. This is our last moment completely alone.' He kissed me long and hard and we loved each other, our child tight between us, calling out in that miserable little room as if we would never love so freely again.

The sky arched wide and high above as we followed the coast road before turning inland. The tide had retreated and banks of mud, where sea birds screamed and swooped, only gradually became a sea that stretched across to the dark mountains of England. To the north, the low hills flickered with patches of green and yellow as clouds scudded across the sun. But there was starvation and dereliction in the villages we passed and I felt pity and fear as dark-eyed women, wrapped in blankets that fell to their feet, held out hands for alms. Their children were listless and had no energy to play. They leaned against their mothers, their eyes blank and their legs thin and bent. William's men rode on either side of us, using their boots to push the women away.

'What's happened, William? Why are the people hungry?'

'The harvest has failed for six years. We do what we can.'

I nodded and fell silent, our imagined sacrifices at St Germain now seemed farcical. We rode on to Dumfries, a fine grey town and crossed the River Nith by a low, elegant bridge into Nithsdale, William's country, paying the toll at the bridge house. William told me that the bridge was named Devorgilla after an ancient Scottish queen and I turned back in my saddle to count its six arches, wondering about a queen with such a powerful name.

Within an hour we were at Terregles, cottages scattered amongst outcrops of rock and gorse. We climbed out of the settlement, following the slate walls of the estate until we reached a wide gate set between high square posts, capped with stone pyramids. William, who had been riding ahead of me, stopped to wait. We looked across the Nith Valley at the path we had come and a sky that seemed to need a wider horizon.

'Are you ready?'

I nodded.

'Welcome to Terregles Castle, darling. Welcome home.'

BOOK THREE

1700–1714

CHAPTER 11
1700

It was dawn and a grainy light seeped into the room. I had already learned that northern countries are deprived of sun and light for most of the winter and to make matters worse, the winter was endless. I felt that Scottish houses ought to have tall, elegant windows to allow as much light in as possible but from the low cottages in the village to castles such as ours, all had tiny windows and low ceilings, as if light and air were something to avoid. I had been told that the narrow windows were for defence, so I could understand the lack of light in the old tower house, where William and I slept. But in the new wing, built around a courtyard, I couldn't see much improvement. At least our windows had glass, unlike the cottages, and we had shutters to keep out the wind and ice.

I rolled onto my side and eased my legs to the floor, pushing myself into a sitting position. One arm rested across my huge belly, the other traced the extended navel protruding beneath my nightshirt. With my foot I tugged at the rug below the bed and pushed myself into a standing position. I was almost upright when my breath was wrenched in one long gasp by a pain that seared from my lower back through to my belly. My hands found the table beside the bed and I leaned into it, panting through the pain. It passed and I waited, pressing my hands into the small of my back until I felt confident that I could pad across to the shuttered window. I pulled the heavy shutters apart and through iced glass, I could see lights in the windows across the courtyard and knew that my mother-in-law, Lucy, was up and a fire would be warming the kitchen. Soon, one of the servants would reach us with glowing coals for our fire and I could curl up against William until we were brave enough to dress.

Another pain, weaker this time, like the pains of my monthly bleed. I walked over to the crib that had been William's and pushed it so it rocked back and forth, creaking like a branch in the wind. Would there be a baby tonight, the last night of the old year, or would the child be born into a new century? I shivered with fear, thinking of the ordeal ahead. The women at St Germain hadn't spared me the horrors of childbirth. One of us might die, or both.

Shivering with cold, I crawled back into bed and curled up behind William, putting my icy feet on top of his.

'William, I think the child is coming.'

'Christ! Winifred!' I wasn't sure if his reaction was to my news or the shock of the cold. He turned to face me, holding me as close as he could. 'The child is soon to be born?'

'I'm having pains.'

'Do you want me to fetch my mother and Grace?'

'Let's wait, as long as we can. Can we pretend it's not happening?'

'What shall I do?'

'Rub my back and sing to me. Sing me the songs you entertained us with at St Germain.'

'I'd prefer to fetch my mother.'

'Then you'll be sent away from me. Stay a little longer. Please, William.'

In the short time before I arrived at Terregles, Lucy had taken Grace as her helper and companion. My new servant, a girl from the village no more than ten years old, knocked and asked if she could set the fire. She stacked the grate high with logs, glancing shyly across the room at the strange scene in the bed. She must have seen what I hadn't noticed in the gloom, the blood in the pisspot that I'd left by the door and being a clever little girl, she had taken it to show my mother-in-law.

Soon our peace and warmth was ruptured by the arrival of light and voices, blankets and hot water. William was banished and I was wrapped and placed by the fire, my feet on a stone bottle filled with boiling water. I was given warm ale, laced with spices and honey. Lucy ordered the bed to be stripped and clean bedding flapped like sails over the wide mattress as the servants shook out the sheets, creating draughts that made the fire smoke. It felt like the entire household crowded the room, cleaning every surface with vinegar. Lucy thought the baby was early but I knew the child was late by many days.

Once the room was clean, the servants were dismissed and Lucy helped me shuffle back to bed. I rested against a bank of pillows and watched my mother-in-law carry hot water and cloths to the table beside the bed.

'I need to wash you down, Winifred. You must be clean for the birth.'

She wasn't my mother. I hardly knew her. 'I can do it myself. Please leave me. I'm not in much pain yet.'

Lucy hesitated, about to argue, but she was a quiet woman who saw everything but said little.

She nodded. 'Very well, I'll ask Alice to sit outside the door and I'll check on you myself every half hour. I'll send Grace up to you as soon as her tasks allow.'

I waited until she closed the door then shuffled backwards out of the bed. I forced myself to wash every part of me, shivering with cold and pain. I heard my mother's voice lecturing Mary Beatrice about the risk of infection and washed and washed as if I could wipe away the pain with each stroke. Lying back in bed, the ripples of labour seeped out of me and I slept. I woke to find Grace holding my hand.

Wonderful Grace, who had turned from cosseted lady's maid to farm hand, without complaint. 'Have you finished in the dairy?'

'I thought of you while I was milking. You're going through what those poor cows suffer every year. And you'll have to make milk, just like them.'

I looked down at my breasts, swollen and ready. 'Where does the milk come from? There's no hole.'

'It just oozes out of the cracks. At least that's what happens with the cows. We must be the same.'

This thought silenced us and we were quiet together as only Grace and I could be. A log shifted in the grate.

'How late is it?'

'Almost time for dinner. I'm not sure if you should eat. How are the pains?'

'That's the funny thing. They've almost gone. As long as I lie here they stay away. I know I have to go through with this birth but I don't want them to come back.'

'I'll go and check with Lucy. She knows what should be happening. I'll fetch you some more warm ale and ask Alice to see to the fire.'

Grace stood to leave but I gripped her hand. 'Stay with me, please.'

'You're on a different path now, Win. I've no experience of this and can't help you. You need Lucy. But I'll come when I can.' She bent over and kissed me on the forehead. The firelight and candles made shadows that leapt and flickered on the walls and I watched the patterns rise and fall. My body felt as if it wasn't mine, as if I had been ill for some time. I had a dull ache in my back and although my limbs were weightless, my eyes felt round and heavy. This would end one way or another.

I lost track of time but hours later there was still no child. I fought against more washing and the forced emptying of my bowel with soap and water. I fought against the walking, the forced march up and down, up and down, my legs dragging behind me. I wanted to lie down and I wanted food. I screamed and bit and yelled for my mother. The pain in my back was like a knife scraping the flesh from my spine and the foul whores that were with me made me walk. They wanted more pain.

And then the worst thing happened. I lost myself. My body was taken over and I shook and roared as if possessed. At last, they allowed me to lie down on my side, my leg lifted wide across my mother-in-law's shoulder. There was only torture. Deep shafts that threatened to disembowel me. And with the agony, a groan and roar that made me bear down as if a boulder would pass from my groin. Again and again.

Lucy shouted. 'Stop pushing!'

'Stop pushing yourself, you ugly old bitch,' someone screamed.

Grace's voice. 'Here's the head.'

Lucy's voice. 'Hold on. Don't push. Pant. Pant. That's right. Good girl.'

'Leave me alone.'

Lucy. 'Push with the pain. Push now.'

Grace again. 'Here it comes.'

A wet slither. Silence. 'He's here. A boy. A great big boy.'

A baby cried. Far way. Lucy passed me a bundle and someone very old and wise stared at me as if he once knew me but couldn't recall my name. He smelt of my body and old blood. I looked at him again and his threadlike fingers clasped the sheet as if someone might snatch it from him. He frowned and yawned, bored already.

'Talk to him. He'll recognise your voice.'

'Hello, baby.' He opened his eyes and searched my face. He knew me.

'Here, I'll help him suckle.' Lucy reached into my nightshirt and lifted out a breast. She squeezed the nipple between her finger and thumb and touched the baby's cheek. He turned, mouth wide and Lucy pushed the dark nipple between his lips. I felt the pull and tug of his mouth, strong and deep and my sagging belly tightened with waves of new pain.

'Help me. I'm hurting again.' I was afraid. I'd heard of women bleeding to death after delivering a perfect child. Husbands left alone with tiny babies. New wives.

'Shush. It's just the afterbirth. Keep suckling the babe and it'll come away the quicker.'

Grace and Lucy moved softly around the room, sometimes in light, sometimes in shadow. They whispered to each other and Grace carried away something dark wrapped in a sheet. I nursed my son, stroking his hair, still sticky from my body. Alice appeared with warm water and Grace eased the child from my breast to bathe him. I heard him cry. The women bathed me too but I wanted him. He was returned to me, clean and warm. I breathed his newborn odour and kissed the deep pillow of his cheek. At the graze of my mouth, he turned towards me and our lips touched. Resting him against my upturned knees, I gave him my fingertips to grasp and lifted his arms. His dark eyes never left my face.

Lucy sat down on a chair by the bed, her apron clean and hair combed. 'He's a fine boy, Winifred.' She brushed her hands across her lap. 'If I didn't know better I'd say he was a child who'd gone past his dates. Look, his skin is flaking. That's a baby who's waited a wee while to be born.'

'No, he's a few weeks early.' I studied the child's fingernails, unable to look at her. My mother-in-law was a devout woman. Telling the truth wasn't possible.

'Ah well, they're all different. All the same and all different. William will be very proud. It's a joy for me to have a child here and he will be glad of a boy to inherit the title.'

'Where is William? Can he see his son? I want him here with me.' I looked at her, my eyes pleading that she break the rules about men and births.

'He's ridden out to Edinburgh, my dear. I've sent a boy with a message. He'll be home soon.'

I tried to hide my disappointment and turned my face to the wall. She was William's mother and he could do no wrong but he had let me down. She patted my hand.

'You're tired. It was a long birth having to deliver that big head. Let's hope it's a girl next time.'

'There won't be a next time. I'm not doing that again.'

'Well, Grace and I won't mind if you wait a while.'

'I'm sorry. I was awful.'

'I've heard worse. Now, you get some sleep. Keep the baby with you. It's cold outside and I think it will snow. He'll come to no harm next to you. Hold him at the breast until he sleeps. I'll ask Alice to bring you some food.'

I'd forgotten about food but the word brought with it a passionate hunger. I watched Lucy move towards the door and a memory of poor Mary Beatrice filled me with horror.

'Lucy ... the queen ... she had to do that in public, in front of the court and envoys from other countries.' Worse, she'd had to give birth in front of my father.

Lucy turned. 'Aye, she's a brave woman. You were lucky to serve her.'

. . .

My spirits darkened and the whisper of desperation I had felt after my mother's death rose inside me. William didn't come home for two more weeks as it had snowed heavily and the roads were impassable. The snow dampened all sound and from my small window I could see only dancing white flakes that drifted against the walls of the house. Day and night were the same. The baby cried and fed and filled the cloths that wrapped him with a foul green shit that smelt like rotting seaweed until turning an alarming yellow that Lucy said was normal. My breasts leaked milk and my nipples cracked. I cried with pain each time he suckled and he always suckled. Lucy brought me lanolin from the sheep to rub on my nipples and said it would pass. I wanted a wet nurse. Sometimes I was angry and wouldn't pick him up and he roared with frustration, his tiny fists screwed up in rage. Alice had been given nursemaid duties and at ten years old, she seemed to know more about babies than me. She would look at me with contempt and lift the hot red child and walk him up and down, soothing him with whispered words. I wanted someone to soothe me. At night I would shout for her, demanding that she see to the baby and change his sodden cloths but in the day I felt ashamed as she fell asleep by the fire, looking like the child she was.

Lucy and Grace visited when they could but there was still a household and a farm to run and many sick and elderly in the village who needed help. When I was alone I cried and raged at my miserable life, trapped in a tower with a tyrannical baby and his nursemaid. I wept for William, needing him and hating him. I imagined him carousing with his friends in Edinburgh, wetting the baby's head in every inn the town possessed. I fantasised about leaving the baby and William and going to my sister's convent in Bruges. I would have some peace and he would be sorry.

Finally, I heard horses in the courtyard, then William's

tread on the staircase. I had no time to remove the baby from my breast. William swept the outside into my over-heated cell, his hands and cheeks reddened with cold and his hair and cloak damp with melting snow. He wrapped us in his embrace, kissing my hair and eyes and nose, whispering my name and begging my forgiveness.

'I wouldn't leave you, Win. I meant to be in Edinburgh just for the old year's night and then the snow fell. I wanted to be with you. I've pined for you every day.'

He was here now. He loved me. I forgave him. 'Here's your son. He's a tyrant and a bully. He doesn't like me.'

William lifted the baby from my arms and the child studied his father with the same steadfast gaze he used to take my measure. 'He's a fine baby. He looks like you. See,' he turned the child towards me, 'he has your eyes.'

William began to undress the baby and I tried to stop him. 'He'll catch cold!'

'This room's as warm as the cows' byre and doesn't smell much better. Let me look at my son.' William stripped the child and laid him down between us. He kicked his legs and cycled his arms, seeming glad to be free of the cloths that bound him. 'He won't disappoint the ladies.'

'William be quiet, he's just a baby,' but I laughed for the first time since the birth.

'Look, Win, he likes you, he's smiling at you.'

I saw the fleeting ripple on the baby's lips. It could have been a smile. I felt hope, like first light on an early summer's day.

William's eyes danced with pride and excitement. 'You won't believe who I met in Edinburgh.'

'I can't guess. I don't know anyone in Edinburgh apart from my sister.'

'Your brother-in-law, the Earl of Seaforth. He took me home

to meet Frances and their children. You didn't tell me he'd fought so many battles with James and was even at the siege of Londonderry. Only ten years ago he tried to start a Jacobite uprising in the north. He's a true Jacobite, not like those old fools at St Germain. He fights for what he believes.' William pulled off his wig and fell back against the pillows. 'God, I was so proud to meet him. I'm so proud to have married into a proper Jacobite family. Your parents, your brother, your sisters, you're all true to the cause. And you, my love, serving our king and queen for so long, I can't believe you chose me.'

There was a great deal I could have said but I kept my counsel. If this myth satisfied William then I wouldn't correct him. But I was interested in Frances and how she managed life with a husband who was a soldier and started uprisings.

'When we were children she was too old to be my friend and she married so young. She seemed to disappear. How many children do they have now?'

'Three, two boys and a daughter.'

'Did they ask about me?'

'Of course, and I told them all I know. They have insisted that once you and the baby are fit to travel, we must all come to Edinburgh. Frances longs to talk to you about your parents' final years and your time at court. She sends her love and a gift for the baby.'

'William,' I hesitated, 'meeting the Earl of Seaforth hasn't given you a taste for fighting, I hope?'

'Not me. I'm too much of a coward. Besides, the Earl has just been freed after four years in prison. I want to be with you and our child, not have you visiting me in a cell.'

I leant across our child and kissed him. 'I'm so lucky too. I can't believe you chose me.'

CHAPTER 12

S ummer had come at last and shafts of light cut through the winter's dirt on the diamond window panes. Baby William sat on a rug, chewing on a bone teething ring, the sun shining on his curls. I thought I would die of love. My husband lay on his back passing toys to his son, having the kind of conversation only parents have with babies. I knelt behind the baby and studied the perfect line of his neck and my husband looked up at me and smiled with pride.

It was possible, at last, to have the windows open and the sound of horses approaching from the village came from the high, small panes. William stood and straightened his wig. We had few visitors at Terregles and I was glad that we weren't three women alone. Voices carried up from the courtyard and baby Will stopped chewing and held up his ring to his father, then turned to look at me, lifting his arms to be picked up.

We heard a male voice, then my mother-in-law speak. A stifled cry. We waited, holding our breath. Even the baby was silent. There were footsteps in the passageway and a gentle tap on the door. I knew it was Alice.

'Sir, madam,' she curtsied. 'Lady Lucy has asked me to convey to you the sad news that the Countess of Traquair's baby has died. She is leaving for Traquair House today and would like you to accompany her. Please, sir and madam, that's what she asks.'

I scooped the baby from the floor and buried my face in his neck. 'We must go and pack. Your mother will want to leave as soon as possible.'

William folded his arms across his chest, 'I'm not going – I can't. Anyway, a baby's death is women's business. I'll arrange for one of the men to travel with you.'

'But William, it's your sister. She's lost her child. And your mother wants you with her.'

William moved into the shadows of the wood-panelled drawing room and I could hardly see his features. 'I don't need you to lecture me on my family duties. I have to be in Edinburgh – it's politics.'

'Charles will benefit from your company, another man to talk to. William, please, this hasn't happened to them before, think how they must be feeling. Imagine if it was our baby, our Will.'

'They've got five children already,' William's voice rose. 'For God's sake, Winifred, this is Scotland, these things happen. Even to people like us.'

I felt a rage that I could barely control. Who was my husband, this stranger who didn't understand that every child lost was a tragedy for its family?

'You are selfish!' I yelled at him. 'You prefer to be with Jacobite friends instead of with us, playing at fanciful dreams of glory. It's just like when Will was born. You should have been here with me.'

William stepped forward into the light and I saw an

expression on his face that was new to me, as if a dark cloud had crossed the sun.

He thrust his face into mine and I felt the spit from his mouth on my cheeks. 'You will never speak to me like that again. Yes, I want to be with men planning a different future for Scotland. I want to be at the heart of things in Edinburgh, not just a Jacobite follower or a nursemaid at home.'

I stepped back from him and held the baby close. 'Your duty is to be with your family. To help your mother make a success of this estate.'

'You smother me, Win. You're naïve and self-centred.'

'And you are lazy and spoilt.'

Our eyes locked in mutual contempt and then he turned away, slamming the heavy door behind him.

The baby's howls echoed around the dark room as I paced, fighting for breath. I couldn't see. I couldn't think. I ran to the kitchen, pushing the child into Alice's arms. At the door to the still room, I forgot to put pattens under my silk shoes and slid across the muddy yard and into the dairy. I leaned inside the door, breathing the smell of sour milk and silage. Our dairy herd had not yet been put out to grass and they shifted in the pale light, gathering together to stare at me like silent observers. I knocked over an empty pail and the sudden noise made the cows anxious and they stepped back in unison. A dairy maid passed me and bobbed a curtsy.

Grace was making butter. She nodded to a stool and I sat watching her thrust the plunger into the churn, my own heart pounding. Up and down.

'Can I have a turn?'

Grace watched my pathetic arms try to match her power and rhythm. 'What's happened to make you so angry?'

'I hate him. He's never here. He does nothing. He lets his

old mother do his work. He should be running this estate, not her. He's nothing but a spoilt child. He thinks he'll be a Jacobite hero. It's pathetic.'

Grace gestured that we change places. 'You forgot to mention that he spends all our money.'

I felt dizzy, as if I might fall. 'What on earth do you mean?'

'Open your eyes, Win. The estate was in so much debt from his stay in France his mother had to send everything he bought in Paris, except the clothes, to be sold in Edinburgh.'

Confusion pressed into my temples. I thought my beautiful linen, porcelain and china had been stored away, to be brought out for celebrations. 'You should have said something, Grace. His mother should have warned me.'

'You didn't notice or ask and Lady Lucy will never say a word against the Earl.'

Grace dislikes my husband, I thought. Perhaps she has never liked him. I felt loyalty to William stir but my anger was fresh and bitter. 'He said I was naïve ... and self-centred.'

'And what did you say to him?' Grace didn't look up but I heard the smile on her lips.

'Nothing,' I lied. 'I just asked him to accompany Lady Lucy and me to Traquair. His sister Mary has lost her baby girl.'

'That's so sad. Of course you must go but I can see how a man might feel he has no place.'

'He'd rather be drinking in Edinburgh.'

'Probably, yes. But you married him for the very reason you hate him right now, his charming spontaneity. That quality doesn't often accompany thrift and responsibility.' I watched her pour whey from the churn into a bucket at her feet. 'Come on,' Grace put an arm around my waist, 'let's go and see the pig. He always makes me feel better.'

We leaned over the low sty wall, scratching the pig's back, smelling straw soaked with rank urine.

'He'll be dead in a few months.'

I grimaced. 'Chopped up and salted to see us through the winter. More salt pork ... don't you ever wish you were back at St Germain?'

Grace poured the whey into the pig's trough. He squealed and thrust his snout into the thin milk, grunting with pleasure. 'I could have stayed – I was asked. I didn't tell you because my place is with you. Always.'

I was shocked. 'I'm sorry, Grace, I assumed too much. I am selfish.'

Grace didn't correct me. 'Lady Lucy and I work so hard to keep a roof over all our heads and allow your husband to lead the life he chooses. His mother will never restrict him and he won't change. But you can help, now that the baby is weaned – take some share of the tasks from your mother-in-law and try to keep his spending in check. This is our home now, we can't look back.'

I looked around at the farm buildings, the smithy and the dairy. 'But what tasks can I do?'

'Ask Lady Lucy, I'm sure she'll be pleased to suggest something suitable. Now, your mother-in-law has to comb the flax in the linen yard before she leaves and I have to finish the butter but then I'll help you both to pack.'

I watched Grace walk back to the dairy. There was sadness in the line of her shoulders and I could see weight around her hips that hadn't been there a year ago. Life had settled on us both.

William was wrong, this wasn't women's work; this was family work and he, as close to his sister as any brother could be, would have brought her comfort. I felt ashamed that for me, there was pleasure in this visit. Out of respect for Mary, my baby was left at home and for a moment, I felt relief mixed with guilt as I watched the maid lay out one of my French gowns. I would dress for dinner.

I walked to the window and pushed the curtains back with the tips of my fingers. Mary's arms must ache for the weight and warmth of her daughter and Lucy would comfort her but what could I do? How was it possible for me to mourn a child that had lived but a few months? I could only regret the loss of the person the baby might have become. I knew I shouldn't wait much longer before I saw Mary but I was afraid. With my French manners and no sense of how to be a real sister to anyone other than to Mary Beatrice, I would be useless.

Standing outside my bedroom door I listened. This house, normally alive with the chaos of five young children, dogs and servants, now felt closed down and in mourning. I tiptoed to Mary's room and heard Lucy's voice rise and fall, singing an old Scots ballad I had heard her sing to baby Will. I tapped on the door and entered. The room was dark and hot and Mary was a white shape on the bed. Lucy met me at the door and whispered that her daughter was sleeping. She held my hand in her own small, dry hands, patted my arm and left to see her grandchildren in the nursery.

I sat down and watched as Mary turned and murmured in her sleep. I pulled a cover over her and she opened her dark eyes but did not see me. In repose, she was so like William I felt my love for him return like a wave breaking over dry sand. The memory of his love for me made me tender and I reached out and touched her.

'Mother?' She turned towards me and tried to focus.

'It's me, Winifred. Do you need anything? Your mother has gone to see the children.'

Mary shook her head and lay staring at the ceiling but she

didn't remove her hand from mine. 'I need my baby. Where have they taken her?'

I hadn't expected this question. I had no idea. 'Charles will have put her somewhere safe,' I stumbled. 'You'll see her tomorrow, at the funeral mass.'

'I want to see her now. Bring her to me, Winifred.'

Her demand dropped into the still air between us. I hesitated. 'I can't do that,' I whispered. 'She's dead, Mary. I'm so sorry you lost her, she must have been a lovely baby.'

'I just want her back. She must be frightened without me.' Mary rolled over and her shoulders trembled with silent, hollow weeping until her shuddering breaths told me that she had fallen asleep.

That night, I slept badly. The bed seemed warm only where I lay and every time I turned, my hands and feet searched for the heat of William's body. Although it was early summer, a wind whispered in the trees of the park and the painful cries of the sheep searching for their lambs made me worried for my own baby. Would Alice comfort him if he cried for me in the night? Would he think I had abandoned him?

I heard a cry and listened. Pulling a shawl around my shoulders, I padded to the door and waited, my chest tight. I heard it again, a desperate calling from the depths of the house. Why did no one stir? I knew it was Mary and that if there was no movement soon, I would have to find her.

The corridors of Traquair filled with long shadows from the light of my single candle. I searched Mary's room first and found it empty, then followed the distant sounds down into the bowels of the house. I kept my eyes focused ahead in case something fearful lay in the darkness but reminded myself that there was nothing around me except furniture that was there every day. Mary was in the game larder behind the kitchen, amongst carcasses of hare and pheasant, holding against her shoulder a stiff bundle wrapped in white cloth. The room smelt of blood.

'I've found her, Win. They tried to keep her from me. I must feed her. She's so cold.'

I sat down next to Mary and put the candle on the table where game was prepared. The wood was stained red. 'Let me see her. Show her to me.'

Mary hesitated, fearing a trick, but I sat very still and folded my hands in my lap, hoping that the failing candle wouldn't leave us in darkness. With great care, Mary rested her baby in her lap and I unfolded the wrapping from the child's face and traced my fingers around the stiff flesh of her cheeks. 'She is a lovely baby.'

Mary nodded and her own fingers followed the path that mine had made. She lifted the baby and kissed her cheek, then cradled the child in her arms and rocked her, humming the lullaby I had heard her mother sing. The candle guttered and died but still we sat, chilled and alone, nursing the dead child. The dark outside the small window turned from black to grey and, finally, she placed the child back in the wooden crate where she had found her. I wrapped my shawl around Mary and together we returned to her room and climbed into her bed. I listened to Mary's breathing, her head cradled against my breast. In another hour the servants would rise and the house would live again.

Later, in the small priest's room at the top of the house, I played with Mary's boisterous children, wondering how I would keep them amused during the funeral mass. Their nursemaids seemed useless, sometimes scolding, sometimes ignoring, sometimes smacking. I thought that I must speak to Mary, once she was well, or her children might become unmanageable. My brother-in-law, Charles, seemed kind but indifferent, regarding his children with puzzled amusement. At last, when Mary arrived with her mother she seemed composed. I had helped her to bind her breasts to stem the flow of milk, as I had learned at St Germain, and her tight black dress and combed hair gave her an unexpected dignity. The sight of the tiny white coffin caused her to stop and bite her hand but her living children distracted her from grief. Mary sat with Charles and the priest began the mass. I paid little attention. My thoughts drifted to my mother and how she had fought the accepted orthodoxy that many babies must die. My miserable faith could not accept that God needed these tiny souls. I didn't know what had killed Mary's baby but I had learned from my mother that it could be stopped. I wished my mother still lived and I found that I was crying.

The child was buried in a distant corner of the estate garden close to the River Tweed. It was a swift and discreet burial but Lucy, seeing her daughter's composure fray, gathered Mary and her grandchildren together and hurried with them to the house. I thought that Lucy's experience must have told her that the children's routine would give her daughter some peace. Alone, I made the long walk back to the house, enjoying the sun on my face and the sound of rooks nesting in the woods. I found Charles at the entrance to the formal garden. We drifted together and, without words, turned onto a path where we walked in silence. I sat down on a marble bench and Charles asked me, with courtly politeness, if he might sit next to me. We remained side by side, staring at the luxuriant spring flowers without speaking. I heard a bee move between blossoms, its drone sometimes steady, sometimes broken, as it searched for pollen.

'Thank you for what you did with Mary last night. I don't know how to manage these things. She's usually such a happy little thing. I was unprepared for her grief.'

'I didn't know what was best. I wasn't sure if it was allowed.

It just seemed the right thing.' I looked at Charles but he kept his eyes fixed on the back of the house.

'It helped her very much and I'm very grateful to you. I wondered if she might lose her mind but now I know she'll come back to us.'

We remained seated but I felt that Charles had more to say. He cleared his throat. 'I'm sorry William wasn't able to come.'

'Oh, Charles,' I apologised for my husband, 'if he hadn't had business in Edinburgh he would have been here. He's getting involved politically with the Jacobite cause.'

'Well they're certainly on the rise again. This country hasn't done well under the rule of William and Mary. It may provide him with some purpose but I'm not sure that his being active in the restoration of James II will sit well with your neighbours.'

I felt unprepared for such a conversation and tried to shift the ground. 'I think he's fallen under the spell of my brother-in-law, Kenneth Mackenzie. Family is very important to him. He's very fond of Mary.'

Charles frowned. 'Yes, they're very alike, both beautiful children. Their mother brought them up to be adored. That's fine for Mary but William must become a man. His mother isn't getting any younger. Do you mind me talking to you about this, Winifred? You seem an intelligent young woman and I worry about the burden that will fall on you.'

I hesitated, afraid of more disloyalty. Charles looked at me now and I saw friendship in the lines around his grey eyes.

'I have only recently learned that our financial affairs are not secure and that my husband's spending is a problem.'

Charles nodded. 'I fear that William isn't here because he owes me money. Had I not lent it to him I cannot imagine how he would have paid his debts. Terregles is a fine little estate, it's not grand but it should make you all a good living. You will have to learn the business, Winifred, before Lucy passes away. It won't be good for your marriage but you must set a limit on William's spending.'

'But I don't know how to do that,' I protested.

'You'll find a way. You have a responsibility to your child and all your tenants to make the estate pay. I will help you where I can.'

Disappointment flushed through me. I wanted what Mary had, to be an adored child. But this kind, thoughtful man said I had to be mature and clever, so I straightened my back and shoulders and whispered my thanks for his advice, my unspent tears binding my throat like a vice.

I left the next day, anxious to see my son, but Lucy decided to remain at Traquair to help her daughter. Time spent travelling on rough tracks gave me the chance to think about how I would become the person that Charles expected and yet hold onto the love and respect of my husband. However, I arrived home irritable and dirty, with no plan. William was there and he lifted me from the carriage by my waist, holding me up and swinging me round as if I was as light as air. He put me down and pulled me close, kissing my cheeks, then led me by the hand to the stable yard, where a small white pony tossed his head in greeting. A lad was busy harnessing the pony to a pretty carriage with high, light wheels and leather seats. Alice stood in the shade of the stable arch, dressed in a bonnet and travelling cloak, with Will in her arms. The child saw me and pulled away from her, opening and closing his hands. I carried him over to William, stroking his head with my lips. The smell of his hair made my newly weaned breasts ache.

William gestured towards the pony and cart. 'Aren't they lovely? I bought them for you in Edinburgh. We can go out for days together, take Will too.'

I saw the delight in my husband's face and felt sense desert me. I kissed him, this generous, impetuous young man and felt the happy anticipation of days to come, roaming the countryside together. I pushed my worries into a cold, empty place and didn't question how they would be paid for.

'Let's go out today, Win, down to the coast. The baby and his nurse are ready. There's food in the cart.' William's eyes were bright with excitement.

'I'm filthy,' I argued but there was laughter in the protest.

William bent to kiss my neck. 'You smell perfect.'

On the coast, the sea foamed and churned between jagged, slate rocks that leaned towards the land as if they had been thrown down like a pack of cards. We found a sheltered patch of sand, cut into the dunes and huddled on a rug, looking across to the brown hills of England. Will crawled around us, exploring the shingle. Tiny shells stuck to his fingers and he held out his hands, like starfish, to share this new mystery. Alice held him by his hands to explore rock pools with his bare feet and when they were out of sight, William pulled a blanket over our heads and kissed my lips, ignoring the baby's howls of fear as icy water rushed over his toes. Worn out by so much that was new, the child slept after we had eaten and we left him with Alice to walk along the beach. William picked a flower and kissed the petals before he tucked the stem into my hair.

'My darling Win, I love you more than life itself. I missed you so much. I was afraid you wouldn't come back to me. Can you ever forgive me?'

I leaned into his chest and murmured, 'Of course I can, I said some awful things too. But William ...' I pulled back so that I could see his eyes, 'Charles says that we owe him a lot of money.'

William studied the seascape, avoiding my gaze. 'He shouldn't have told you, that's men's business.'

I placed both hands on his upper arms and faced him. 'We

must live within our means and pay back everything we owe. I'll help you.'

But William's eyes dropped to his feet and I let go. We walked on together side by side, back towards our sleeping child, our hands not touching. The joy of the afternoon washed from us and the only sound was the crying from the gulls above.

CHAPTER 13

This was my fourth Christmas at Terregles. I knew it wasn't possible to have a Christmas like those of my childhood. As the Kirk frowned on celebrations, there would be no decorations or music. My mother-in-law insisted that we follow the same rules as our neighbours, so that we didn't draw attention to ourselves. I had fought her at first, resenting a creed that seemed steeped in misery rather than harmless fun.

It was early evening and we sat together in the panelled drawing room that became warm and comfortable in the winter months, with its low ceilings and small, narrow windows. I placed my hand on my stomach, confident that another child would be born in the summer. Grace and Lucy sat by the fire, talking in low voices about the possibility of snow. My son was asleep, unaware that tomorrow he would be given some nuts and dried fruit. Although it was a working day, we would have a special meal as Lucy had fattened a goose through the autumn and I had made a pippin pie from the last of the apples. The itinerant priest we shared with other families had already visited and there would be no mass on Christmas Day.

Lucy's only concession was to maintain the Scots tradition

of placing a candle in every window, to light the way of the holy family. Tonight, we lit the way for William too as he had promised to be home on Christmas Eve. I worked at the table on the accounts, the ledger lit by a rush light at my elbow and the candle in the window behind. I listened, in part to the murmurs of the other woman and in part for the crash of the gates and the ring of hooves in the courtyard. My additions showed that we were in credit by the smallest margin. Our difficulties in finding a market for our cattle, wool and linen were as severe as for any other Scottish farm. Our tenant farmers struggled to pay their rents and the fit, young men from the villages were taken to fight as mercenaries, rather than work the land. I sighed and threw my pen down, smearing ink across the page, recalling my argument with William about his spending.

'You don't understand,' he'd shouted at me, 'I need to be able to maintain a position in Edinburgh as the Earl of Nithsdale. That takes money.'

'No, William, you must understand about living within our means. The more you spend in Edinburgh the less we have here. We thought we were frugal at St Germain but that was nothing compared to the savings we have to make now.'

'Ah, St Germain, of course. I'd forgotten your perfect life at St Germain. You're as mean as your father and, from what I've heard, as controlling as your mother.'

'That's so unfair, William. I'm simply trying to make sure we live without debt. And you are nothing like your mother, more's the pity.'

'Don't bring my mother into this.' William had swung his cloak around his shoulders and walked out, calling to me from beyond the parlour door, 'I'll return at Christmas and not before.'

My mother-in-law interrupted my thoughts. 'Are you

alright, Win? Come and sit by the fire. Leave those until tomorrow.'

I joined them by the hearth and warmed my hands. Lucy spoke to us both in a low voice, as if she feared being overheard. 'Our neighbours have asked a few questions about William's activities. I'll talk to him once he's home and remind him to take care. We don't want trouble.'

I rose and pushed at my stiff back and felt my bodice tighten over my breasts. I yawned, covering my mouth. 'William says that since James II died and the French king recognised his son, the Jacobites are more hopeful of a restoration.'

'Aye and that's stirred everything up, made people around here angry.'

'Whenever I visit our neighbours I hear nothing but respect for you, Lucy, so I'm sure it's safe. I'm feeling very tired and a little sick, so I'll go to bed and wait for William there. I'll be so glad when this nausea passes.'

'He'll be with us soon, don't you fear. You get some rest. I'll check on the little one for you before I go to bed.'

I kissed her and Grace and climbed the narrow stone stairs to my room, the candlelight creating a tunnel of light with nothing but emptiness behind. I felt a prickle of fear and a surge of unexpected loneliness. I slipped into the room that my son still shared with Alice and held the candle close to his face so that I could see the fine blue veins in his eyelids and the dreams flickering behind. I watched his chest rise and fall and the candlelight shift against his breath. Alice snorted from her bed beside the wall and I left. I needed to check they were alive but I didn't want them awake.

In my room, I was irritated to see that the little girl who tended to the fires had allowed mine to burn low and knelt down to add more logs and gently blow on the grey embers. Satisfied that the wood had caught, I crossed to the window to close the shutters, shivering and pulling my shawl tightly around me. I could see nothing outside except night and heard only the cry of a fox but still I watched. He would come back tonight. He had promised.

I thought I saw a light but it was only a moth dancing outside the window, then I saw it again, a light on the brow of the hill. Then many lights, dancing lights, moving. Men with torches. The men with torches were here again. I stopped breathing. I thought the blood from my heart would burst through my ears. I stumbled to the door and called out, 'Alice! Grace! Lucy!'

My voice sounded hollow and distant. I ran to scoop Will from his bed and shook Alice roughly. 'Wake up! Wake up!'

I stumbled down the staircase and burst in on a startled Grace and Lucy. 'Bring blankets to the game larder, as many as you can, we're under attack!'

Time slowed. We secured the heavy door to the larder, which was one of the few rooms in the house with a lock. Between us we dragged the oak table across the flagstones and turned it so that even if the lock were forced, the door would not open. There was no window, only a small hole to allow air to circulate. We huddled on the floor, wrapped in blankets, shaking with cold and fear. Will clung to me and sucked his thumb. I prayed he wouldn't cry.

Suddenly, I sat upright and whispered into the dark. 'We've forgotten the kitchen girl!' No more than eight years old, she had been among the many children that roamed our countryside, stealing what they could to survive or dying, quietly and forgotten in the ditch, picked over by crows until their bones sank into the undergrowth. William had told Lucy to throw her out but Lucy refused and she slept in the kitchen by the fire, without a name, learning simple tasks and hiding stolen food under her blankets until the smell forced us to steal everything back from her and throw it away.

'We have to leave her, it's too late,' Grace spoke. 'We can't risk fetching her. I hope she's got the sense to hide away.'

The waiting was the worst. The cold seeped into my bones through the stone floor and I retched at the smell of dead meat and blood from the game birds hanging above us. I heard everyone's breathing above my own pounding heart and the click, click of Lucy's rosary as she prayed for our lives.

Like a storm in the night, the mob hit the house with a hail of breaking glass and splintering wood. Footsteps stamped above and we heard the sound of our heavy furniture being tossed aside in anger. We listened to the braying laughter of men beyond control, drunk on power and rectitude. I smelt the sweat of fear in our cell and urine that may have been from Will but might have been from any one of us. We clung together and I pressed my child to my breast, covering his ear with my hand. This would pass. It would be over. There would be morning. I closed my eyes and thought of waves crashing onto rocks, I thought of forcing a child from my body, I thought of the squealing anguish of the pig as he died. I began to tremble and then shake. My stomach cramped and I groaned with the pain. I felt a hatred for these men that rose in my throat like vomit. I would not stand for this.

Feeling for Alice in the dark, I passed Will to her and pushed myself up from the floor. My stomach cramped again. I breathed until it passed then brushed down my robe and smoothed my hair. I was mistress of this house and the mob were only villagers who sold me food and worked in my fields. I heaved the table away from the door, feeling the strain on my belly and squeezed into the narrow space to unlock the door.

Lucy and Grace spoke together, their voices trembling from the darkness. 'What's happening? Are they breaking in?'

'No, it's me. I'm going to speak to them. They've no right to be here. Lock the door behind me.'

'Win please,' Lucy pleaded, 'think of the baby.'

'I must go. If I don't, we'll always be afraid. Push the table back behind me.'

I strode through the wreckage, the worst of the destruction hidden from me by the night. In the drawing room I found a straggler, helping himself to candles and I slapped him soundly on the back of the head. He startled and turned around, his eyes burning with panic and then he ran. I followed the sound of voices to the hall, where the men were gathered. In the light from their torches I saw that there were four ministers of the Kirk, waiting to address the mob. I recognised the minister from Torthorwald. I had only recently helped his wife with a potion for her child's fever.

'Good evening, gentlemen, I hope you are pleased with your night's work.' My voice rang out, sharp and clear, and I heard my mother's cold authority. In the shadows the men huddled, small and thin-faced. I was taller than most and pulled myself to my full height. Some of them turned away, afraid that I would see their faces. Others, out of habit, removed their hats and nodded to me. I heard some at the rear of the pack shuffle out of the hall, muttering. The ministers of the Kirk looked at me with contempt as if I was horse muck on their boots.

'And what purpose did this serve, frightening women and children, left alone? You should be ashamed of yourselves, to treat your neighbours so.'

'We believe that you are harbouring a priest and conducting idolatrous worship. We are within our rights to search your house.'

'And did you find a priest? Did you find evidence of worship?' I spoke with icy clarity.

'You know that we did not. You have hidden the evidence.

But we will be watching you and we will come again. Your husband's father,' this last word was spoken with contempt, 'persecuted the families of these men for their beliefs. Now it is their turn. An eye for an eye.'

'And does your righteousness include this,' I gestured to the faeces smeared on the walls, 'or this?' I held up the arm of a broken chair. The men stepped back as if I was about to hit them. There was silence. We stood facing each other, uncertain who should move next. I heard a small child cry. A high, keening, wail, like a rabbit caught in a trap. I pushed through the men. They parted to let me pass as if I might strike them dead if they touched me. At the back of the hall, leaning against the stone arch to the kitchen, I found our stray child. She was dressed in a white shift that Lucy had cut down for her, so that she might learn not to sleep in her clothes. She lifted her shift and her cries deepened when she saw me. Her thin legs were streaked with blood. She had been raped.

I lifted her into my arms, smelling the fluids of men who had torn her for their pleasure and carried her to the front of the crowd. I pointed to the blood so that all of them could see her violation. 'And is this part of your righteousness?' I heard more men leave from the back of the crowd and those trapped at the front shifted from foot to foot and loosened the cloths around their neck.

One of the ministers took on a pulpit voice and addressed the remaining men. 'The men who did this vile act will be caught and punished. Go home now, all of you.'

The remaining men disappeared into the night and an incongruous group remained, the four ministers and the child cradled by me. The minister from Torthorwald turned towards me and spoke, still using the tone of a preacher. 'Far worse than this was meted out to the people of these parts by your husband's family and those like him. You have no friends here.

Go back to England, or better, to France. And warn your husband that scheming to restore a Catholic king only serves to unite those who would impose upon us a union with England. He cannot win. Goodnight, Lady Nithsdale.'

William arrived just before midnight and I had to hold him back from riding out to the ministers' homes and seeking revenge. Instead, he paced the rooms that we had attempted to set right, pushing furniture aside and kicking anything that lay in his path. He filled our home with more male anger and we had already had our fill. I saw the look that passed between Grace and Lucy. They were waiting for me to deal with him.

'Shut up, William, and sit down,' I shouted. 'Or help us to clean. If you can't do either of those things then go to bed.'

William looked at me, puzzled and uncertain, and fell into a chair, holding his head between his hands. Lucy and Grace slipped from the room.

'Can't you see how I feel?' he pleaded, not raising his head. 'My wife, child and mother attacked while I'm not at home. I could kill them with my bare hands. We know who they are. Surely you must let me gather some men and right this violation.'

I pulled a heavy chair to his side and felt, again, a deep, low ache in my belly. I was drained of feeling. I didn't want to have to look after him, suffering the shameful anger that arises from guilt. He deserves to feel this pain, I thought. I tried to keep impatience from my voice and spoke with a measured and reasonable tone that I hoped would keep my scorn in check.

'If you do that, more harm will come to us. You might be hurt. If you kill one of them, you will be arrested and hanged. Despite the evidence I see around me, I believe that this is a civilised land. You must go to the law.'

'And what would have happened if they'd done to you or my mother what they did to that kitchen maid, or if they'd killed you?'

'I don't know, William. It didn't happen. I'm so tired. We were all so frightened. Please leave it alone, just for tonight.'

I listened to his breathing, fast and hard, but still he didn't lift his head to look at me. 'What do you want from me, Winifred? How can I make this right? I mean with you. You were so brave and I'm proud of you. But it should have been me.'

'Just stay with me and hold me. Help us rid this house of the taint, so that it's our home again. Play with your son tomorrow. It's Christmas.'

I lost our second child the following day. Rest made no difference and the contractions grew deeper and more frequent until I passed a bloody mess into some rags that we burnt on the kitchen fire. We couldn't speak about our pain. William's face smiled whenever he was spoken to but when we fell silent he chewed his lip and twisted his hands. Lucy made us eat and she and Grace whispered around us and took our son out for long walks.

William stayed with us until Hogmanay, but his eyes looked inward. I returned to my duties, to the care of my boy and the work of the estate. But in my mind I saw only the missing child, a little girl I had already named but who would never be spoken of again.

CHAPTER 14

William indeed found some purpose within the Scottish parliament as a respected member of the Jacobite party and I felt relieved that debate was his battlefield, fighting with arguments rather than swords to prevent a parliamentary union with England. William of Orange had died and Anne, the new queen of England, Scotland and Ireland, was equally determined to create that union, along with many Scottish noblemen who should have known better.

I understood these things after listening to William. I felt proud of him, watching his eyes alight with passion as he described the web of political intrigue in Edinburgh. I accepted his absence because there was nothing in Terregles except a quiet estate, run by his mother and his wife and a small village full of people with narrow horizons. William had not been raised to be a farmer. Unlike our brother-in-law Charles, he found no satisfaction in discussions about crops and yields. Besides, Charles had his growing family to keep him at home while we had failed to fill our empty house with children. I was now thirty-three and there had been no more pregnancies. I was not my mother's daughter after all.

While the years of famine were behind us, making a living from farming became more difficult as the English continued to tax our exports and forbade trade between Scotland and the colonies. William had a small allowance to support his life in Edinburgh and I had to trust that he borrowed no more.

But if William wouldn't stay with us, I was determined to go to him in Edinburgh whenever Lucy could spare me. At last, it was a fair spring day and warm air drifted through the open window of the carriage, carrying the stink of effluent from the streets. We were on our way to visit my widowed sister Frances in Cowgate but the crowds on the street were dense, even for the over-populated Edinburgh, and the carriage slowed to walking pace. I closed the window, for without movement, the stench became unbearable. The high tenements closed in around us and it was as dark as a winter's afternoon. As a distraction we talked in a desultory way of our son's education, rehearsing old arguments.

'There's nothing suitable for Will in Dumfries,' William repeated. 'He needs to be with other children. We should send him to Paris, where he could be with other Catholic boys, perhaps to the Scots College?'

William knew that I wouldn't consider it. I didn't want to send my only child away and besides, we couldn't pay for it. 'We'll have to engage a priest, there is no other choice,' I replied.

The carriage stopped moving and I asked our agile son to lean out and see what was happening. However, before I could stop him, he had climbed out of the window and onto the roof of the carriage. Next, we saw his red face and fair curls hanging upside down in the frame of the window.

'The driver says it's an execution. I want to stay up here and watch.'

I reached across to snatch him but he was too quick. 'Will, come down at once!'

'Do you see what I mean Win, he'll soon be beyond your control. It's not good for him to be at Terregles with three women.'

Despite my intentions, critical words spilled from my mouth. 'If you were home more, he'd have a man to discipline him and teach him.' I wanted to apologise but the crowd started to chant. The sounds of 'Darien, Darien' became audible, repeated again and again.

'Ah, I know what this is,' William looked out of the carriage window. 'It's the execution of those English traitors, the crew of a ship – I think it was called the Worcester. They've been found guilty of piracy against one of the ships in the Darien scheme. They had to find someone to blame for the failure of our investment and these men just happened to get in the way.'

'Bring Will down,' I pleaded, 'he shouldn't see this.'

'On the contrary, I think I'll climb up and join him. It'll do him no harm to learn that the English are selfish bastards, out to screw the people of this country.'

'But these men are innocent! You said yourself that the Darien scheme failed because of incompetence.'

'We must keep the civil unrest going. The English have to think we're ungovernable and then they'll send in troops. If they do that no Scot will accept the union of parliament, no matter how well their own pockets might be lined. Then we'll have a chance of restoring a Stuart king.'

The crowd roared and the chant became a song. I could imagine what was happening on the platform, in full view of my young son. 'He's only five, bring him down!'

William pushed the carriage door into the backs of the crowd and pulled himself onto the carriage roof, using the open window as a foothold. I heard him moving above me. There was another roar from the crowd then a cheer and the singing started again. I closed the door and windows and waited in the unbearable heat. Gradually, the crowd thinned and individual voices, discussing everyday affairs, filtered up to me as the crowd went home. I heard movement above and watched William climb down from the roof and reach up for his son.

'Mother,' Will scrambled up the step, 'they were like this.' He pulled a face, his head lolling to one side, his tongue protruding. His father glanced at me, like a guilty child.

'Father, why were they like that? Will they stay like that?' The child looked between us, excited but fearful.

'William,' I said, 'tell him what happened to those men.'

'They're dead, Will. The rope around their neck killed them. People thought they had done a very bad thing and this was their punishment.'

'And will they be with our Lord in heaven?' His grandmother had taught him well. I saw William hesitate and interrupted.

'Of course they will,' I stared at my husband, 'but their wives and children will be very sad and will miss them.'

Will put his hand on his father's knee. 'What was the bad thing they did?'

William sighed and pushed his brows together with his fingers. At last, our carriage began to move and we tried to continue our journey, jolting and shaking as our driver followed the crowd.

'What was the bad thing, Father?' Will whined.

'We all saved up a lot of money to send some ships far away. We wanted to explore and find new things to grow and make the people here very rich. At first the English promised money but then they didn't give us any. And when our brave men and women fell ill and had to fight with the men who already lived in the faraway place, the English didn't come and help. Those bad men stole things from one of our ships, even though we're very poor. They said they didn't do it but our courts found them guilty. So they had to die. That's the law.'

Will was silent and his thumb crept into his mouth. His father pulled it out. 'Only babies suck on their thumbs.'

I watched Will struggle to think of a way to make things right with his father, to show him that he wasn't a baby.

'Father,' he pulled at William's sleeve, 'I don't like the English either.'

He was not alone. Once we had returned to Terregles, a draft proposal in favour of union was presented to both the English and Scottish parliaments and rumours of growing civil unrest made the people of Dumfries fearful of an invasion of English forces from across the water in Ireland.

William began to spend more time with us but my hope of involving him with the estate was futile. I tried to interest him in his son's education and his mother's failing health. Instead, men called at the kitchen door, furtive and in shadow and he would talk to them, often late into the night.

I became more afraid. I was Catholic and English and I stopped travelling alone to Edinburgh and Traquair. I felt uncomfortable even in the town of Dumfries, where men gathered in groups and stopped talking when I passed, spitting on the ground where I had just stepped. Lucy went with Alice and the kitchen girl we had now named Isobel to buy our provisions, as our English accents made Grace and I feel unsafe outside the high walls of the estate. I spent my time in the garden and it became my escape, as it had been for my mother. I grew enough vegetables and fruit to feed the household through the year but I no longer tried to make potions and cures. I was fearful of our neighbours. I was watched and only barely tolerated and didn't want the charge of witchcraft to be added to the reasons I was not to be trusted. Isobel had grown into a sturdy girl, with a round, pale face and fair eyelashes that were invisible except in sunlight. She was a presence, who listened and watched but rarely spoke. She was afraid of men and having William at home unsettled her. I tried to interest her in the garden, training her in any simple skill that might offer her a future but William had insisted on getting dogs for the house and Isobel hated them. Our pack followed me everywhere, barking at every sound and raising rather than quietening my anxiety.

It was still mild in the middle of the day and I encouraged Isobel to leave the warmth of the kitchen to help me clear the last of the root vegetables for the animals. I worked fast, enjoying bending and stretching and the smell of the earth. I noticed that Isobel stopped working whenever I did and stared at me with her pale eyes. Her lips moved as if she had something to say. I waited, eyebrows raised, expectant and encouraging, but eventually I had to ask. After several false starts, Isobel leaned towards me and whispered something I hadn't wanted to hear. I left Isobel in the garden and went to find William. He was in the smithy, waiting for his horse to be shoed.

'William, I've heard that you're holding meetings with the Presbyterians.'

'Who told you that?' He didn't wait for a reply. 'I know, it's that girl, the one who's always listening in corners. So, Winifred, you believe the gossip of a kitchen girl. And one who's not too bright. And you wonder why I prefer not to spend time at home?'

'Promise me you're not, William. Those people attacked us. They raped Isobel. They hate us.'

He stared into the blacksmith's fire. 'Sometimes our enemies must become our friends. The Kirk hates the idea of union as much as we do. They're afraid that England will impose

Anglican practices upon them. I'm surprised you don't understand this or find it exciting. I'm afraid you've become dull, stuck out here with my mother.'

'And you've become stupid through not spending enough time with me or your mother. If you lie in the same bed as the Kirk, what will happen if you succeed in preventing the union and then you try to impose a Catholic king?'

'There will be a war?'

'Yes, a civil war that will cause terrible destruction to this country and will likely destroy our family.'

William smiled, as if we were playing a game and he held the winning card. 'The French will invade and impose James Edward Stuart by force. We won't lose.'

'So Isobel is right. You are consorting with the people who subjected us to that terrifying night, who took weapons from this smithy and might have killed us.'

'I'm not saying I'm colluding with them. I'm simply saying that it's a sensible idea. It may have to happen. It's politics. And get rid of that girl, I can't risk her hanging around and listening at keyholes. The next time, she might not tell you – it might be anyone who offers her a bit of food or money.'

The next day, Isobel was gone and so was William. I tried to do my normal tasks but my palms were slippery with anxiety. I dropped a jug of milk on the kitchen floor and when I tried to sew, the needle slipped from my fingers. I played with Will but he grew tired of me as I forgot my turn and spoiled the game. I smiled as I spoke to Lucy and Grace but my lips felt tight. My fears grew as daylight faded. We ate our supper at the long oak table in the kitchen but I couldn't swallow.

'Where do you think our Isobel has taken herself off to?' Grace asked.

Lucy poked at the food on her pewter dish. Her eyesight was failing. 'I expect she's gone to try her luck in Dumfries. We couldn't expect to keep her here for ever. We made her work too hard. She might even think she can find her family but if she doesn't, she'll support herself in the way girls her age always do.'

I pushed back my chair. 'I'm going to look for her. I'll take two of the stable boys with me.'

Grace stood up too, tipping her chair backwards onto the stone floor and gripped my arm. 'What's the matter, Win? You look terrified.'

'I have to go. I'm afraid something's happened to her.'

'Then I'll come with you.'

I couldn't allow this, not if my worst fears were true. 'Grace, please stay here with Will and Lucy. They can't be left alone. I'll be fine. Please, Grace.'

I had to act. I had to search for them. Waiting wasn't possible. I ran from my startled family to the stables and harangued the boys, who had thought themselves settled for the night, to saddle three horses, for two of them would accompany me.

There was a clear sky and every star was visible. My breath caught in my throat as I inhaled the frosty air with every panting breath. We galloped across the heath and down into the town, dismounting as we approached the first houses. Candles flickered behind dark cottage windows as the sound of our horses echoed on the cobbles. I instructed one of the lads to find an inn where the horses could be stabled. I covered myself with my cloak and took the other stable boy with me. I had no idea where to begin to look for William but sent the lad into each alehouse we passed to scan the drinkers inside.

The servant, to his credit, asked no questions and carried out his task.

'No-one in there my lady. To be honest they've all been almost empty so far but this landlord,' he nodded towards the inn he had just left, 'said there's something happening in the town, a rally against the articles of union.'

'Let's go. Your master may be there.'

He hesitated. 'It may be dangerous, my lady. He would be angry with me if I led you into trouble. Perhaps we should go home.'

I wanted to go home too but we would continue until my search proved fruitless. 'Take me to the gathering now.'

We could smell burning and hear the roar of the crowd well before we reached the fire. The sky was lit as if it was day and ash drifted like snow. The people massed in an angry crowd, much fuelled by ale. Someone was haranguing the mob, waving a document above his head that flashed white as it caught the light from the flames. The crowd jeered, their upturned faces reddened by the heat. Men and women jostled for better positions and I could see sporadic fighting erupt like a wave, rippling through the packed bodies. Children ran around the edge, darting between legs, screaming with excitement.

We watched from the dark, fearful of going forward. I pulled on my manservant's arm and pushed into the crowd. I felt bodies press around me and smelt sweat from their clothes and sour ale from their breath. I gripped the boy's arm with one hand and kept my hood tight around my head with the other, scanning the crowd for William. If he was here, he would be near the front. The crowd began to chant, 'Burn! Burn! Burn!' A wave of bodies heaved backwards and my feet were crushed by the heels of those in front. I staggered and lost my grip. In seconds I was parted from my companion. The crowd moved as one and I was carried with them. I held on to strangers to stay upright. It became hard to breathe. My lungs filled with smoke.

A man caught me by the waist and pulled me back through the crowd, brutally pushing past anyone in his path. As he dragged me across the grass and into an alley, my feet barely touched the earth.

He pushed me against a wall and tore back my hood. 'For Christ sake, Win, what the hell are you doing?'

I couldn't speak. I rested my forehead on his chest and cried. William lifted my chin and kissed me, gently at first but then more urgently. 'I'm going to take you home,' his voice was hoarse. 'We'll talk there. Where is your horse? I'll sack whoever it was brought you here and if you came alone, I'll sack Grace.'

'Please. It's my fault. Don't blame anyone else.'

I had no idea where to find my horse. William's was stabled close by and I was lifted up by strong arms to sit in front of him. He wrapped his cloak around me and we made the journey home together, allowing the horse to pick his way through the boulders and gorse so that he was not too burdened by the extra weight. I leaned back against my husband and we talked in low voices, the horse's ears strained back to catch our words. I was glad of the dark and to be facing the shadows of the heath. It was easier. I didn't tell the whole truth. William bent over my ear, kissing the lobe as I confessed that I thought he had run away with Isobel for sex. I had feared for our love. I was afraid of the chasm between us. I'd been replaced in his heart by political ambition.

William whispered that he desired only me but too often I seemed disapproving. I made him feel like a schoolboy. He was fighting for the independence of our country and if I would only try to understand, I would be proud of him. He was no longer the dilettante from St Germain, he whispered, but a hardened politician on the cusp of great things.

Upstairs we tore at each other's smoke-stained clothes before we fell onto our bed. I could taste the ash on William's face and neck and the charcoal from his hands left black smears across my breasts. Our love came fast, fired by fear and rage as well as passion. I prayed for another child, even as my desire rose and I became lost to all but the waves of pleasure that broke across my body.

William's breathing quickly became even, woven through with the gentle sounds of sleep. I lay awake, curled against him, smelling the fire in his hair. I listened to the sounds of the house waking and heard the horses returning from town, enjoying the comforting rhythm of daytime routine and my release from fear. The night seemed far away and I was safe. I could never tell him the truth. Last night, I had believed that my beloved husband had taken Isobel away and killed her.

CHAPTER 15

The dog was the first to stir. Bea had an unfortunate mix of parents, with her short legs and a long tail on a body that would have been better suited to a larger dog. She lifted her head and sniffed the air, then gave a low growl, which woke the other two long-legged hunting dogs who stretched and yawned. Bea began a peal of barking that drove the other two into a frenzy. I was hoeing rows of newly sprouted vegetables, working hard and fast to warm myself against a March wind that made mockery of the spring sunshine. I'd loosened my stays, like the women who work in the fields, and was keen that no one should see me in such disarray.

The noise of horses was unmistakeable and I raised my hand so that I could see who approached the gates. I recognised the coach from Traquair and felt alarm clutch at my belly. Something terrible must have happened. Lucy and Grace were already at the entrance, wiping their hands on aprons and smoothing their hair. The coach halted, spraying tiny pebbles and earth from beneath the wheels as the horses slowed their pace. The footman climbed down, bowed, and opened the carriage door. My son ran from the house and took my hand.

One small girl after another climbed out of the coach and stood solemn and wary.

'It's my cousins!' Will cried. 'But where are the boys?' He turned to me in disappointment as Mary's two eldest sons failed to appear. At last, Mary's head appeared at the carriage door and she was helped down the steps, heavily pregnant and from her size I guessed it was twins. I'd lost another baby, one who had lived only a few days, and there had been no more.

Mary kissed me and I felt her swollen belly press into mine. Will capered around his small cousins and a game of tag erupted, making the dogs bark again. I asked Alice to take all the children to the garden and they trooped in a line after her, followed by the dogs. We supported Mary into the house and settled her by the fire in the drawing room. A servant was sent to fetch warm ale and we watched Mary swallow each mouthful, leaning forward in case we missed a word of her news.

'Dearest Win,' she turned her reddened eyes to me. 'Your husband and mine are in prison. They're being held in Edinburgh Castle. I didn't know what else to do. The babies are soon to be born.'

Lucy looked at me, her face drained of colour. I felt my hands start to tremble and gripped the arms of my chair. I couldn't speak. *Prison.*

Lucy took her daughter's hand. 'Hush now, you did the right thing to come here.'

'They're accused of betrayal, of plotting with the French to restore James Stuart to the throne. I don't know anything else. Men came for my husband and took him away.'

Mary's lips twisted as she fought to hold back more tears.

'I must see William,' I spoke at last. 'I'll have to go to Edinburgh and find out what's happened. Mary, you and the children are welcome to stay here with your mother.'

'It's best I return to Traquair,' Mary interrupted. 'The little ones will be better off at home and the two older boys shouldn't be alone without their father. It's not safe. What if more men come and the house is searched? I should have sent a message but I panicked.'

'Then I'll come with you and stay until the babies are born,' Lucy nodded, looking around her for agreement.

Grace folded her arms, chewing her lip as she always did when she made plans. 'We'll all go to Traquair. Will can stay there to play with his cousins and we'll take the carriage on to Edinburgh and find a lawyer.'

I clapped my hands. 'And we leave as soon as we've packed up some food.'

Edinburgh felt quite different. The Scottish parliament had closed its doors following the act of union and the wealthy had hurried south. The streets seemed narrow and empty, the shops mean and the bustle of clerks and servants diminished. As the high tenements loomed above the carriage, the sense of desolation made my fears grow. Had William and Charles been tortured? Were they being held in a damp cell, their legs and feet clamped in irons?

I struggled up the long, steep climb to the castle and stopped to catch my breath and stretch my aching calves. Grace paused too and scraped her foot against the stones on the path, making patterns in the dirt. She wandered close to the edge and waited, her hands pressed into her back. I followed and we stood side by side, looking down on the city and its clustered rooftops and chimneys. The North Loch lay beneath us, dark and stagnant.

I was glad that Grace was here. Only she would understand how frightened I was of visiting another prison where my family were captive. I could see lines around Grace's eyes and in the unexpected sunshine above the city haze, I noticed a heavy down on her upper lip. I realised that I had no idea what Grace had wanted from life. I had never asked and she had never said.

The guards were reluctant to let us through the gates but Grace was at her most authoritative, insisting that her mistress was in poor health and had travelled for many days to see her husband and brother-in-law. I did not need to act a part. The climb had left me breathless and sweat prickled through my hair and down my neck. I knew I looked pale, with an unhealthy sheen that would convince them of my perilous condition.

Thankfully, William and Charles were not held in a dungeon but in comfortable rooms, well furnished and with high windows that looked across at the hills behind the castle. Charles looked the worse, thin and grey, with new deep lines that ran from his nose to his lower lip. My husband led me to a chair, my brother-in-law brought me wine, and we sat together and spoke of the children and our families. Charles asked so many questions about Mary that my eyes pleaded with William to intervene. Finally, I became impatient.

'For goodness' sake, why have you both been arrested? What have you done?'

William put a finger to his lips and cupped his ears. Of course, our conversation wasn't private.

'I believe that the French fleet attempted to land near here with James Edward Stuart on board,' William said in an unnatural voice. 'They were intercepted by the English and ran back to France. Charles and I were arrested on the assumption that we were in some way complicit.'

'Which I was not,' Charles growled.

'There was an invasion… almost.' I gasped.

'I wouldn't say invasion,' William continued in his schoolmasterly tone, 'I understand it was a pretty half-baked affair. I know very little about it.'

Charles interrupted. 'Win, you must go and speak to my

lawyer and try to get us released. I have to get home to Mary. This is an absolute travesty. And another thing ... we have each been asked to pay several thousand pounds as a bond. Tell the lawyer to find the money.' He looked at William with contempt. 'I'm afraid I can't pay yours.'

I knew immediately that William was guilty and Charles was almost certainly innocent. I rose and pulled William over to the window.

'Could you find nothing better to do than play war games?' I hissed. 'We're one country now, whether you like it or not. There's nothing to be gained. We'll never be able to find this money.'

William shook his head. 'It's worse. Fear of the invasion led to a run on the banks. All my debts have been called in. There's nothing left – I think we might be bankrupt.'

I sat down on the window seat. 'Debts,' I hissed. 'Bankrupt! How could you do this to us, how could you, William?'

'This was our moment. I'm fighting for Scotland, for what's been lost. The people are with us, whatever their faith. It's not about restoring a Stuart king any more but about regaining our country. If it had worked, my debts would have meant nothing. It should have worked.' He leaned his palm on the shutter and wiped his cheek against his shoulder. I had never seen him look so tired. He raised his eyes, red and veined with exhaustion and whispered to me. 'We missed the moment. We missed it, Win, and I don't know why.'

He aimed a slow punch against the shutter with his free hand and pressed his forehead against the wood. From behind, I put my arms around his waist and lay across his back, speaking softly into his ear. 'I'll get you out of here,' I whispered, 'but the cause is over William. It's finished.'

· · ·

From shopkeepers and landlords Grace and I learned more of the botched landing of the Stuart king. The people of Edinburgh were cynical and resigned. Young James had run from battle like his father, they said. What more could you expect from a boy brought up in St Germain by a widowed mother? I remembered the isolated little boy I had cared for, a child who had always been given his own way. It seemed that in the intervening years, he had learned nothing.

My sister Frances told us more about the beautiful plan, foiled by circumstance. James had been too ill to travel because he caught measles and, before a single vessel set sail, the English had all the time they needed to arrest all known Jacobite supporters. Many scores had been settled, Frances said. Anyone of significance who had failed to vote for the union had been imprisoned or threatened with the payment of punishing bonds to stay free.

The following day, Grace and I trudged back up to the castle but were met with news that all the prisoners' cells were empty. We were not the first that day to demand the warden's time and an explanation and while his manners were without fault, he could not hide his impatience.

'They've been moved to London, Lady Nithsdale, all apart from Charles Stewart. It happened through the night. The decision was not mine, I can assure you.'

I felt a pang of jealousy. 'Why was my brother-in-law released and not the others?'

'He'd paid his bond ... and I'm still the warden of this prison, whatever our so-called leaders in England might believe. I knew he was needed at home.'

'They're all needed at home,' I argued. 'What on earth can be gained by this, except to give their families more trouble and expense.'

'London believes that there isn't a viable judiciary left in Edinburgh or Scotland.'

'But that's because everyone is either a prisoner or under suspicion.'

The warden nodded. 'Or has taken their wealth and business south.'

'So this is how our new country works – humiliation and bullying masquerading as security?'

'Yes, my lady, my own humiliation is nothing compared to that of the prisoners and theirs is nothing compared to our former country. Now, if you'll excuse me, I have to complete the prisoners' documents today.'

Unable to secure a loan to pay my husband's bond in Edinburgh, I decided to follow him to London and leave Grace at Traquair. I would take Will with me to London, hoping that my charming eight-year-old, so confident and engaging, would encourage my estranged family to lend me money. Before we left, I realised that my struggle with the walk up to Edinburgh Castle was not the result of months bent over the estate accounts but that I had been feeling unwell for several months. Grace encouraged me to try to contact our physician, Dr Pitcairn, and request an urgent appointment.

We were asked to wait for the doctor in his study but I couldn't sit down. Instead, I paced the room, pretending to read the titles of the leather-bound volumes that lined the walls.

'Ah, Lady Nithsdale, my pleasure indeed, do take a seat.' Dr Pitcairn gestured to a chair next to Grace. 'And how is your mother-in-law, Lady Lucy?'

'She's well, doctor, very well, but I'm afraid for my own health. I can't be ill – not with my husband in prison.'

'A terrible business,' Dr Pitcairn lowered his dense eyebrows and shook his head. 'I too was questioned by the authorities. But what is troubling you?'

In a rush of detail, I explained about the pains in my belly, feelings of dizziness in the morning, my lack of energy and Grace confirmed how exhausting I found any physical activity. Dr Pitcairn asked me to lie on a couch behind a screen and throughout the discomfort of the examination, Grace held my gaze and pressed firmly on my shoulder.

The doctor waited on the other side of the screen for me to dress and as we found our seats, I thought I saw a smile flicker across his lips. He studied me before speaking, his eyes alight with good humour. 'Lady Nithsdale, I am pleased to give you the news that you are with child.'

I gasped, 'But I can't be, I'm still having my monthly bleeds.'

'It can happen, particularly with women who don't easily retain the unborn child. I understand that you have to travel to London but after that you must go home and rest.'

Grace looked at me, her face creased by a smile of relief. 'I'll make sure she does.'

Dr Pitcairn stood to shake my hand. 'Now, away ye go and have another baby, and tell Lady Lucy that I'll see her again within the month.'

We stayed with our old friends Mr and Mrs Mills, who were still resolute in their belief that the Stuarts were the true heirs to the thrones of both England and Scotland and that this would be achieved with the support of the French king. I tried to explain how unlikely this was, given that the French fleet had turned tail at the sight of English men of war in the Firth of Forth. I told them what I knew about Scotland; how much the people continued to suffer under English rule, with unfair taxes and restrictions on trade and that most lowland Scots had little patience for the romantic fantasy of the Stuart cause. What we needed were jobs, decent agriculture and the chance to trade freely with the colonies and that anyone who could deliver this would be supported. They listened politely but I was not heard and I learned to curb my opinions for fear of alienating such dear friends. I said nothing about the expected child, either to my friends or to William, fearing that if spoken of, my hidden and determined child might be lost.

When I visited the Tower, I left my son with my brother at his home. I did not wish upon my own child the horror of an imprisoned parent. Returning to that evil place, I felt as if I had no past; no St Germain, no Terregles, no husband or child, just a never-ending journey of imprisonment, fear of execution and grinding demands for money.

Money was the one thing I didn't have. Mrs Mills was patient about payment for the rooms but I knew her hospitality would have to end. My sisters and brother were sympathetic but they had nothing to lend. Didn't I know that our scheming with the French had brought suspicion on all Catholic families and my sisters' husbands had no hope of advancement in George of Hanover's court? Didn't I care that my brother had suffered another spell inside a prison, Newgate Prison in fact, a facility quite unlike the rooms enjoyed by some in the Tower of London? Wasn't I aware that our estates and titles were still not ours? Everyone except me knew that young James had recently visited his old governess, our sister Lucy, at her convent, surely evidence of another act of betrayal. Our family were believed to be nothing but spies and conspirators. *Didn't I know these things?*

My friends recommended many different lawyers but the rush of impoverished Scots lairds to the south meant that Jacobite funds were scarce. At last, my brother made contact with a sympathetic lawyer who specialised in debt and estate management.

A week after my first appointment, I was immediately shown into Mr Blackstone's study. The document was in Latin but I had retained enough reading knowledge to understand the main points, without having to ask for a translation. I tossed the parchment across the lawyer's polished desk. 'He will never accept this. He's already humiliated. He's lost everything. You can't do this to him.'

Mr Blackstone frowned and steepled his fingers, brushing the tips over his lips. 'Lady Nithsdale, there is no other way. If there was, I would have explained it to you.'

'He's lost his role in government. He's lost the chance to end the union of parliaments. He's lost the chance to restore a Stuart monarch to the Scottish people. You can't ask me to tell him that he'll now lose his estate to his son.'

The lawyer pinched the top of his nose and closed his eyes. 'He'll lose the estate anyway. You're facing bankruptcy. If he can't pay his bond, he won't be released. In time, they'll get tired of feeding and watering him in the Tower of London and they'll seize your estate and kick him out. My lady, it is far better that the estate remains secure in your son's name, rather than held in government hands.' Mr Blackstone tipped his head slightly, in deference to me, but I could see he was becoming impatient. He was treading a well-worn path at the end of which was always the client's defeat and acceptance.

'But what price self-respect? Is there no way we can avoid this further shame? Explain it to me again.'

The lawyer rubbed his eyes. No doubt he was thinking of his dinner, already in preparation, if only he could get rid of me. 'We set up a trust in your son's name. I recommend that your brother-in-law Charles, Earl of Traquair, be one of the trustees. He's a reliable sort.' His eyes looked into the far distance and misted slightly. 'The others are your choice. The trustees will pay your husband's bond and service the debts using income from the estate. The Earl of Nithsdale will receive a small yearly allowance on which you must all survive. When the debts are paid, all income will go to your son and his father will continue to receive an allowance. When your son comes of age, he will inherit the estate.'

'So a father must crawl cap in hand to his son? Beg for money?'

'My lady, this is your only hope of borrowing money to secure your husband's release. As regards your debts, banks will lend to the trustees but not to your husband. He's not a good risk. And may I remind you that the interest on your debt mounts daily.'

'He's a good man,' I whispered.

Mr Blackstone reddened. 'I'm sure he is. Bankruptcy isn't about personal worth but loans are always about profit. This plan will hold the estate for your son, whatever happens. If I may speak plainly, I'm sure your husband will not be content to farm quietly at Terregles Castle. What if he is imprisoned again or even killed? If he signs this, no one will be able to confiscate your land.'

'But what of my son? William may resent him.'

'I'm a lawyer, Lady Nithsdale,' he sighed. 'Those are matters that you must resolve.'

BOOK FOUR

1715–1716

CHAPTER 16

On this perfect day in Braemar, after eight years of broken promises, muddle and disappointment, I allowed myself to believe that perhaps this was our time. Men from the highlands and lowlands of Scotland gathered for a hunting party, united in their hatred of English rule and the betrayal of the Articles of Union. It felt like an occasion of crystal joy, giving hope for what might yet be achieved.

William and I walked arm in arm on the edge of the gathering, looking for Mary and Charles. I wore one of my finest gowns, a leftover from St Germain, let out and trimmed with new lace. William carried our little daughter Anne on his shoulders, supporting her with his free hand. Our son was at school in France, paid for by my widowed sister Mary. Anne pushed William's wig over his eyes and he pretended to be cross with her but she wasn't afraid and she tried it again until he had to be firm. Her bottom lip protruded in a pretend sulk and I tickled her bare foot, making her giggle.

From where we stood, on a bank slightly above the crowd, we could see across to Braemar Castle set low by the river, like Terregles but much grander. The mountains circled us, those furthest away dark brown with a dusting of snow. Behind us, a gentle hill rose, sculpted like a mature woman's breast. The highest ground was purple with heather, studded with outcrops of grey stone and stunted trees between the rocks. Away from the crowds, curlews rose, their rising call burbling, reminding me of the heath at home. Grass carpeted the lowest slopes in the fading sepia of early autumn and the hillsides flickered from brown to gold as the sunlight scattered in the path of the scudding clouds.

I felt a fierce mix of love and pride as I leaned against William's shoulder and watched the mass gathering of the clansmen and lowland lairds, with their families and servants, in front of the castle. For me the Highlands were a new land and the men who belonged there, the fabulous chiefs, were as exotic as any foreign prince. They wore their hair long and loose, with plaid over their shoulders and belted at the waist. Their wives were strong, dark-haired women with blue eyes who watched their husbands closely as they bent over to kiss my hand, a gesture that somehow combined chivalry and flirtation in a single sweep.

'Win, look, it's the Earl of Mar.' William pointed to a small man in full highland dress circulating in the crowd, shaking the hands that reached out to his and slapping the chiefs on the shoulder as if they were his brothers. He carried a sword that ran the length of his shoulder to his ankle.

I had expected a more romantic figure on a grand horse. 'So that's our leader. He doesn't look powerful enough.'

'He's the best we'll get. Remember he was only a civil servant in Queen Anne's government but he has the money and connections to pull this off. He doesn't have to be a fighting man himself.'

'But wasn't he one of the commissioners who worked for the union with England?'

'Mar's on whichever side puts butter on his bread. I heard he'd been snubbed by George of Hanover, who didn't want him in his new government. Never scorn a small rich man.'

'But can he be trusted? Won't he just change sides again?'

'Who can we trust here?' William swept his hand across the crowd. 'How many of these are spies for the English or the French or the Spanish? We can only use the moment for our own ends. Once it's over we'll see who's loyal.'

I heard our names called from below and we climbed down the bank to meet Mary and Charles. Someone began to play a flute and I could smell roasting meat as the venison from yesterday's hunt turned on spits. The men had hunted in the Forest of Mar and William told me of brandy served from a deep hole in a boulder by the side of a rushing burn. It was surprising that so many deer had been killed, I thought. When they returned from the forest, William and Charles had been in no state to ride, let alone hunt.

'This is so exciting,' Mary clasped my arm. 'We've seen Rob Roy MacGregor. He's in a tent over there.'

Even in Dumfries we had heard of the famous Rob Roy. Charles linked arms with us both. 'Come on, I'll introduce you.'

We pushed through the crowds, Charles and William pointing out the clans McLachlan, Rollo, Drummond and McDonald who had set up camps around the edge of the field, their servants and dogs guarding their territory as if part of their fiefdom. Banners proclaimed their clan loyalty, their support for King James and the end of the union. Between the highland camps, local people were selling food and drink and jugglers entertained groups of children. One tent seemed busier than most; a crowd gathered outside hoping to catch sight of the hero within. Charles pushed confidently through and into the tent. I was blinded by the unexpected gloom but saw a tall man pull away from a group to slap Charles on the shoulder. The two men hugged in the fierce, embarrassed way that men do and they came into the light of the entrance where we stood, hesitant. Rob Roy snapped his fingers and a servant brought wine and a rough Scots bread to a table outside, in view of the adoring crowd. Squeals of delight and whistles encouraged Rob Roy to give a full bow to the crowd, who roared their approval. He turned to me, his eyes roaming over my body. Finally, he held my eyes in a deep, experienced gaze that made William move to my side. As we sat around the table, the crowd fell silent, hoping to catch a word from his lips.

'So, Charles Stewart,' Rob Roy sprawled in his seat, 'are you going to shift your lazy arse and fight for your country?'

Charles indicated William with a nod of his head. 'I'll leave that to you younger men. My brother-in-law will be fighting with the lowland men.'

Rob Roy raised his pewter tankard to my husband, and William flushed with pleasure.

'And what will your role be?' I asked our host, unsure whether to call him Rob or MacGregor.

'The wee man over there,' Rob Roy indicated the Earl of Mar with a backward jab of his thumb, 'wants me to help bring out the clans.'

'You mean, to be a sort of figurehead?'

'That's it, lassie. I've no fighting experience but he thinks the chiefs will come out for me. He's no fool, the Earl of Mar.'

'But he does need some experienced soldiers, don't you think?' William interrupted. 'Who do you think he'll recruit?'

As the men fell into a deep discussion of tactics, I studied Rob Roy's long red hair, burnished in the sunshine, and his fine tanned features, and thought he was quite the most desirable man I had seen since we left France. A clansman joined us and leant on Rob Roy's shoulder, whispering in his ear. MacGregor rose and bowed deeply to the women. 'I'm afraid I must go. I've kept my good men waiting long enough.' He shook hands with Charles and William and we were left to finish our wine. The crowd sighed in disappointment and I felt myself do the same.

'Charles, how do you know him?' Mary's cheeks were flushed with pride.

Charles grinned and put his hands behind his head. 'He owes me money.'

'Don't we all?' I heard William mutter.

The men spread their coats on the grass and we sat close to one of the roasting spits where a small band of fiddlers cajoled the cooks to keep turning the handles, although they were already stripped to the waist and streaked with sweat. Men and women began to dance, stepping and turning to the music. As more wine and brandy were drunk, the laughter rose and the pace of the dancing became faster, more tumbling and chaotic. Charles and William followed a rumour that flagons of brandy were being served behind the castle. Anne pulled me over to join the dancing and by the time the men returned my hair had fallen loose across my shoulders and I felt the excitement of laughter and music as if I were a young girl and not a matron of almost forty-three.

We bit into tender slices of meat served on slabs of potato bread, the juice running down our chins and onto our fine clothes. The Earl's brandy burned our throats and throbbed through our veins. The music was the sweetest ever heard, the people the most beautiful, the smell and taste of the food the finest. I loved every person that shouted and swayed in the crowd. We were a band of heroes, brothers and sisters united. Everyone was my friend. Mary began to sing a ballad that Lucy had loved and I joined her, our voices rising in what I believed was beautiful harmony until we both began to cry, as we remembered her mother. Lucy had died two years before, her final years spent at Traquair House with her daughter.

Privately, I believed that disappointment with her son had hastened her end but I knew that she was happy with Mary, helping with her many grandchildren where she could. Will had spent much time there too, sharing lessons with his cousins and having the companionship of older boys. Our home was no longer a comfortable place for our son since his father could not hide his resentment that the estate now belonged to Will.

I pulled my knees towards my chin and resting my cheek there, turned my face to look at Mary. 'I miss your mother.'

'Yes, I do too ... every day,' Mary replied, her eyes glistening.

'When I was in labour with Anne, she sat with me for three days. I thought I would die. But she called for a woman from the village and between them they turned the child. Anne was born within minutes.'

'Ah, I never heard that story.' Mary closed her eyes and began to rock gently, humming the song again.

I remembered how Lucy had wept with relief and joy after the birth and knelt at my bedside, asking me to join her in a prayer of thanks. Although I had closed my eyes as I cradled my newborn daughter, I gave no thanks to God but only to my mother-in-law. If God was given credit for Anne's safe birth, I reasoned, he must be responsible for all the babies lost and I could have no truck with a God so cruel.

A shadow fell across me. A young man's body blocked the sun and I struggled to see his features.

'Aunt Winifred?'

I struggled to my feet and peered at him. It must be my sister Frances' eldest son. How did I look? I wiped a hand across my mouth in case he kissed my cheek.

'Mary, Charles, can I introduce my nephew, the 5th Earl of Seaforth.' I spoke with care in case I slurred my words.

He sat with us on the grass and accepted some brandy. 'I'm here to bring the Mackenzie out to support the cause. I'm the head of the clan.'

I couldn't remember his age; but he was surely not old enough to be fighting? 'Of course you are,' I agreed, wondering why my tongue didn't shape the words in the way I wanted. 'My husband, the Earl of Nithsdale,' I struggled with Nithsdale and had to repeat it, 'is going to fight with the lowland lairds.' We looked at William, asleep on the grass, his mouth open, with Anne spread across his chest.

My nephew exchanged a few polite words with Charles and Mary, and I remembered to ask after the health of my sister. After these pleasantries there fell a tense and disapproving silence. My nephew finished his brandy and excused himself, brushing down his smart new uniform before striding away to join his clansmen.

The sun had set behind the mountains but there were many hours of daylight ahead. We found water to drink and washed our hot faces in bowls of scented water carried through the crowd by servants from the castle. The Earl of Mar was a thorough man, who knew how to throw a party.

We decided to walk again, attracted by the call of highland pipes from across the green. In the fading light, the jugglers had replaced their balls and hoops with flaming torches and the tumbling embers rose and fell against the dark backdrop of the hills, sending out sparks like fireflies. A familiar face, like us somewhat the worse for the Earl's brandy, clasped William's arm and we gasped in delight to see one of our companions from St Germain. He asked for news of my sister Lucy and I felt proud to tell him that she was now the Prioress of her convent. He told us of the loneliness suffered by Queen Mary Beatrice since the death of her daughter from smallpox. This shocking news had failed to reach me at Terregles and I felt sadness for the old queen. She would find comfort in her religion but fate had dealt her too harsh a blow in taking her daughter. I reached out for Anne and pulled her close.

The men boasted of the hunting party. Who had killed the most deer? Who had drunk the most brandy? Anne became fractious and tugged on my hand so Mary and I took her to find a puppeteer. No doubt to the relief of their parents, he had gathered around him most of the small children. A pretty woman stood to one side with three children hanging from her petticoats and another, a baby, in her arms. Mary, who was attracted to small children like wasps to end of summer fruit, tickled the baby and Anne peered out from my petticoats at the other woman's eldest child. In the unspoken way of children, the two joined hands and ran to sit and watch the puppets. The remaining two clasped their mother's skirts for only a second or two more before they waddled away to sit with the older children

'Thank goodness,' the young woman sighed, 'my nursemaid is lying in the castle with a fever and my husband has left me to make plans with the Earl of Mar. I'm Mary and my husband is Viscount Kenmure. He's been asked to command the lowland force.'

I saw the skin on her neck redden with pride.

My husband had hoped that he would be asked to lead these men and I tried to swallow my disappointment. I felt a band tighten around my throat and moved away knowing that my eyes must be bright with tears. One day William must have the chance to show his worth. Even if he dies, let him be proud in death.

As the light fell, the clansmen, the lowland lairds and all the families gathered around a platform which had been constructed for the day. Servants lit torches on three sides and we waited, the drunken laughter and loud voices rising and falling then gradually softening until a hopeful and expectant silence held our tongues, interrupted only by the lowing of distant cattle on the hills. The sad notes of a single highland piper drifted towards us from the castle and we turned, watching, waiting.

The sound of pipes soared then retreated with the wind but gradually became more substantial, until we were able to see the piper, followed by the Earl of Mar and behind him, a standard bearer. Three pipers on the stage joined the lament as Mar climbed onto the platform and stood before us, his hands crossed before his chest. He remained with his head bowed until the music stopped. A moment of breathless quiet was followed by a roar of welcome from the crowd. Bonnets were thrown and men whistled their approval.

One by one the clan chiefs and the lairds were called to the stage, including my husband, his back held straight with pride. The men joined hands above their heads in a chain of loyal brotherhood; Highlanders, Lowlanders, Catholics, Episcopalians, Protestants, united in common cause against the union. The crowd gave an ecstatic roar. One of the young men on the stage smiled at the fair young woman we had met by the puppets. She waved at him and blew a kiss. So that was Kenmure. He stood on the Earl's right and to his left was a middle-aged man who, unlike everyone else, was dressed for battle.

'Who's that man?' I whispered to Charles.

'It's Mackintosh of Borlum. He's to lead the men down from the north to join the lowland forces. He's a very experienced soldier.'

We were shushed by the crowd. The Earl of Mar had produced a parchment and waited for silence. I should have listened more closely but I was watching William, searching his face. Did he know that he had been usurped by Kenmure? Had he guessed from his place in the line what the positioning on the platform meant?

But in the almost darkness, as bats fluttered around our heads the hush was broken by these words, spoken by the Earl.

'Now is the time for all good men to show their zeal for His Majesty's service, whose cause is so deeply concerned, and the relief of our native country from oppression, and a foreign yoke too heavy for us and our posterity to bear; and to endeavour the restoring, not only of our rightful and native king, but also our country to its ancient, free and independent constitution under him whose ancestors have reigned over us for so many generations.'

The flag bearer stepped forward and unfurled the Standard of King James III of England and VIII of Scotland. The flag-bearer was a young man, not quite grown, and he struggled with the weight of the pole. He tugged at the flag to allow the wind to catch and unfurl its bold message. As the standard was raised the orb toppled to the ground and rolled across the stage, settling at the feet of Viscount Kenmure.

I gasped and bit my hand to stop myself from crying out. I had a vision of Kenmure's head lying on the earth at Tower Hill. I heard my voice, 'No! No!'

Kenmure's precious wife covered her mouth and stared at me. Fear crumpled her innocent features. I saw William shake his head and frown.

Charles called out, 'No Union! God save King James!' and the crowd bellowed with relief.

CHAPTER 17

'My darling boy,' I wrote, 'I am glad that you are finding your Greek lessons a little easier. We miss you so much, especially Anne who pines for her big brother. We have some very exciting news. The king's standard was raised at Braemar in September and there is a great army assembled in the north, ready to fight for the restoration of King James and put an end to the despised union with England. Your father is to fight too, leading our local men, and he has spent many weeks preparing ...'

I put my pen down and watched Anne playing with one of the puppies by the fire. How could I tell our son that his father had struggled to persuade but twenty men to join him? We couldn't lose men from our fields or we would starve and our tenant farmers and neighbours were no different. From the estate itself, we had found only the blacksmith's assistant and two of the stable boys, one of whom was a child in a man's body, willing to join the fight. Other local men had been pushed to join; men who drank too much or who were too slow to learn a trade and their families were glad to be rid of them. This was William's army.

I wouldn't tell the boy of the long wait, six weeks now, for something to happen with hope fading at the end of each day when no message came. I stared out of the narrow window panes, as if by watching I could create the sound of a horse cantering towards the castle. I picked up my pen and chewed the end of the quill.

'... *with the blacksmith making swords and daggers and the village women making uniforms. We have asked the blacksmith to make you a dagger like the ones he is making for the men but you must promise me to be very sensible and not let Anne play with it when you come home. Bea has had her puppies, six of them born alive, and we are letting Anne keep one. A fox got one of our chickens last night and I am very cross because she was meant for the pot on Sunday.*

I will write to you again with news of your father and his bravery. Pray for his safety in the battles ahead and be proud of him.

Your loving Mother.'

At last, the call to arms came and William and the other lowland peers hurried to meet with Jacobite forces from the north of England. In letters, my husband spoke warmly of the bravery of their leader, the young Earl of Derwentwater, but he complained that the English Jacobites had failed to take Newcastle and missed their rendezvous with the French fleet, who were bringing precious arms and supplies. William described how they had roamed through Scottish and English towns, receiving a mixed welcome, without any clear direction from the Earl of Mar or further news of the French. As I read his words I heard his frustration and felt my own familiar loss of hope in the Jacobite cause.

My spirits revived as Charles arrived at Terregles with his men from Traquair, bringing news that Mackintosh of Borlum was on his way south with two thousand men and I joined Charles on the ride to Kelso and Jedburgh. Villagers seeking adventure on a warm October morning ran out from their mean, dark cottages as our troops marched past, pursued by wailing women. Charles and I rode at the rear to make sure that stragglers stayed with us and that any boy who looked younger than my son was sent back to his weeping mother.

At Jedburgh, my husband and Viscount Kenmure inspected their troops in the meadows below the ruins of the abbey. From horseback, we watched them ride up and down the ranks, their numbers now quite respectable. William said that this was the third time the men had been inspected as there was little else to do but he hoped to get them moving before the inns of Jedburgh became too much of an attraction. Some of the men were in uniform but the latecomers wore their ordinary working clothes and some carried pitchforks or scythes, whatever they had been able to find in their rush to follow.

Charles and I secured food for the men in the town and several innkeepers joined us on the meadow. A large fire was burning to roast a pig, the innkeepers' wives had made a fresh batch of bread and there was enough ale to keep the men mellow but not drunk. It was clear even to me that the men needed to be moved on as soon as possible but there was still no sign of the highland force. Before it was quite dark, we were joined by a few hundred men from Northumberland and their approach had raised our hopes until we realised that the sound of their pipes was from the south and not the north.

The abbey ruins rose stark and black against the fading light. Smoke from the bonfires around the camp twisted lazily, barely able to rise above the tents without help from even the gentlest breeze. A murmur of voices and fragments of music played together in a quiet rhythm of contentment, as well-fed men turned to thoughts of sleep. Those who had a change of heart had already slipped away through the dark shadows and the remaining men were ones who could be relied on to fight. We sat with William at his fire, mesmerised by the rise and fall of the flames and the shifts of embers. There was nothing more to say.

I caught the first sound. I thought it was a sheep bleating, lost and alone. More sounds drifted, rising and fading, then pipes, unmistakably highland pipes and the tap, tapping of a drum. I touched William's arm. He had heard too. We all heard and stood to listen. The camp fell silent. A rattle of drums, then a roar from the town and our men roared in reply and threw their hats above their heads. The Highlanders had come at last.

In the early morning, before the first rooks were awake, I watched the sturdy Mackintosh, flanked by William and Kenmure, lead what seemed like a never-ending line of men out of town. I felt a joyful pride as William passed, sweeping his hat from his head. Finally, as the last man became a wavering mirage on the horizon and the skirl of the pipes a memory in my ringing ears, I felt empty and alone. The silence was acute, filled only with sounds from inside my head. Slowly, the town awoke. People swept their doorsteps and talked to their neighbours, hands on hips. Mothers scolded their children. Food was bought and sold, coins exchanged. I stood for a long time, watching ordinary life return. Charles touched my shoulder and whispered. 'You have to go home, Win. All you can do now is wait.'

Our quiet life at Terregles irritated. The days, growing shorter and darker, were filled by mindless tasks. I couldn't sleep at night and in the day I struggled to move my heavy limbs or organise thoughts in the thicket of my brain. Anne pestered me to entertain her and I snapped, only to hug her close minutes later. I tried to concentrate as Grace raised endless details about the house, garden and estate but my mind drifted to the sound of highland pipes and William perhaps fighting for his life. I thought I should go to Traquair, where Anne could play with her cousins, but I stayed because news would come first to Terregles.

I had expected a messenger or a letter from William but in late October, the day before the pig was to be slaughtered, Grace and I stood by his sty and scratched his back for the last time. He grunted and shifted so that I could reach the bit he liked, just behind his ear, and I turned my head to avoid inhaling the stink from his sty. We had paid a farmer to come with his men to do the murder and we needed to talk about the gory aftermath of butchery and preservation.

We had just agreed that I would take Anne out for the day, when Grace pointed towards the smithy. 'Isn't that the blacksmith's boy, the one who went off with William?'

I looked closely as a familiar young man strode towards the smithy as if he had been on an errand and was simply in a hurry to get back to his master. He looked dirtier, thinner and more ragged and he stared at the ground, his head bent forward, as if by not looking at us he wouldn't be seen.

'Come on, Grace, let's find out what's happened.' I lifted my petticoats and skidded on my pattens across the muddy yard and into the workshop, Grace close behind.

The blacksmith and his newly returned assistant bowed. This was not women's territory and I felt the unfamiliar burn of the furnace on my face and the stinging charcoal in my nostrils. It was hard to breathe. The boy's face was lit from below. His cheeks and chin shone translucent pink but his eyes and mouth were dark hollows.

'Henry, why aren't you with your master?'

He tugged at the cloth around his neck. 'I came home, my lady.'

'I can see that, but why are you home? Is your master well? Tell me everything.'

'Aye, madam. The master is well. They're marching towards ...' he struggled to remember. 'Aye, that's it, Preston.'

'Why aren't you with him? Wasn't it your duty to stay?'

'My lady, the men from the north, the Highlanders, they said the king's not going to come from France. So they went home. And I did too.'

I leaned my forehead on Grace's shoulder. 'How many men have deserted?' I asked, raising my head.

'Many. We didn't like it down there. The people wouldn't join us. And the king's not coming. So I came home.'

The blacksmith was as protective of his apprentice as he was cruel when they were alone and his tone was hard but polite. 'He's said enough, Lady Nithsdale. Leave the boy. Can ye no see he's worn out.'

The door slammed closed behind us as we left the smithy to walk back to the pig. Grace put an arm around my shoulders but I shrugged her away.

'How could they leave him? This isn't going to end well.'

Grace shook her head. 'You don't know that. The boy was trying to justify his own desertion. It's bound to be an exaggeration.'

'I want to go to him. Other women follow their husbands into battle.'

'But you have a duty to your children and to the estate,' Grace reminded me.

'So we have to wait,' I protested, spreading my hands in despair, 'always to wait. Why is it that men can act but women must wait?'

Grace lifted her head from the pig's broad back, her brown eyes bright. 'But, Winifred, only some women are allowed to act and when they do, they rely on other women to wait. I will not be left here alone, managing the business and raising your child.'

News followed swiftly after the blacksmith boy's arrival. While he had strolled home on his solitary journey to Terregles, we learned that he had left his friends, neighbours and my husband to barricade the streets of Preston. I heard that William and Lord Kenmure had fought, stripped to the waist, until they had been forced to surrender on November 13th.

These unwelcome details came from Lady Kenmure as she sat in my library, with light from a high window falling on her pretty face, torn with grief. At the moment of her telling me, I hated her and my hatred blocked out the words she spoke. I studied her red eyes and dry lips and her curls hanging loose and wild like damp weeds. Her hands gripped each other tightly, as if she needed someone to hold her. She was not so grief-stricken as to fail to notice that I wasn't listening which led her to repeat herself. I understood how much the detail mattered to her but all I wanted to know was whether William was safe. Both of our husbands had been taken prisoner, along with other peers, and they had last been seen in a carriage, presumed to be on its way to London. Other officers had been arrested and twenty-two ordinary soldiers had already hung from the scaffold. Hundreds more had been corralled in a church and left to freeze and starve to death. Many were already herded together at the ports for deportation to the colonies. Breathlessly, Lady Kenmure told me that our urbane host from Braemar, the Earl of Mar, had wasted our advantage by dithering and was now hiding in Perth. Our blacksmith's boy was right, there had been no backing from the French.

Her story told, she fell silent and I shivered as the cold night seeped into the room. Like the last of the light, I felt any shred of hope drain from me. Alice crept in to light the fire and whispered that we could join Grace and Anne at the table for some supper. Out of duty I had to offer the heartbroken young woman hospitality and my coldness towards her softened when I watched her play with Anne and saw her struggle to put her grief aside to answer Grace's questions.

Once Lady Kenmure and her servants were settled for the night, I sat sewing by the drawing-room fire with Grace, as was our habit. This was our time to share the small details important to those who manage large but impoverished estates. Tonight we sat in silence and my needle rested on my lap. It was impossible to plan until we had more news. I found I couldn't speak my thoughts. So much had been lost. The future was empty. And William might yet die at the executioner's sword.

Word came in time. William's letter was business-like and he assured me of his good state of health and mind. He asked me for money, which was the one thing I couldn't find. My scrupulous management of the meagre amount the trustees allowed us every month meant that we had a well-stocked larder and cupboards of clean linen but there was never any money. He pleaded that I come to London at once, as he expected to be imprisoned again in the Tower but, without money or a friend to plead for him, his situation would become intolerable.

I knew that my own small drama was far outweighed by the loss of the Jacobite dream but selfishly, I could only grieve for us. Without the glory of victory, how would my husband ever lift his head again? I knew I should go at once to Traquair and seek advice from Charles but I felt reluctant. Once given advice I would be expected to act and unlike before, when fear and fury would have driven me to William's side, a strange, leaden despondence settled on my limbs and I wanted nothing more than to curl up on my bed with my child, smell her odour of freshly mown hay and sleep for ever.

CHAPTER 18

The moment I arrived at Traquair, Anne and Alice were swept away to the nursery and I joined Charles in the new library, the heads of philosophers glowering from a painted frieze over the bookcases. Charles was agitated, anxious for his own safety. The government's spies must have known that he had not been active on the battlefield but they would have guessed at his complicity in other ways. Charles paced before me, cracking his knuckles.

'I've had very bad news, Win. My contacts in London are certain that William and the other peers will be accused of treason and a date will quickly be set for their execution. George of Hanover will want to make a spectacle of them but he'll be keen to settle the matter without delay.'

Fear growled in my belly, as if I might empty my bowel. 'What can we do, Charles? What's for the best?'

He wasn't listening. 'I know you'll want to get down there as quickly as you can. William will need money and a good lawyer. I've arranged both for you. You must close up the house, dismiss the servants and leave as soon as you can.'

'But I'm not sure ...'

'Don't worry about the money. I won't want it back. The carriage is waiting to take you back to Terregles. Leave the child here, with her nurse. That's one less thing for you to worry about. She'll be happy here.'

Back in the nursery, I watched Anne play. She stood with her hands on her hips, her back to me, lecturing her cousins, trying to organise the game. She had no idea. A solitary child, one who has adults for companions, must think that this is how games are played. Her cousins, mindful of my presence, were sullen but cooperative. It wouldn't last and poor little Anne would have some hard lessons to learn.

Mary entered and drew the curtains. The room was warm and comfortable with the smell of children and nursery tea. Mary would help her children eat, read to them and watch the nursemaids bath them until she had to dress for dinner with Charles. I wished I was Mary.

She whispered to me, 'Win, the carriage is waiting. You must go. Please try to save my brother.'

I put my hands on her shoulders and looked into her eyes, so like William's. 'Please care for my little girl. Be kind to her. Be patient with her. Talk to her about me, in case she forgets.'

'Win, you must say goodbye to her now. Delay no longer.'

I bent to kiss Anne's cheek but she was distracted by the table laid with milk, cake and honey. I turned her around to face me.

'Anne, I have to go away for a while. I'm going to help your father. I will come back for you.'

Anne hesitated and for a moment I had her attention. I held her close and smelt her end of day, dirty child's body. She pulled away from me, calling goodbye over her shoulder, waving as she ran to her place at the table.

. . .

The moon was full and bright above the battlements of Terregles. Thin strips of cloud gave the moonlight a temporary fragility but did not diminish its strength. At the end of the terrace I waited for Grace, my long shadow reaching into the darkness. I had two packages at my feet. One was a leather box containing legal documents, proof that Terregles and all its farms and land belonged to my son. The other, a bundle of stiff cloth, contained the body of our old dog Bea.

Grace appeared from the direction of the blacksmith's workshop, dragging behind her two large spades. I watched Grace cross the grass and her shadow touched me well before she was close enough to speak. Looking back at the house, the windows were shuttered and blank, like the eyes of an old woman.

Grace passed me a spade. 'You dig the hole for the dog. I'll dig the hole for the box because it will have to be deeper. Make your hole on the other side of the terrace,' she pointed into the darkness, 'because if a fox digs her up, we don't want the box of documents to be exposed as well.'

We separated and began to lift the turf. The ground was hard with frost and our spades scraped and rang so loud against the earth that I feared we would be heard in the village. Everyone was gone from the house. The last of the servants had left and only two horses remained, saddled and fed, so that we could leave at dawn. We couldn't trust anyone to help us.

I dropped my spade onto the grass, having lifted only a few inches of soil, and walked back to Grace. My throat hurt from breathing in the frost. With her strong dairymaid's arms Grace was making better progress and I watched her dig. She stood up and leaned on her spade, steam evaporating from her body as if she was on fire.

'It's strange in the yard, Win. No sounds from the cows, the blacksmith's fire so cold. Do you think we'll ever come back?'

'I hope so,' I said, then hesitated. 'Maybe not us. My son might return, with his family. I can't see a future here, not right now. Not for you or me or William.'

'It feels like we're abandoning Lucy. This was her home. She would have hated to see this.' Grace wiped her cheek, leaving a smear.

'I'm glad she's not here to witness any of it, her son's ordeal or this flight from Terregles, but when things are resolved you could come back. I can't manage this journey without you but you don't have to stay with me for ever.'

Grace turned away and attacked the frozen ground as if she hated it. I trailed back to my patch and chipped at the frosted earth, scraping layer after layer, thinking of Grace and her life with me. She had been my mother-in-law's closest friend and companion and yet I had barely considered how she must have felt after Lucy's death. I saw that I had been blind to Grace for many years, yet I owed her so much. This house and garden were more hers than mine, if hard work and commitment counted for anything. I saw that Grace must be desolate. Whatever happened next, I would release her from my service if she wanted to go. This must be the last thing I asked of her.

I lifted the hard, frozen rags into the grave and scraped earth over Bea's body. Unwanted by any of the servants, we had found her shivering under the horse's drinking trough in the yard. A stable boy had despatched her as his last job. She lived on in the puppy that had gone to Traquair with Anne. As I stood over her grave, I reflected that her life had been the same as any other female. We try to breed, sometimes we lie down in a patch of sun, then we die. I replaced the turf and pressed it down with my boot.

In the kitchen, Grace pulled me close but our cheeks didn't touch. We said goodnight, hoped that each other might sleep, and Grace took a candle and went to her room. Her light

186

vanished as she turned into the passage. I took my candle and wandered the empty rooms. Some of the furniture was covered with old bed linen, hostage to our possible return. Other furniture was earmarked for Traquair, to be kept for our children should they lose us. Where was my home? Was it this house and its cold, sparse interior? I'd lived here for fifteen years yet had never felt that I belonged. In a flickering pool of light I climbed the stairs to Anne's room, missing the tap of the dogs' claws following behind. I sat down on her small bed and looked around me at her familiar things, dark silhouettes in a palette of grey. Would she want her doll's house or her puppet theatre? Perhaps Charles could fetch them with the furniture.

Until the dawn smeared the sky an ominous red, I lay curled on Anne's bed. I had given up my child. If I died and William was beheaded she would belong to Charles and Mary. I'd made this decision because of the assumptions of others. I hadn't found the courage to say, 'No, wait. I haven't decided whether to go. Let's talk about it. What's best for the children? Is there another way to help William?'

I heard Grace in the kitchen; for the last time, she had lit the hearth and boiled water so that we could wash. Porridge bubbled in a pot hanging from a trivet.

'Did you sleep?'

'Not a wink. Did you?'

I shook my head. 'I don't like the look of that sky. I think it might snow.'

'As long as it's not too heavy it will be safer. People will stay by their firesides. We won't attract any attention.'

I washed my face and hands in a bowl that Grace had set upon the kitchen table. A clean, folded cloth lay beside it. I thought of these objects lying undisturbed for months, perhaps years. I would come back and the towel would be lying, curled up and dry exactly where I had left it.

I trickled honey across my porridge and took my first mouthful, dragging it from the spoon with my teeth because it was so hot. 'We should be in Newcastle in a few days. Charles showed me a route that avoids most towns and there are inns where we can rest overnight. Once we're on the coach to London, the worst will be over.'

'Charles should have provided us with some men to see us safely to Newcastle.'

I thought this too but felt it disloyal to agree. 'It would be too obvious with men. We're better on our own.' I carried on eating, spooning the porridge down fast. We cleared our plates and poured water on the fire then wrapped ourselves in layers of our warmest clothes.

Grace laughed. 'No one will recognise us like this. You look like that fat woman from the village.'

'And you look like her sister,' I replied. 'Come on, Grace,' I linked arms with her, 'it's time for one last journey.'

CHAPTER 19

It took us five days to reach Newcastle. The snow fell in plump, heavy flakes, swirling around us like feathers burst from a torn pillow. Our horses were slow, sturdy animals with thick winter coats, not easily alarmed but not easily hurried either. They lowered their heads and shook their harnesses, pushing through the blinding flurries on paths that were still familiar. When we reached strange territory, the sun came out and we stepped softly across countryside empty of animals or people, only the wisps of smoke rising from cottages reminding us to keep quiet. We passed through secretly, protected by the blanket of snow.

The innkeepers showed little curiosity about two middle-aged, sturdy country women on their way to Newcastle. The assumption was made, time and time again, that we were farmers' wives, used to travelling alone through the Borders. We avoided conversation but if we needed to speak, our English accents raised no alarm. Around us we heard grumbling about the heavy tax burden on farming communities imposed by the government but the failure of the recent uprising was met with resignation and cynicism. The union with England seemed to be disliked but accepted with a shrug. I wondered whether William and his friends had been misled about the level of popular support for their cause and whether we hadn't deluded ourselves by mixing only with those of like minds. The people drinking in these inns seemed to want fair government and food in their bellies and anyone who delivered this would be respected. There was certainly no enthusiasm for a Catholic king.

In Newcastle, we hurried to the offices of the coaching company. The man who sold tickets took an agonising time to scan his lists but looking over his shoulder I could see that all the coaches to London were full until Christmas. A man behind me in the queue suggested the three of us ride on to York together, as there would be more coaches from there. I thanked him but I knew we needed to rest and our horses fed and stabled. He bowed to me, accepting my decision but offered to book seats for us all when he reached York.

I had another reason to make sure I took a night's rest. The night before William left to fight at Preston we had made the sort of love that can produce a baby. My monthly bleed was late and my breasts were swollen and tender. This brought me no joy. We had tried so hard to fill our house with children but now, with no home and William in prison, another child would be unwelcome.

I had to tell Grace as soon as we were huddled over the tiny fire in our room. Her silence was uncomfortable and then words spilled from her mouth, cruel words that only echoed my shame.

'You ought to have told me this before we left home. If you're with child, we could have stayed. Neither Charles nor William would ever have expected you to travel to London in winter if they'd known.'

'We couldn't have stayed. After what's happened, how long before the troops arrived at Terregles?'

'But we might have sought protection at Traquair,' Grace argued.

'And involved Charles and Mary? Charles would have been arrested and what then?'

Grace fell silent, then spoke again. 'For goodness' sake, Winifred, you're forty-three. How do you know it's not the change?'

'Because I have no signs of the change. My monthly bleed is regular, my skin is smooth and unlined, there's no hair on my face. I'm having another baby.'

'This is a bad thing, Win. We have a perilous journey ahead of us. You need your strength to fight for William. I can't act for you if you're laid up in bed. You should have thought about this before you did the act.'

I studied my hands. 'If they'd won, if he hadn't been taken prisoner, another child would have been glorious,' I whispered.

Grace said nothing more but turned her face from me. Was she thinking that the chains that bound her to me grew tighter with this news, that she wouldn't ever be able to leave me if the worst happened to William? I would set her free, I told myself. I was determined.

The weather turned bitterly cold with a hard frost but our ride from Newcastle to York was without incident. There was only one seat on the coach from York to London, reserved for us by our friend from Newcastle, but he was not so gallant as to give up his own seat for a lady, or at least a lady he assumed was a servant. I argued with Grace that she should take the seat first and I would hire a fresh horse and ride alongside the coach. I hoped to shame our hero into offering his seat when he saw me mount the horse. From his fawning good humour, I guessed that he was looking forward to my company to pass the long hours ahead and I hoped to spoil his plans. But Grace was stubborn and wouldn't agree, since she knew that I was probably with child, even though I reminded her how sick the rolling movement of the coach would make me.

We had been travelling for less than a day when snow fell in deep, blinding drifts. From the window there was only a grey light, filled with darting white arrows. The other passengers complained as I opened the blinds, struggling to keep Grace's dark shape in sight. Her new horse, panicked by his temporary blindness, made certain he kept close to his companions but there were times when I couldn't see her and I called out for the carriage to stop in case her horse had stumbled and she was lying in a ditch. I was terrified we would lose her. There were moments I was so fearful that the other passengers joined me in banging on the roof for the driver to stop.

We were delayed many times. The wheels sank into deep drifts in the ditches at the side of the track and we had to climb out so that we could free the coach. Some of the passengers were elderly and there was nowhere for them to shelter, as those of us fit enough to thrust a shovel into snow were put to work. This wasn't the beautiful snow of the Borders. There was a penetrating wind that froze the nose and fingertips in seconds. Nothing of the landscape was recognisable and it was as if the world had stopped. I felt certain that someone would die; from cold, from lack of food or from exhaustion. When we moved, the carriage was silent. Everyone was afraid and I imagined that we all thought of death and were preoccupied with the manner of our dying. No one would give up their seat for Grace.

My own thoughts were troubling. I believed I was being asked to pay too high a price for my husband's foolish ambition. *This is completely and utterly pointless, ill-judged, reckless and foolish*, I raged. In my anger I dropped the back of one hand firmly into the upturned bowl of the other, making a smacking sound that startled the terrified passengers. We should have considered other ways to fight for William's freedom. What were the other wives doing? Grace was right, perhaps I could have stayed at Terregles and held onto our home for the children's sake. If we lost William, better that they should still have their mother and their home.

But I could never say these words. It was too late to turn back. We were committed to the journey and it had to be endured, day after endless day. The snow now fell on ice and the horses' hooves slid, making the carriage swing and sway. We stopped hourly, to dig out the wheels or for a passenger to vomit. I begged Grace to let me ride the horse. I could barely see her eyes through the ice that had settled on her hood but she persistently refused. We stayed at whatever inns we found open along the way as the horses were exhausted after only a few hours of travelling.

After six long days our carriage turned over in a ditch. We knew exactly where we were because, at last, the blizzard stopped and a sign told us that in sixteen miles we would have reached Grantham if our carriage wasn't broken and one of our horses dead. Two of the elderly passengers, both women, were confused and one had a cut to her head. We could see smoke rising from a settlement across open land and after some argument, we pushed through snow that was thigh deep, digging our way out from the deepest drifts, so that the old women could be carried by the men. Finally, the horses were led to safety behind us. There was a small hostel, a low-ceilinged dark hovel with smoking fires and rooms that smelled of dogs. The landlord was persuaded to find space for our large party and stable our horses while we waited. No one was quite sure what we would wait for but there was a general consensus that we would wait.

I found Grace in one of the bedrooms, cleaning the wound on the woman's forehead. She saw me peer around the door and hissed 'Winifred, wait!'

She lifted the shaken old woman's hand and pressed it

against the cloth to hold it in place, then joined me at the open door. 'We can't stay here, Win. Let's go on, alone.'

I was horrified. 'Go on! You can't mean it.'

'I do. What's the point of this journey if we don't get to William as quickly as possible? He must be desperate, with no word from you, and your family will be beside themselves with worry. Anyway, if we hang around here we'll be left in charge of these two.' She swept her thumb backwards to take in the two old sisters, now dozing by their smouldering fire.

'But you've ridden for days, in the bitter cold. Surely you want to rest?'

'Look at the weather, Win. It's not snowing. Let's take our chance and go. If we stay we're wasting money that you'll need in London. The landlord is certain to overcharge.'

I crossed the room and looked out of the dirty window at fresh white snow, like sweet, sugar icing and a fierce blue sky.

'You're right, Grace.' I agreed. 'Let's hire new horses and leave this lot to fend for themselves.'

On Christmas Day we reached the George Hotel in Stamford. We stayed for one night, demanding hot, scented water and bath sheets and dried our hair before the fire in our room. We ordered food, roasted pigeons with vegetable broth, and ate with our fingers, letting the gravy dribble from our fingers onto the shifts we'd borrowed from the hotel. We insisted that the hotel find a washerwoman to make our clothes fit for London. In our shared bed, we giggled at stupid things; how Grace had looked with icicles hanging from her eyebrows and the selfish men who had shared our coach. Now we were safe, these things were funny. I could smell Grace's warm body and twisted between my fingers a strand of her hair that spread across my pillow. I moved over to rest my head on her chest. We fell silent, listening to men and woman calling to each other in the street. My thoughts were of William, without visitors on Christmas Day, and Anne, without her parents, and Will, in France, without news. No doubt Grace thought of Terregles, standing cold and empty without her.

The snowbound countryside vanished as we travelled south, and late the next day we arrived at the Mills' house in Duke Street. The servant was reluctant to let us in but we persuaded him to lead our horses round to the stables and allow us wait in the hall while he sought Mrs Mills. In the mirror we saw what he had seen, two rough-looking women, with dirty riding cloaks and faces reddened with cold. Mrs Mills rushed into the hall, flapping her hands.

'My dears, we've been so worried about you. Thank goodness you wrote from that inn or we would have thought the worst.' She led us up the fine oak staircase to the drawing room, where Mr Mills put aside his book and stood up, holding out his hands to us in welcome.

'Winifred, Grace, come in and get warm. I've tried to see William but he's allowed no visitors. Thank the Lord you're here and safe.'

Our travelling robes were carried away and we were encouraged to sit close to the fire. I had forgotten how elegant English houses could be and while our hosts fussed arranging food and warm ale, both Grace and I gazed at the plasterwork ceilings and the tall marble chimneypiece and overmantel. The walls were coloured a deep pink in the latest wall covering which I remembered was called wallpaper. We had only heard of such things in rural Scotland. Our hosts wanted to talk about the terrible defeat at Preston and how bravely our men had fought but I stressed that I must go to William at once. They saw that arguing was pointless and Mr Mills offered to take me to the Tower as soon as we had eaten. I left Grace in the company of Mrs Mills, pleased she could rest at last. I would rest once I'd seen my husband.

Access to the Tower was only possible through narrow pathways lit by rush torches that created dark corners and threatening shadows. The cobbles shone, wet with melted ice that would soon freeze. Mr Mills waited in the carriage as close as he could to the nearest entrance for William's prison. Alone, I hurried past the Bloody Tower, where men and women had once been tortured, when our country was a little less civilised, and Traitor's Gate, where the executed bodies had been disposed of in silent boats at night. I turned past the green and ran down the path to the Lieutenant's Lodgings.

I was prepared to be refused and had enough money with me to guarantee a change of heart in the most ethical warder. But to my relief, I found that the Lieutenant's Lodging was now guarded by wardens who had once been in charge of rooms where titled women had been held prisoner. I was recognised immediately by the warden's wife, once employed as a girl to do my mother's washing.

'Heavens!' She squealed with delight. 'I'd know you anywhere! When you were a little girl you used to visit your mother. Every week you came and a right sad little thing you were too.'

I smiled as broadly as I could manage and, to my surprise, I remembered her name despite my exhaustion. 'Marian! My mother always said her clothes were washed perfectly.'

My ingratiating words were ignored, as Marian called her husband to see the little girl who had once visited the Countess of Powis.

'Tom, come over 'ere,' she bellowed. 'Guess who this is? It's that little girl who used to visit her mother. Yes, that's right, it were years ago. Do you remember? The lady from Wales who had the castle.'

As Tom hurried over, Marian studied me. 'Such a good little girl you were. Always a polite and grateful child.'

'You were such a good little girl,' Tom repeated, 'and a pleasure to serve your mother.'

I shared the sad news of my mother's death, hardly unexpected given my all too evident age, but their sympathy meant that only a few coins had to pass between us before I was allowed to see William. Tom escorted me up familiar stairs, through the guards' hall to a room close to where I had once visited my brother.

I pressed my clammy hands together as the warden explained to the guard who I was. The door was unlocked and I was announced, as if this were a social event. William had his back to me but he spun on his heel as he heard my name.

'Winifred, at last. I've waited every day for you.' William held me close and I pressed my forehead into his neck. I could smell his familiar scent, a mix of vanilla and earth but there was an overlay of old, anxious sweat. He felt thin through his clothes which were sticky with grease.

My new friend Marian brought us ale and slices of thick, rough bread and I thanked her many times.

'Marian, please may we have a fire?' The room was damp with a clammy, penetrating cold.

'He can't pay for fires,' she announced, hands on hips.

'He'll pay for fires now I'm here, and better food, please. And Marian,' it was important to keep using her name, 'how much does it cost to have clothes washed?' I used my mother's gracious tone, the one that expected no argument.

Marian's eyes narrowed and she curtseyed. I watched the thought track across her open face that, at last, someone was in charge of this prisoner. Even better, someone with money. It would be worth her while to look after him.

Once we were alone, William and I studied each other in

the candlelight, holding hands. His skin was pale and deep shadows fell beneath his cheekbones.

'I'm sorry I couldn't be here sooner, my love,' I whispered. 'The journey took over two weeks. The weather was appalling and there were times when I thought we'd lose our lives. I've money from Charles and the name of a good lawyer in London. Now I'm with you, we can start fighting for your release.'

William shook his head and sat down at the table. He poured ale into two pewter tumblers and began to tear at the bread. I sat facing him and waited for his reply.

'I've been charged with high treason, along with the six other peers. We're to be sentenced in early February. It's certain to be execution, what else could it be? I'm preparing for my death, Win. I'm ready for it.'

I grasped his hand. 'No William, we must fight. You will not die.'

William looked at me with his hooded eyes and shrugged. 'What is there to live for? Do you know that our so-called king has finally arrived in Scotland, too late of course to give any help to that fool Mar. He landed at Peterhead just before Christmas but I'm told he was too ill to meet anyone. The guards love giving me such news.'

'But we could move abroad, perhaps to Rome. Think of me, our children, your family.'

William wiped his hands over his face, stretching back his cheeks and allowing them fall back. His lower eyelids were reddened and the skin below his eyes dark and pouched.

'I'm tired of failing,' he sighed. 'I don't want to run. The Jacobite cause has been my life.'

'You can have a life without a cause,' I reasoned.

'They've already hung the officers. Why should I live? Because I'm a peer? What sort of country is this, where a title makes a difference to whether a man lives or dies?'

He leaned forward, became animated. 'Do you know what they did to us when we reached London?' He jabbed at the table. 'We were trussed like chickens and blindfolded. They led us through the streets on horseback, so that everyone could see us. People threw rotten food. The worst thing was the jeering.'

William took a deep draught of ale and wiped his mouth. I sipped at mine to stop the tears. I had a pain low in my belly and I had started to sweat.

'But if you live you could still make a difference.' I tried to keep my voice low and reasonable but it caught and trembled as frustration and rage flushed across my face and neck. 'There is much to put right in our new country.'

'And how would that work if I was hiding in Rome?' William sneered.

I felt exhaustion wash over me. I stood to leave and pulled my cloak around my shoulders. 'I must go, William. I'll speak to the warden's wife and make sure you have what you need. I'll come again tomorrow, but now I must rest.'

CHAPTER 20

I returned from the Tower and splattered my unborn child into a porcelain bowl after hours of pain, shaking like a dog in whelp. I developed a fever and lay in Mrs Mills' perfect guest chamber, sometimes lucid but at other times hovering in a world where sound and time obeyed no ordinary rules. The bed had drapes of kingfisher blue and sometimes the colour shone so brightly it hurt my eyes. Above me on the ceiling swooped a plasterwork eagle which I saw preen its feathers and pause, staring at me as if I were a mouse on the ground.

Grace and Mrs Mills visited William and it seemed I had paid Marian enough to secure adequate food and warmth. In my conscious moments I went over our meeting and tried to understand how it must be to face death in full awareness of your fate. Most of us slip away without planning and are not reprimanded for a self-centred attitude at the point of death. I must not judge him, I decided. Until I faced my own death before an executioner, I couldn't possibly know how I would behave.

I was desperate to see William on the day of sentencing and persuaded Grace and Mrs Mills to allow me to rise from my sickbed even though I was still weak from a month of fever. After hours of waiting to be admitted, the families of the peers were crushed into seats at the back of Westminster Hall. I tipped my head in recognition of Lady Kenmure, like me thin and pale. The other wives, who looked as distraught and anxious as I felt, I didn't recognise.

We could not have doubted that this was a grand state occasion, that our husbands' fate was a spectacle, as the members filed silently in from the Commons and the Lords from the Upper House. The presence of the Prince of Wales reminded everyone, including the judge Lord Cowper, that the fate of these prisoners was of great interest to the king. A rumour swept through the women that all the prisoners had agreed to accept a guilty verdict and were hoping for the king's mercy.

My head ached and I struggled to hear William's plea. His voice was unrecognisable and he persistently cleared his throat as if he hadn't spoken for some time. I wanted him to see me, for him to know that I had come. I tried to stand but an usher signalled that I must sit down.

I listened to William beg for his life. Something shifted beyond my understanding, as I heard my husband deny that he had ever plotted to overthrow the monarch. It had all, somehow, been an accident. Our glorious days at Braemar, at Jedburgh, had been nothing more than William falling in with a bad lot, accompanied by only a few servants from our estate. It was nothing really, nothing at all. George of Hanover could count on William's loyalty, most definitely.

Again, I reminded myself that I should not be quick to judge. I too had persuaded him to fight for his life. But how would we live together with this between us? He would hate what he had said and he would hate me for having heard it. My ears buzzed and I felt my scalp tingle as the fever crawled back inside me. The judge's words sounded like an echo, as if he had spoken from the depths of a cave. I heard the words 'cut down alive' and 'bowels taken out and burnt before your faces' before I fell across Mrs Mills in a deep faint.

The next day I was allowed to sit up in the library, wrapped in a blanket, to receive Lady Kenmure and Lady Nairn. I listened to their plan for a joint petition to parliament and agreed to help fight for our husbands in any way my health would allow. Time was short. The date would be set for the execution in a matter of days and we had already received word from the Lieutenant Governor of the Tower that if I visited William again I would be held with him until the execution.

I sat alone, looking out on the February garden. It was unusually cold and the bare branches and statuary melded into a pattern of grey and brown. Nothing moved. The door opened and Mrs Mills, followed by Grace, pushed backwards into the room with a tray. Grace sat down next to me and placed cups of steaming chocolate on a small table between us. I noticed how pretty the table was, with its pie crust edge and inlaid wood of different colours.

'How are you feeling?' Mrs Mills asked.

'Frightened,' I replied.

'It's an awful sentence. The judgement was very harsh.'

I took a sip of chocolate to help me speak. 'There's brandy in this.'

'Just enough to give you some strength. There's much to do.'

'I can't face it. I can't face his death, not like that.'

'Then we have to fight to save him. We only have a few days. You have to contact everyone you know of influence.'

'Perhaps we can't live with this either, hiding for the rest of our lives in France or Rome, without our children or any income. We'd be better dead.'

'Win, you have to snap out of this,' Grace interrupted. 'You don't have to live abroad. You don't have to live without the children. If William survives, those are choices you can make. But at the moment William has no choice but to face being hung, drawn and quartered. You must try to save him. If you don't, you will exist but not live, wherever you are. William means everything to you, he always has ...'

'What can I do?' I pleaded. 'The other women have the petition in hand.'

'We should try to tap into the disgust the country feels at the way the ordinary men were treated at Preston. The sentence given to William and the others is barbaric. The king won't want to be regarded as an animal. If we can generate enough disapproval, he might be persuaded to show mercy.'

I thought about this, sipping my chocolate, feeling the warmth of the brandy creep into my limbs. Grace was right, I must act. No one else could save my husband. I had to try to see him again in the Tower.

Marian required a very generous bribe and cake from Mrs Mills' kitchen before she agreed to let me see William and give me her word that I would be allowed to leave. I needed her on my side, so I lingered with her.

'Your mother healed me when I had a fever,' she poured me some warm ale. 'My old mum was ever so grateful. She had time for people, your mother did. She was special.'

'Many people thought so,' I agreed. 'I'm afraid I haven't inherited her qualities.'

Marian peered at me. 'You look very peaky if you ask me, but no wonder, what with everything that's going on.'

'I was with child when I came before. The child was lost but I'm lucky, I have a healthy son and a little girl ...' I couldn't find the words to continue.

Marian lifted her skirts to warm her knees in front of the fire. 'Gawd, we lose too many. I've had twelve but only three living.'

'You must ask my husband about his sister Mary. She's had seventeen births with thirteen living.' I saw Marian's interest in her prisoner stir and at last, she offered to lead me to his room.

William was crouched at a table, his back rounded and his neck sunk between his shoulders. He was reading the Bible and raised his eyes from the text with reluctance, as if he minded being disturbed.

'Winifred,' he stood to kiss me, 'you're recovered at last. Grace told me you'd lost another child. I'm so sorry.'

'The baby was conceived in hope. It's best he wasn't born to live in despair.'

'I'm preparing for my death,' William indicated the Bible. 'The priest comes every day. It's allowed. They're being generous at the very end.'

We sat on opposite sides of the table and I reached across for his hand. 'There's still hope. Help me with a plan.'

William sighed and shook his head. 'The lawyer says that Terregles has been sequestered and is now in the hands of the government. They've confiscated all our land to pay for the cost of the trial and execution.'

'But they can't do that,' I stammered. 'The estate belongs to our son and he's done nothing wrong. We must fight this.'

'You'll have to fight alone. I know you will. You're beautiful, clever, strong. I'd have been nothing without you. I'm sorry if I haven't told you often enough.'

'Your love has meant everything to me,' I whispered. 'We've made a family together. We still have a home. I'm sorry I've been so sensible. I haven't always been able to share your ...'

'But you helped me fly, Win. I found a purpose. Without you I'd have been a Scottish dilettante, hanging around whatever court would have me. My only regret is that I pleaded for my life in Westminster Hall. I hated every word I said. It made a mockery of all the men who died at Preston, the men who were executed or frozen to death and those who now slave in the colonies. I have to be executed.'

'Listen to me, William, we must fight this even if all we achieve is a better death for you and future prisoners. This country must learn to act like the civilised land it pretends to be. We could try to persuade the king that it's to his advantage to be seen as a modern man. You might still be able to help others, even at the moment of your death.'

'I'm not afraid. It won't be painful. The priest has assured me I'll quickly lose consciousness. But if you want to fight I won't stop you. I know you well enough not to try. If I were you, I'd try to meet the king and plead your case. You're still a very handsome woman and he's just a man. Use it to your advantage.'

CHAPTER 21

Mr Mills listened to me explain William's plan as we travelled home from the Tower. 'He thinks I should try a personal approach to the king, since it's tradition that the king must listen to a petition from a woman. Is it possible for me to meet with him in the short time we have left?'

He frowned and took time to answer. 'I'm not sure if a petition from you would be accepted under the circumstances. You might be arrested. It's very risky.'

'But if I was willing to take the risk, can you think of any way the king might be persuaded to meet me?'

Mr Mills rested his elbows on his knees and thought. Finally he spoke, 'We have a friend, Mrs Morgan, who attends social events at the palace. I believe there's a gathering tomorrow night. You might be able to slip in with her.'

After dinner, I was introduced to Mrs Morgan, a tall, handsome woman, the wife of a respected Jacobite sympathiser. We sat in a circle, Grace and Mrs Mills included, and my gaze swept over the group before I spoke. 'I know I'm asking too much of you all but I have to grasp every chance until William's fate is certain.'

Mr Mills explained the plan and Mrs Morgan listened, never taking her eyes from his face. I couldn't read her expression. Would she agree? These gentle people had to live here after Friday's execution whereas I would be gone, either executed like William or fleeing from capture.

Mrs Morgan hesitated before she looked at me. 'I will have to ask my husband but if he agrees, be ready for my carriage tomorrow evening. I will make sure you meet the king, one way or another.'

Although I was introduced without challenge to the drawing room where invited London society met to play cards, flirt and plot, I doubted that Mrs Morgan would ever be asked again. Voices lowered as we entered and people whispered, glancing at me before dropping their eyes and turning their backs. I was the wife of a condemned man, dressed in black as if already a widow. I carried the aroma of death and no one would dare make the social misjudgement of acknowledging me.

We scanned the room for the king but he wasn't present. Rather than waste more time, we found our way to a passage where the king must pass. We walked and talked in low voices, trying to look interested in the paintings and tapestries, as if we had left the party only moments before to take some air. Mrs Morgan sat on a window seat and fluttered her fan but I paced the floor and bit at the corner of my nail. I was dressed in black because the dress was borrowed but I knew that black suited my pale skin and dark hair. I wore Mrs Mills' best jewellery. The king must notice me. If he did, there was a chance.

After an hour or more I heard the sound of German accents. The king was coming. Here was my chance. As the sounds grew close and he entered the hall, I threw myself on my knees in front of George of Hanover. He recoiled as if he had been bitten. I spoke rapidly in French, begging him to read the petition held out in my hands. He stepped over me, staring ahead as if he could neither see nor hear me. Still kneeling, I snatched at the tails of his coat and tried to push my petition into his pocket. The king walked on and I was pulled over, flat on my face and dragged behind him. A servant caught me by the waist. Another prised my hands from the king's coat. I saw the petition fall from his pocket and roll under a window seat. I tried to reach for it but a servant was there before me. The king and his entourage passed on, leaving me prostrate on the floor. A smell of dust and polished wood and baying laughter from young men told me I had failed.

In the morning, the news was all over London. At Duke Street we had many callers. My sister Mary was the first. Widowed again following the death of Viscount Montague, she was now betrothed to Sir George Maxwell. Her expression left me in no doubt of her horror that her younger sister's behaviour had so shamed and humiliated the king.

'How could you, Winifred? Everyone is laughing. My future husband and I will no longer be welcome at court.'

'I must do everything I can to save William. I didn't intend to shame the king. The shame was mine.'

'The rumour is that he behaved like a boor. It's exactly the image the king's trying to avoid.'

'I can't help how he's seen. People have interpreted my story to feed their own prejudice. If he wants to be respected as a civilized monarch then he should pardon William and the others.'

Mary's eyes narrowed. 'You might be better, young lady, to let the execution happen.'

'How might it be better, to lose my husband and in such a terrible way?'

'If he dies, you'll get your widow's settlement. If he lives, you'll have nothing. Be realistic, Winifred, and plan for your future as a widow with two children.'

Seeing that I wasn't in any way penitent, my sister refused Mrs Mills' offer of chocolate and swept from the room, saying that she would show herself out. I promised myself that I would never speak to her again.

The Duke of Montrose was our next visitor. He was anxious to protect his reputation and was brought into the house through the servants' quarters. His news was better. The servant who picked up my petition had given it to Lord Dorset, Lord of the Bedchamber who had read it with interest and passed it to the Prince of Wales. Montrose explained that the prince was keen to distance himself from his father's reputation as an uncultured man and after Mrs Morgan and I had fled he had read the petition aloud to everyone in the drawing room, many of whom were lords. Montrose reassured me that it had been received well. I clapped my hands. Surely this was excellent preparation for the women's petition to the House of Lords?

The other wives were not convinced. Lady Nairn and Lady Derwentwater were our next callers and they rebuked me for acting alone. I felt for their determination to stay calm and use measured arguments, despite the evidence of distress in their pale faces and red-rimmed eyes. They seemed too young to be facing such tragedy and Lady Derwentwater was evidently with child. I was left in no doubt that they believed my action had been selfish and they wondered aloud about Mrs Morgan's judgement in agreeing to help. They feared the king's resentment would ruin any chance of reprieve for all our husbands. We had already failed to present our petition in parliament and they worried that no peer would now dare to risk his reputation to present a petition to the House of Lords. I gave them the news from Montrose and promised to ask the Duke to present the petition on our behalf.

Once alone, I paced the library. If Lady Nairn was right and our petition failed, our husbands would die in two days. Stung by the women's accusation of disloyalty, I knew that I should do nothing further to risk the success of the petition but I couldn't allow William's fate to depend upon a lords' debate. I needed a plan, one I would execute only in the most desperate of circumstances. The one advantage I had over the other wives, I reasoned, was my ease of access to the Tower of London and, finally, I could use that advantage. I sent for Grace and Mr and Mrs Mills, joined later by Mrs Morgan, and we conferred long into the night.

As head of the household, Mr Mills spoke on behalf of his wife and their friend. 'I have heard that James returned to France earlier this month. Sadly, I must report that he burned the land behind him as he retreated, leaving ordinary Scottish people to freeze and starve to death. We must accept that the young king does not have the disposition to lead us to victory. At least for this generation, the Jacobite cause is finished. I can't speak for our friends in Scotland but here we must learn to live under George of Hanover.'

Mrs Mills interrupted her husband. 'I heard that two young supporters, foolish enough to proclaim James in public as the rightful king, were pulled from their horses and stripped naked in front of a jeering crowd!'

Mr Mills frowned at his wife. 'But we're not giving up on William. Winifred is right, his situation is worse than the others, particularly after the incident with the king.'

Now Mrs Morgan interrupted. 'It was worth the risk. The circumstances were unfortunate.'

Mr Mills sighed and continued, avoiding our eyes. 'That's what I was about to say. No one is to blame. But we are agreed on one thing, Winifred. All we must know is our part of the plan, exactly what you need us to do. It's safer for us all if we know as little detail as possible.'

Mrs Morgan agreed. 'Well spoken, Mr Mills. My husband is keen that I bring no further attention to our household but should the petition fail, we will help William escape. No man should face such a death.'

I felt relief and gratitude and thanked them all for their bravery. 'Let us hope that the petition succeeds.'

The day before the execution, a bitter wind whipped from the Thames. We waited outside Parliament House for the Lords to assemble, shivering, blowing on our hands and stamping our feet. The atmosphere was almost convivial as all the wives were there with their children and there were many friends too, highly regarded women who, being female, only had to worry about disapproval rather than loss of rank. As the lords filed past we shouted and cheered, demanding a reprieve for our husbands. They stared straight ahead, even our friends amongst them would not acknowledge us, but we were not moved on by the soldiers who guarded the entrance. I took this to be a sign that ordinary people, servants, guards and soldiers, wanted our men to live.

We crushed into a gallery to hear the debate. One lord protested angrily that the king had no right to reprieve men that parliament had found guilty, another that it was only parliament who could ask the king to have mercy on prisoners. This carried weight and it was agreed that parliament would petition the king that very evening. We sighed and clapped, hugging each other. Our husbands might still live.

But an elderly peer stood, leaning on the bench in front of him with one hand on his hip. Surely all the men did not deserve to be reprieved? He seemed puzzled, disappointed. Was no one guilty? Speaking for himself, he said he could only agree to a request for mercy for those who deserved it. This brought a murmur of approval.

I rose and pushed my way through the other wives. I wouldn't stay to listen to this. William would not be one of those pardoned; my humiliation of the king had made that a certainty. I had to act, quickly and alone. I paid for a carriage to the Tower of London. My entrance was barred at every gate but I smiled at the guards and told them my wonderful news. The imprisoned peers would be reprieved the very next day. I feigned a relieved and excited cheerfulness which was infectious on a bitter February afternoon and I was allowed to pass. The council chamber in the Lieutenants Lodge, where the wardens and their wives gathered around the fire on slow afternoons, was full of women. Marian was holding court with the younger wives and I could see they were all the worse for ale.

She greeted me enthusiastically, as if I were her closest and dearest friend. 'This is Lady Winifred Herbert,' she announced to the others, raising her tankard. 'Her mother was lovely when she was here, a real lady. The best prisoner we've ever had.' She turned to address me. 'You here to see your husband? He isn't allowed visitors. He's for the chop tomorrow.' She made a cutting motion across her neck and cackled with laughter.

'Marian, I wanted you to be the first to know. My husband is to be freed. Here, have another drink.' I reached into my bag and drew out a handful of coins.

'You're a lady, like your mother. Your father was a rum 'un, a bit like your husband.' Marian took a deep draught of ale and laughed from her belly. The other women, who seemed a little wary of her, laughed too. The room was incredibly hot and I felt that my skin must be glistening with sweat.

'Can I see Lord Nithsdale, just for a short while? I'll tell him the news and leave.

''Ere, you,' Marian shouted to the armed guard at the door to William's room, wiping her lips with her sleeve, 'Let the lady in, you lazy shite.'

William startled then rose to greet me and we held each other close. If my plan wasn't successful, I knew this might be our last time together. I kissed him softly on the lips then pushed him towards the window, where we wouldn't be overheard.

'The House of Lords has agreed to petition the king to pardon some of you, but not all. Those who deserve to die will still be executed. I think that's you and probably Kenmure,' I whispered.

William nodded. 'It's fine, Win, I'm ready. Here,' he led me to the table, 'I've been working on my speech. Can I read bits to you? I'm not sure they work.'

'No, I won't look at your speech!' I hissed and dragged him back to the window. 'I'm here to tell you that I'm rescuing you tomorrow. You must cooperate with me or several of our friends will end up on the scaffold alongside you, including me.'

'Win, this is foolish.' William sat down at the table and picked up a sealed envelope. 'We need to make plans for after my death. I've written to ask Charles and Mary if you can live with them at Traquair. Please take this letter to them.'

I sat down next to him and took his thin face between my hands and turned him to look at me. 'This horrible place, this Tower of London, will never take one of my family. I will not be beaten by this travesty of humanity. You will be ready for me tomorrow morning. If you resist me, I'll kill you myself.'

William's eyes widened with surprise then softened. He smiled. 'I'm thinking of the night I rescued you from the mob in Dumfries. There's something mad about you, Win. You'll do this thing whether it kills us all. Don't tell me any more. If you're here tomorrow I'll go with you like a lamb. But I will spend tonight writing letters to the children. And if you don't mind, my precious, loving wife, I beg you to look at the pathetic words I've scratched on this parchment before you go. I'm particularly worried about the bit where I try to explain why I lied to the Commons and the Lords to get myself off.'

I gave Marian a few more coins to thank her for her leniency then hurried back to Duke Street, taking a hackney carriage from the many that lined the streets outside the Tower. Business was brisk under the new king.

At dinner I could eat nothing and when I heard the Duke of Montrose announced, I threw my napkin down and ran into the hall. The Lord's petition had been presented to the king but his response had been unhelpful to those of us who were looking for a clear answer. The king had been unwilling to make an immediate decision but had reminded those present that he had a duty to guarantee the safety of the people. There would be no executions in the morning but nothing else had changed.

That night in the drawing room, I checked my plan with Grace and she slipped away under cover of darkness to warn Mrs Morgan, while I prepared Mr and Mrs Mills. I couldn't sleep and could hear Grace pacing in the room next to mine. I knew the layout of the Lieutenant's Lodging, I knew the routines of the guards, I was trusted by the wardens. Throughout the long night I rehearsed every detail. I couldn't dwell on the consequences of involving dear friends in my terrifying scheme because if I did, it would have to be abandoned. Throughout my life I'd asked too much of other people and tomorrow would be the greatest test of their loyalty. I didn't even write letters to my children. To fail was beyond my reckoning. We would not fail.

I opened the window of my room and listened to the night

sounds. An owl swept down from the trees and something rustled in the bushes. If I could have found any faith, I might have prayed, but instead I fell on my knees and thought of my sister Lucy, secure in her convent in the company of women. I clasped my hands together and looked into the face of the bright, smiling moon and asked whoever might be listening to keep us safe.

CHAPTER 22

W e met in the grand drawing room, a strange little group: Mrs Morgan always elegant, Mrs Mills short and preoccupied. Grace stood by the fireplace and Mr Mills, also small and busy, paced the room filling and emptying his pipe. These were my co-conspirators, as yet innocent of the shocking things I would ask them to do.

I spoke to them at last. 'My dear friends, thank you for being here with me. Without your help over the last two months, I think I would have turned my face to the wall and given up hope. But today, I'm going to ask you to do a most courageous thing for me. It will be the last.'

It was as if everyone had stopped breathing. 'I will do everything I can to make sure you come to no harm and that your identities are protected,' I continued. 'We must leave soon for the Tower of London.'

I turned to Mrs Morgan, 'Please wait in here for a few minutes with Grace while I check that we have everything we need. Grace has some clothes for you to change into. Mr Mills, I'm afraid I had the audacity to ready the coach. Could you ask the coachman to bring it around to the front of the house and wait there with Mrs Mills?'

My trusting friends asked no questions as the coach pitched and rolled through the dirty, rutted streets to the Tower. The driver had been instructed to make great haste and we struggled to maintain our balance. I chattered nervously, distracting them with nonsense about the weather and the number of beggars and whether the new king would do anything to make London a safer city. Mrs Morgan, in her extra petticoats and cloak, began to look hot, her cheeks burning with fiery pink patches and I worried she might faint. I passed her my handkerchief which had been dipped in lavender water. I saw Mr and Mrs Mills exchange a quick glance, as if they thought they might have become involved in the desperate antics of a woman driven mad by grief. I think only Grace's calm smile prevented Mr Mills from asking the coachman to turn around for home.

The coach stopped at the first gate to the Tower, and Grace put a hand on Mr Mills' arm to prevent him from stepping down from the coach with his wife and Mrs Morgan, who were to accompany me on foot. Grace said that she needed him to continue alone with her but he protested, anxious for the safety of his wife.

My tone forbade any further argument. 'It will just be like an ordinary visit to my husband. I will keep her safe. You must go with Grace to secure a lodging for William and myself. Only a man can do this. You will return here very soon.' Mr Mills settled back into his seat, his expression forlorn.

Grace climbed down from the carriage and hugged me. 'Be brave and take great care,' she whispered before shaking Mrs Mills and Mrs Morgan by the hand. 'Listen to Winifred,' she instructed. 'Do exactly as she says.'

At each gate, we were received with sympathy as news of

the king's prevarication had already reached the wardens. Like me, they had guessed that William would not be one of those reprieved and they allowed me the wife's privilege of access to a prisoner facing execution. My explanation that my women friends, their heads lowered and eyes masked by handkerchiefs, had come to support me in my farewell to William, was accepted with kindness and I was nodded through. I was lucky that grief is an embarrassment and no one wished to look too closely.

At the Lieutenant's Lodge I asked Mrs Mills to wait downstairs. She looked afraid, as if she had finally grasped that she was to enter this place of imprisonment and execution. I was fearful she might choose to run.

I pressed my cheek to hers and growled. 'I will come down for you soon, I promise. If anyone asks, you are waiting to say farewell to the Earl of Nithsdale. Keep your face down and covered.'

I turned to Mrs Morgan. 'Upstairs I will call you Mrs Catherine. You must stand tall but cover your face.' She nodded and I saw her swallow. Her face was pale and dappled with sweat. 'Follow me now.'

In the chamber, the guards sat around the fire but the mood was quiet and solemn out of respect for the condemned man. As I had hoped, there were only a few women. Women notice details.

'I've brought some friends to say goodbye to my husband,' I addressed them as a group, speaking over their heads. 'We won't stay long. I have to go to the House of Lords. There's to be another petition tonight. My servant will call for me when the carriage is below. Will one of you let me know when she arrives?' I tried to swallow but I had no saliva. I felt Mrs Morgan as a shadow at my shoulder.

The head warder, Marian's husband Tom, pushed himself out of his chair and came towards us, tucking his shirt over his belly and into his trews. 'The women all got a bit drunk last night,' he folded his arms and smiled, then looked down at the floorboards. 'They're a bit poorly today.' He walked in front of us to William's door and pushed the guard's halberd away. 'Let Lady Nithsdale and her friend in. Where's your manners?'

William jumped as we entered. He hadn't expected me and certainly not Mrs Morgan, who he had never met. I put my fingers to my lips and William raised his eyebrows as I asked Mrs Morgan to strip off both of her outer cloaks and the extra petticoats. I kissed William on the cheek then steered my friend back through the door and past the guards, now dressed in only one layer of clothing.

'Has my servant called to say the coach is ready?' I called out to Tom. At my side, Mrs Morgan feigned great distress and covered her face.

He didn't look up from his game of chess. 'No, my lady, no one's come for you.'

'That's ridiculous. I'm going to be late.' I feigned irritation. 'Come on, Mrs Catherine, I'll take you downstairs.'

To my relief, Mrs Mills still waited for us, chewing on her glove and staring anxiously up at the staircase when she heard our footsteps.

'Is it my turn?' she whispered.

'Cover your face and come up with me,' I barked. 'Don't look at anyone. Pretend to be heartbroken but no obvious weeping or wailing.'

We hurried back through the wood-panelled guard's chamber without more than a friendly nod from Marian's husband. The guard on William's door let us pass and I closed it behind us.

'What next!' William grumbled but I could see he was interested. 'Why is Mrs Mills here?' He remembered his manners and bowed to her.

I whispered to them both. 'I need to create confusion about how many women there are and who's gone in and who's gone out. Luckily, they're not paying much attention. Mrs Mills you must put on the clothes Mrs Morgan left behind. Hurry now!'

'I thought those were for me.' William interrupted, looking away as Mrs Mills stripped to her petticoats.

'Just do as I say. Don't argue. I'm going to take Mrs Mills down to wait with Mrs Morgan. You'll be next.' I pointed to the clothes Mrs Mills had dropped on the floor. 'While I'm gone put these on.' I glanced out of the window at the fading light. 'Good, it's almost dark. I want you out of here before they light the lamps.'

I turned and saw that Mrs Mills was crying. 'It's nearly over,' I pressed her shoulder. 'Your husband should be waiting at the gate with Grace. I'll get you out of here now. This time, stand erect but cover your face.'

Rushing Mrs Mills through the chamber that was lit only by embers from the fire, I felt hopeful that the warders wouldn't notice her trailing robes and petticoat. I walked behind her, complaining about my carriage and loudly begging Mrs Mills to try and find out what had happened.

Downstairs, I pushed Mrs Mills and Mrs Morgan outside the Lodge and we hurried past the guards to the gate where their coach would collect them. It was a cold evening and the guards barely lifted their heads from their glowing braziers to nod in greeting.

'Wait here for Grace and Mr Mills,' I commanded them. 'If I'm not back in ten minutes with my husband, save yourselves. If your carriage doesn't arrive, hire a hackney and get home. No one knows you were here.' If I failed at least they would escape.

Back at the Lodge, the young lamplighter was starting his duties. I had but a few minutes of dusk to get William out. I ran up the stairs and walked briskly through the chamber. The guard dropped his halberd lazily and yawned. He didn't look at me. Inside, William was dressed in Mrs Mills' clothes. Since she was a plump woman, they fitted his girth but the petticoats were too short and showed his big, manly feet. There was nothing I could do. His cloak would have to hide the worst. I pushed William into a chair and tried to lighten his heavy brows with powder. It was useless.

There was a tap on the door. We looked at each other. My stomach turned to liquid. Was it over? Was I a prisoner too?

'Lady Nithsdale, I'm told your carriage has arrived. It's waiting outside. You must hurry.'

'Just a minute,' I called. 'My friend is deeply upset.'

Our moment had come. William and I looked at each other and he pulled me towards him and whispered, 'Win, you must be the bravest woman ever born.'

I pulled the hood of the cloak over his head and pushed a cloth into his hand. He covered his face and I coaxed my distressed woman friend through the chamber and down into the hallway, clasping her hunched shoulders. I felt as if my chest would burst but no one stopped us. No one called out.

I pushed open the heavy wooden doors to the outside and strode back through the gates, with William clinging to my arm. My tall and ungainly companion attracted no attention from the guards but I heard kindly greetings from those who noticed me pass, 'God bless you, Lady Nithsdale.'

Grace waited in the fading light next to the Mills' carriage, her pale face suspended in the dusk like a mask. The other two women were secure in a hackney carriage and Mr Mills sat next to his coachman. Walking after William to prevent his shoulders and feet being visible to the guards behind us, I heard Mr Mills swear. 'Gadzooks, she's done it!'

I shouted to Grace, 'Get him out of here, now!' She pushed

William into the Mills' carriage and I turned to the others and flapped my arms, 'Go now, all of you!'

The next bit was the worst. I trembled at the thought of returning to the Lodge, taking the risk of being present at the very moment William's escape was discovered. But our success depended upon the deception being played out for longer and I had to gain more time. My instinct told me to run, to try to leave with my husband, but my friends were gone. I pulled my cloak around me and with my head bowed, reached the Lodge unchallenged and hurried up the stairs, breathless, towards William's empty room.

'Here again?' His guard lowered his weapon. 'You can't stay away. I thought you were rushing to meet a carriage?'

'Yes, you're right but I must say one last farewell to my lord, alone.' My genuine tears were those of terror, not grief, but he let me pass. Inside I paced and pushed chairs, as if we were moving around. I feigned a deep voice that I hoped sounded like William comforting me and then I fell silent. The horror of the empty room crept under my skin. I feared the sound of voices, of a key turning in the lock. I felt trapped. I couldn't breathe. I could bear it no longer. I pulled my hood around my face and left, pretending to whisper a desperate farewell to William through the open door. Out of respect, the guard looked away.

I dropped the string of the viewing hatch over the top of the door, trapping it inside and keeping my head down, walked slowly back through the wardens. Their voices dropped to whispers, wary of my distress. On the stairs I met the boy lighting candles and stopped to speak to him. I pushed some coins into his hand.

'My lord is praying. He's not to be disturbed. He wishes to be left in darkness, for darkness is his future. Do not light his candles tonight.'

The boy nodded, his back to the wall, more afraid of me and

imminent death than he was of the wardens. I knew that he would eventually light the candles as expected but perhaps he would wait awhile. I had to get away.

I ran through each gate as if demons snapped at my heels but was allowed to pass unhindered. These good men, who felt sadness and guilt at their necessary involvement in my husband's incarceration, would feel duped and bitter in a matter of hours. I hated that I had abused their trust.

In my solitary journey from the Tower, shock at our extraordinary deception overwhelmed me and I allowed myself to wail, biting on my gloved hand. If Grace and William had been caught, when dawn came my husband would be hung and disembowelled. I would be imprisoned with Grace and perhaps my loyal friends. I felt no sense of triumph and trembled with fear, as if I were ill with fever.

At Duke Street, I was met with excitement and relief. Everyone was present apart from Grace but Mr Mills reassured me that within the last hour he had seen her at the safe house with William. Everyone wanted to talk at once. We felt cold, although the servants built up the fire until it roared like an inferno. We were exhausted but no one wanted to rest. It was only five o'clock but years might have passed since we met in the drawing room. Not even Mrs Morgan wanted to leave us to be with her husband. It seemed impossible that these were the same rooms, the same furniture. Soon, the cook would ask Mrs Mills to check on the dinner organised only that morning. These humdrum matters could not exist because we were utterly changed.

We had achieved something that was believed to be impossible and every detail, every fear, every minor triumph had to be turned over and inspected. Mr Mills quietly admitted that once he realised the nature of the plan and had no faith in its success, he had left Grace alone to try and seek refuge for

William with her aunt. He had been desperate to return to the Tower, he breathlessly explained, to rescue his wife and had expected poor Grace to return to the Tower in a sedan chair. But once he had seen that Mrs Mills and Mrs Morgan were safe and when my husband had appeared with me, the ugliest woman in the kingdom wearing his wife's dress, he had not hesitated to take Grace and William in his carriage to find a better safe house. This was where William lodged and where he now waited for me.

Mrs Mills pretty face crumpled when she remembered how she had feared for her life walking through the guards and Mrs Morgan admitted that she had been terrified waiting alone downstairs, risking discovery and capture. I cried out my own admission that I feared I had risked their lives for the sake of William and we might all have ended on the gallows.

This dark truth, that I had disregarded their safety and without their consent, silenced us. When our deed was discovered, we would not be safe. I was confident that my friends hadn't been recognised but suspicion would certainly fall on them. They were loyal Jacobites and it was widely known where I had been staying. I had to leave at once, for their complicity would be certain if I remained. But the night wasn't yet over; there were further trails I had to lay before I could be with my husband.

CHAPTER 23

Under cover of deep night, I returned at last to Duke Street in a sedan chair and Mr Mills took me by carriage to the room he had finally found for William. It was a miserable little house in Wapping and my confidence ebbed as the coach dropped me at the end of the street. I tapped on the door and waited, watching rats feeding on the day's refuse. Shuffling came from inside and light from a candle appeared in the window. A shadow checked my presence and heavy bolts scraped against wood. The door opened a fraction and an old woman peered at me, her face covered in moles, some darker than others and her cheeks and chin sprouted wiry hairs.

'You must be the wife,' she sniffed. 'His lordship's upstairs. He's expecting you.' I squeezed in through the barely open door, pulling my bag behind me through the narrow gap. She looked out at the street then closed the door, repeating the complex locking sequence.

Finally, she turned and spoke. 'There's to be no candles upstairs. I live on my own, so people might notice a light. I sleep downstairs.'

'Of course,' I agreed.

'There's to be no walking around. My daughter visits in the day. She'll be suspicious.' I wondered how much our friends had paid her, hopefully enough.

As we climbed the stairs, I pulled back from the smell of mildew and something else offensive from her clothes. 'I've put some bread and ale in the room. There's nothing else.'

She pushed me into a room that was in complete darkness and the door closed behind me.

'Win, is that you?' Oh, the joy of William's voice from the dense, black space. I felt my way towards him and my hands found his face. I touched his lips then kissed him.

'You're safe, my love,' I whispered, 'you're safe.' I kissed his face and cold hands.

'Come into bed, you'll freeze.' I felt William lift the covers. The bedding smelt damp. I stripped off down to my undergarments and removed my stays. William was wearing only a shirt and I felt the rough hairs on his legs against mine. We twined our cold feet and shivered, holding each other close. William began to kiss my face and ears and his hands lifted my robe and cupped my breast. I felt a familiar searching ache and we made deep, gentle love, each tender moment like the finest wine sipped from Venetian glass.

We slept for a while, my head on William's chest, breathing together. I woke to movement and in the faint light from a small, high window I could see William's face, propped on his elbow, watching me.

'You are the bravest, cleverest, most beautiful woman on God's earth. I love you, Winifred Herbert. Please, please never leave me.'

'I couldn't let you die. I had to rescue you. If you had been executed, I, too, would have died. You are my one true love, William Maxwell, and the Tower would not take you from me.'

We were silent. Shapes formed in the thin light that filtered

226

through the dirty window. The bed was narrow and across from us there was a table with the bread and ale. The churning in my gut wasn't fear but a desperate craving for food. I couldn't remember when I had eaten last.

We sat up in bed, tearing at the bread and drinking ale from a pewter goblet. We talked over every detail of the rescue. I still couldn't believe I had managed something so daring, that luck had been with me and our true friends. I wanted to laugh out loud and dance on the bare floorboards.

'You should have seen Mills' face when I stepped out of the Tower, wearing his wife's dress.' William roared with laughter and I had to quieten him with a kiss.

I swept my hand around the dismal room. 'He didn't believe I would pull it off but once he saw you he had to find this awful place in a hurry.'

'What was the alternative?'

'Grace had asked her aunt to hide you.'

'That wouldn't have been safe.'

'Not for you or for Grace, so thank goodness Mr Mills had a change of heart.'

'My dear there was just one thing wrong with your plan. You should have swapped the women around. I ought to have worn Mrs Morgan's clothes.'

'For goodness' sake William, it worked, didn't it?'

'I'm teasing you, Win,' I heard the smile in his voice. 'But why did you take such a long time to come to me?'

'There was unfinished business. The Duchess of Buccleuch had offered to try to petition the king again on my behalf and she was going to present it tonight. I had to contact her and ask her not to. If your escape had already been discovered, she might have been caught up in the backlash. I didn't speak to her but left a message with a servant giving the excuse that I'd reconsidered and ought to present a petition together with the other wives.'

'Did the wives object to you trying to petition the king?' William asked.

'They thought we should have acted together. They felt I'd humiliated the king which made him more likely to be vengeful.'

'I wonder how they'll feel when they hear about this? You won't have made many friends.'

'If I'd thought about the consequences for our friends, for the wardens at the Tower, for the other prisoners, I couldn't have done it. I had to close my eyes. Anyway,' I continued, keen to finish my story, 'I then hurried to see the Duchess of Montrose, who had offered to use her influence with the king. She asked that I shouldn't be shown in, not wanting to risk being with the wife of a condemned man but her servant showed me in anyway. The Duchess was so shocked by my appearance I told her everything. She said she'd go to court tonight and find out whether the king knew you had escaped and how he was reacting. She begged me to hide myself as soon as possible. Mr Mills brought me here as soon as he could. That's it, the end of the story.'

'So far,' William grunted. 'We've still got to get out of the country. I don't trust the old witch downstairs.'

'Nor me, but I think we're safe as long as she's being paid well. I've no money to give her, have you?' I felt William shake his head.

William got out of bed to use the slop pot and I brushed the crumbs from the sheets. 'This reminds me of St Germain.'

'If only,' William laughed and we curled up together in the narrow bed, his arms tight around my belly. I felt so tired. Sleep threatened to overcome me, yet I wanted to stay awake.

'William,' I spoke to him over my shoulder. 'Are you glad you're free?'

'Of course I am, my sweet love. To spend the rest of my life with you and our children will be the purest of joys.'

I slept but dreamed of a bell, a single, monotonous tolling and when consciousness arose the sound persisted, ringing on and on like the death toll, until I wanted to cover my ears. I turned over to William but he still slept. I felt sick. The bells meant that someone had been executed. Dawn slipped through our small window and I could see he was wakening. He opened his eyes and put his arms behind his head. I rested my head on his chest and smelt the stale sweat from his armpits. He put one arm around me then stroked his hand up and down against my bare arm. I raised myself on my elbow and looked at him.

'It could have been you, William. You might be dead.'

'I wasn't afraid. If I'd had to die I was ready.'

'I know that. I never doubted your bravery.'

'It wasn't about being brave, just being ready. I felt I'd tried to do everything I could for the cause but nothing worked. We were let down by our leaders and by young James. Such a golden opportunity missed. There was so much support. Scotland was behind us.' I thought about the ordinary men and women who had spoken to me as I travelled through the Borders with Grace but decided to say nothing. We had the rest of our lives to pore over such details.

'Do you regret being here with me?' I was fearful of his response and wished I hadn't asked.

'Not at all.' He smiled his perfect smile. 'We'll try to live an ordinary life. I'll find you a home somewhere. I'll be awful to live with but you're used to that.'

We were interrupted by a sound on the stairs and the door opened. The old witch didn't bother to knock and carried in some lit coals on a shovel. I saw her sniff and wondered if the room reeked of sweat. She bent over the grate and piled logs on top of the hot coals.

'What's the news, mistress?' William asked her.

'There's two lords executed, Kenmure and Derwentwater. They're saying Derwentwater stood in for you, my lord.' She seemed pleased with this and watched for our reaction, her hands on her hips. Fear clutched the back of my neck. I asked her for hot water and she backed out of the room carrying the slop pot, her eyes never leaving William's face.

William lay back on the pillow and groaned. 'This is the worst thing, that young Derwentwater should die for me.' He covered his eyes.

'You don't know it's true,' I whispered.

'What's not true,' William hissed, 'that he's dead or that he hung for me?'

'That he hung for you. It's just gossip.'

'Why would he die except as revenge for you and me? Kenmure and I were marked because we were the leaders of the lowland army. Derwentwater was nothing but a boy, with a young wife who's expecting a child.'

'William, he was one of the leaders of the Jacobites from the north of England, there was every reason for him to be chosen. I won't accept your arguments until I have proof. I had to save you.' I sat up and wrapped myself in a sheet. The cold was intense. I wanted William's arms around me.

'You shouldn't have interfered, Win. You always interfere. I was ready to die!'

'Well I wasn't ready to let you die, you selfish bastard.' This was not how it was meant to be.

'You're the selfish one,' William spat the words. 'You do everything from selfish motives. You involved our friends in a plot that could still lose them their lives. Treason is always punishable by death. Your antics could result in your execution as well as mine, leaving our children orphans. A young man has died because you saved me. A child has lost a father. I wasn't worth saving. The price was too high.'

Our landlady walked in again, with a bowl of hot water. 'There's five wardens lost their jobs,' she announced primly, 'their wives and children thrown onto the streets.' She clicked her tongue and wiped her hands on her dirty apron.

We struggled to appear composed and by the slight upturn of her wizened, dry lips I could see that this had been noticed. 'Thank you, mistress,' I tried to speak with authority, 'we'll not trouble you for long. Our friends will be here soon.'

William turned his back on me and I climbed over him and tiptoed across the room in my bare feet to the table. I washed every part of myself with the rank, sour cloths. I wanted every trace of him gone. I dressed and sat on the chair, my arms folded in my lap. My mind searched through our long marriage, looking for evidence of my selfish behaviour. I was too angry to cry.

I tore into him. 'You asked me to come. You begged me, commanded me. I didn't want to. I wanted to stay safe at Terregles with Anne and bear our child. Your sister and her husband practically blackmailed me into making that journey. Charles provided me with money but no escort. Grace and I nearly died and I lost our baby. I've made every sacrifice for you, William, and so did your mother.'

'And I've never been allowed to forget it. Martyrs are no fun, Win. I simply wanted you here with me at my death. You should have asked me what I wanted.'

Accusation and counter-accusation cracked across the cell until Mr Mills walked into an acrid silence between us.

'Have you heard the news?'

We nodded miserably.

'Is it true that Derwentwater hung for me?' William asked.

'They weren't hung, they were executed, which is a blessing. He certainly wasn't expecting to die. He had no suitable clothes and he hadn't written a speech. The poor lad was quite tongue-tied, I'm told. But I wouldn't listen to the gossip. We won't know why he was executed until we see the papers. You must remember that he was quite a favourite at St Germain and had spent his youth as a companion to the prince.'

I felt some comfort from these words but I could see from William's preoccupied expression that he preferred his own truth.

Mr Mills blustered on. 'The good news is I've secured a passage for William across the channel. You'll be travelling as a manservant of the Venetian ambassador.' In the gloom I felt Mr Mills turn towards William. 'You'll have to hide in a servant's room for a day or two. To be honest, we have to get you out of here fast. I don't think the old woman's to be trusted. Mrs Mills is downstairs plying her with cakes and ale but if anyone paid her more than we're offering, she'd take it. I've come to take you to the embassy now.'

'And what about my wife?' William spoke about me as if I wasn't there. 'When does she come to France to join me?'

'*If I come at all*,' I thought.

'Ah, that's the problem.' Mr Mills rubbed his chin. I heard his beard scratch. 'Winifred is, if anything, more wanted than you. She's not the king's favourite person right now and he's said he wants her head for yours. I think she'll have to lie low for some time. You've got a better chance of getting away safely without her.'

'That's fine. It's a good plan,' I interrupted. 'I've business here, a daughter left at Traquair House. Of course William should go on alone.' I turned my back on them both and with my finger traced the path of water spilt on the rough table. 'One last thing, my most loyal friend,' I added, 'have any of you been approached as suspects?'

'Not so far,' he whispered. 'Your plan was so brilliant I don't think anyone has a clue who assisted you, or how many women went in or out of the cell. All that's being said is that you didn't act alone. The story that's circulating says you left a poor woman behind in William's cell to hang for him.'

William gave a bitter laugh that was just audible.

'Come on,' Mr Mills chivvied William, 'I can't hang around here. Get out of that bed and get dressed. Here's another of my wife's dresses and a hat.'

'Here we go again,' William muttered.

After my husband left, with only a dry, cold kiss between us, I climbed back into the stinking bed, fully dressed. I couldn't rest. My mind churned over every word of our bitter row, answering William's accusations with quick responses that would have shown him how wrong he was. I never wanted to see him again. The words that had passed between us could not be undone. Every joyful moment of our past, St Germain, our little boy's first steps, our daughter's birth so late in our marriage, was tainted by this revelation of his dislike for me.

At last, there was a tap on the door and Grace whispered. 'Winifred!' She had come... I wouldn't have to lie here in darkness until the old woman sold me for a price. I sat up and finding Grace's arms around me, I cried.

For weeks, we were moved from house to house, relying on the charity of friends and Jacobite sympathisers. I sent messages to my sisters and brother, seeking some financial support and had no reply but at least they didn't betray me. My situation was very serious and Grace was at risk too, since it was well known that I rarely acted without her at my side. News came that William had arrived safely in Paris and I had a letter from him, asking me to join him. There was no word of forgiveness and I learned that he had recruited a servant, despite having no money to pay his wages.

Grace and I spent hours in our solitude talking about our perilous act. When I told her about William's reaction to the death of Lord Derwentwater we both fell quiet, sharing thoughts that couldn't be spoken. *He wasn't worth it.*

The reaction from London society was mixed. We heard that in private, many found the humiliation of the king amusing but few expressed such a view publicly. It was widely reported that William's name had actually been included on a list of those to be reprieved, so my rescue had been pointless, but others told me that the document looked as if his name had been added as an afterthought, in order to make my actions seem reckless and unjustified. I was reassured that the execution documents confirmed that Lord Derwentwater had always been facing the axe. I heard a lot about my bravery but not much about my sense and there was resentment amongst Jacobite women about my disregard for the safety of the other husbands. The older women shared my sister's view that I might have been better to stay my hand and wait for society to forgive a wife who had played no part in her husband's misdeeds.

However, time moves on and in the political mire of London society, my story was quickly forgotten. Loyal friends began to petition for my safety on the grounds that there was no evidence I had been involved. Everything was circumstantial, they argued, and no-one should be kept a prisoner in society without being charged with a crime. The Solicitor General decreed that active searching for me should cease but if I was found in either England or Scotland, I would be arrested. I had been given liberty to flee the country unhindered. However, ungrateful and stupid as ever, there was one more journey I had to make, risking the lives of both myself and my loyal companion Grace.

CHAPTER 24

The distant Cheviots were dusted with snow. Our little horses, still heavy with their winter coats, pricked up their ears as we picked our way along the banks of the Tweed. The river sparkled as it coursed over shallows and folded deep and brown under the roots of trees. The lambs here were newborn, pure white and fragile. Their mothers were protective and alert. It was the middle of April and we were almost at Traquair. My brother had lent us money to make this journey to Scotland but he expected to be repaid by my brother-in-law Charles.

Once again we had travelled the hidden paths of England and Scotland, avoiding all but the most remote inns and seeking lodgings in farmhouses and cottages. With the reluctant consent of my sister Anne, we were accompanied by John, our young companion on our flight to France over twenty years ago, now a middle-aged man. We faced no trials like those encountered in the winter but we made a quiet group, each too preoccupied with what had been and what the future might hold, to concentrate on the present. Poor John found us sad company and he also fell into thoughtful reflection. Emptiness had settled on me like a weight.

This wasn't the panicked terror of old, where fears jumped out at me in daylight and haunted my sleep. I travelled through each day certain that I would always be William's wife but we would now live apart, even though I was several months with child. The irony of my late burst of fertility brought more sorrow, as we had once shared a dream of a house noisy with children. I knew that Grace had much to reflect on too, not least the bitter words we had sometimes exchanged in our enforced isolation. I was facing a life without my husband and a future without my dear Grace but I reminded myself that each day brought me closer to Anne.

Grace had needed persuading to be with me on this journey, breaking every law in the land, but I promised to release her once I had secured my daughter and the estate papers. She yielded to my desperate pleas for a female companion to accompany me, since I was with child, and finally agreed to come. My brother had promised to find Grace a home after I had left the country, since I argued that our mother had taken Grace from her family as a child and we had a duty to her.

We avoided the villages of Innerleithen and Traquair and crested a hill. The land fell away into a hollow where the ancient house of Traquair rested solid and patient as it had for six hundred years. I stopped my horse and the others waited for me, turning back in their saddles. I wanted to look at the house, to fix Traquair in my mind as a memory. It was a beautiful house, like my own Terregles but better. It was still a home.

Our horses became impatient, suspecting that stables were close and without a signal, they cantered together down the hill. As we approached, we laughed and called out and John did his amazing two-fingered whistle. This was madness, as magistrates may have been waiting for us, but we were lucky, as ever, when foolish bravado overcame sense. The door opened to a tumble of children and dogs, including my perfect little girl.

I couldn't stop touching her and crying and she grew impatient with a mother who wouldn't pay attention to important things like her new ribbons or the amazing servants' bells that rang a different sound for every room. Charles and Mary hurried Grace and I away to the drawing room upstairs. There was too much to say, so we were silent. I couldn't stop looking at my child, who was healthy and grown. I wanted her on my knee but felt uncertain to ask. She circled the furniture, banging the keys on the harpsichord and stealing glances at me when she thought I wasn't looking. We were brought cakes and sweet wine and Charles talked about crops and the weather. When I thought of the rescue I felt that an aura of shame hung over me. I suspected Charles and Mary caught my mood, so apart from a hug and a whispered thank you from Mary, neither of them questioned me. That night, Anne slept in her own bed in my room and in the morning I found she had crept in beside me.

Charles asked me to meet him in the library and I waited for him there, pulling books from the tightly ordered shelves and smelling the new leather binding. The library was almost complete. There were sections for philosophy, history and the great writers of the day and I wondered whether Mary or Charles ever sat here to read. I thought of Anne having lessons in this room with her cousins, part of her everyday routine I was about to destroy.

I heard Charles' footsteps on the stairs and he appeared without his wig, as he often did on days spent only with the family. He pushed a hand through his thinning hair.

'It's too hot in here,' he fussed. 'Why do they lay fires in April?'

'You asked to see me, Charles,' I reminded him.

'Ah yes.' Charles made a point of trying to remember why.

He frowned and paced the room, one hand on the back of his neck.

'Look here, Winifred, you must know how incredibly grateful we are to you for saving William. You were so very ...' he hesitated.

'Brave?' I helped him.

'Yes, that's it, brave, of course. The thing is, how long do you think you'll stay? My friend, the Lord Lieutenant, will tip us off if soldiers are on their way but I think it's only a matter of time.'

'I only came to pick up Anne and say farewell to you and Mary. I plan to leave for Terregles tomorrow.'

'My dear sister, you don't have to leave so soon. Stay with us a few days. I'm sure Mary's told you how much we have enjoyed your daughter. We'll miss her. And is it wise to go back to Terregles?'

'Thank you, Charles.' I bowed my head towards him. 'But I must retrieve something. Only I know where it is. Also, I must try to save anything that's left at Terregles. William and I are in desperate need of money. If I could trouble you for horses for Anne and Alice, her nurse. I'll try to sell them to a stable in London and return the money to you.'

'Nonsense!' Charles roared. 'Keep the money. You're absolutely right. The government don't own Terregles, whatever they might think. Get over there and sell what you can but don't hang around. They'll be watching out for you. Your tenant farmers did well this year, so I'll give you all of the rent money. The trustees can go hang.'

'Charles, I'm grateful to you. You've done so much for us already.'

Charles studied the terraced garden below. His voice was quiet, almost a whisper. 'We haven't done enough. It was never enough.'

The following day we arrived at Terregles in the late

afternoon, untroubled by soldiers or brigands. I was beginning to feel safe. It was unlikely that our passage had been unnoticed but perhaps there would be enough time to rescue what we needed. Anne rode in front of John on a large horse from Charles' stable and she was the first to see the turrets of our home. She squealed and bounced with delight and I found my own excitement rise as the familiar landscape unfolded.

But the bustle of life and work was, of course, gone from the estate buildings. Where things had been made and grown, there were weeds and decay. Apart from us, there was no sound beyond the screaming gulls. Anne turned to me, her young face full of dismay. 'Mother, where is everyone?'

The house was worse. Broken glass scraped on the floor as I forced open the thick oak door and the smell of smoke and urine swept me back to the destruction of my family home at Lincoln's Inn. I didn't want Anne to see this. I gave Alice some money and asked her to find rooms in the village for herself, John and Anne. Grace and I would have to stay.

We worked for many hours before dark, identifying anything left intact that could be sold. I was glad that Anne didn't see the doll's house broken and scattered across her bedroom floor. We lit a candle in the kitchen and burned some broken furniture in the grate. Our supper was bread and cold bacon, carried from Traquair.

'I'm going to call all our neighbours to the house tomorrow morning,' I mumbled, so hungry I couldn't wait to empty my mouth.

'Isn't that asking for trouble?' Grace answered.

'They must already know we're back. I'll try to stop anyone informing by pretending we have the government's permission to be here. They can then pick over the things we're selling.'

Grace shrugged. 'It might work. We shouldn't stay long though. We must get out into the garden and dig up the papers.'

I nodded, my mouth too full to speak, and wiped my hands on my petticoat. Grace was already at the passage that led to the pantry and still room and I hurried after her. The spades were where they had been left, just inside the door of the estate workshops. Our thieving neighbours clearly had no need for such mundane items. Tonight there was no moon but we knew exactly where to search. The ground was soft from the spring rain and only a few deep shovels of earth revealed the top of the leather case. We brushed the soil away with our hands and reached down, lifting it onto the grass. I knelt to open the lid then hesitated. Something had moved behind me. I felt rather than saw the presence. Grace stood up. I knew she had seen it too. We waited. My heart hammered in my chest. There was a sound, a thin wail.

'It's a rabbit,' Grace laughed, 'probably caught by a fox. Open the case, Win. Those papers better have survived.'

I picked up the box and held it close to my chest. I didn't feel safe. 'Let's go inside.' I peered into the dark. 'We don't know who might be watching.'

Inside, we built up the kitchen fire and I prised open the lock with a knife. The papers were intact, dry and legible. I hugged Grace and we laughed with relief. This was my proof. The estate belonged to my son, not to William, and could not be taken away.

That night, I rested on the bed I had once shared with William, the case next to me. There was almost no bedding and what remained was soaked with rain from the broken windows. I knew sleep was impossible and I lay and stroked my belly, swollen with pregnancy, and wished for the safe delivery of one more child. Dawn would come soon and I had no desire to linger. There was nothing for me here.

I must have dozed and woke, startled. Someone had stepped on broken glass. Again, the high, thin wail. I cursed that I'd let

John sleep in the village. I'd been too confident. It might end here after all. I picked up the broken rocker from the child's crib at the foot of the bed and crept from the room, raising it above my head as a club. There was no sound, just someone small and quiet moving through the rooms downstairs. I followed the wraith, catching a glimpse of a figure ahead of me, flitting from room to room. They knew the house. Finally, I found her in the kitchen, pushing the bread and bacon we had saved for the morning into her mouth and her pockets. A tiny baby, almost newborn, lolled on her shoulder. If I didn't immediately recognise her, I recognised the greed. It was Isobel.

Before dawn, Grace crept downstairs into the kitchen and seeing me already there with Isobel, stepped backwards, her hand over her mouth. 'What on earth is she doing here?'

'I found her in the house last night. She has a newborn boy. I've sat with her all night trying to help her feed the baby but she can't. She hasn't the strength. And she's eaten our breakfast.'

This was too much for Grace. 'I'm cold, dirty and haven't slept. I will not go without breakfast. I'm going to one of the farms to buy eggs, bread and milk. I don't care if it's dangerous. I've had enough. While I'm gone would you please ask her,' she flapped at Isobel with her hand, 'to lay a good fire and boil some water so that we can wash.'

I stood up and searched in my purse for money. 'Could you ask the farmer's wife if anyone in the village is nursing a baby? We could save this child.'

Grace straightened to her full height, nearly as tall as me. 'Sometimes you have to let things be.' She lowered her voice, so that Isobel wouldn't hear. 'The child will die soon. Surely that's the best thing.'

'But who knows what this child might become?' I whispered. 'We can't decide who lives and dies. We must give him a chance.'

'Winifred, we've got other things to think about. Getting back to London safely must be our only ambition. You are a meddler. Leave this!'

I also pulled myself to my full height, glad I was taller than Grace, and put my hands on my hips. 'Yes, I'm a meddler. Yes, I interfere. I don't believe we have to meekly accept things. That's how I am and I'm not going to change.'

Grace and I glared at each other, our eyes almost level. Grace's expression softened and she shrugged. 'You've become just like your mother.' She slammed the door behind her.

Our neighbours gathered in the formal gardens, already smothered with weeds. It was a beautiful day, almost summer, and many had arrived with their children and food and ale. I watched Grace move among them, shaking their hands, and I saw that she had once been part of this community, whereas I had always been a visitor. John rang a bell he found in the stables and gradually the voices and laughter became a murmur and then stopped. I addressed the crowd from the steps of the terrace.

'My dear friends and neighbours, you may have heard rumours that I am implicated in the escape from the Tower of London of the Earl of Nithsdale. There is no evidence to connect me with this deed.' Even the children were silent. 'I have the permission of the government to be here and I will leave tonight. Please enjoy today and buy whatever takes your fancy. Everything is laid out in the stables.' I gestured towards the yard.

A man raised his hand and stood up, twisting his hat in his hand. I nodded to him and all heads turned. 'My lady, if I may be so bold, I have a question for you.'

'Go ahead,' I smiled encouragement.

'Is it true that the Earl wears women's dresses?'

The crowd roared with laughter but I waited for silence. Eventually, they wiped their eyes and looked at me expectantly. 'I can confirm that he does but only when the occasion demands and certainly none of mine.'

The crowd whooped and cheered and a fiddler began to play. We were about to have a magnificent party.

I took my chance to slip away with Isobel. Grace had found a young woman in the village who had given birth to twins and one had died. Suspecting I was going to snatch her child, the only thing she had ever owned, Isobel trailed behind me but I dragged her along by the wrist. We found the cottage and knocked on the door. A woman without any teeth peered out.

'Can we see your daughter?' I asked.

She held open the door. News belongs to everyone in a tiny village like Terregles and we were expected. My eyes adjusted to the dank interior. There were two rooms downstairs and the woman, probably no older than me, beckoned us to follow her into the back. A young woman was nursing a baby, her expression blank. I knelt down and looked into the empty crib. 'I'm so sorry that you lost your baby.'

She nodded and looked up at me, waiting to hear what I had to say. Isobel pressed her child against her shoulder and he gave a barely audible mewl. The young woman's eyes widened. I spoke simply, so that Isobel would understand.

'I want you to nurse this baby. I will pay you. Once he is weaned his mother,' I pushed Isobel forward, 'will come back for him.'

I opened my bag and brought out some of the gold coins given to me by Charles. The older woman stepped forward and pushed them into her pocket. The deal was done. She nodded to her daughter. The girl placed her own child in the crib and raised her arms for Isobel's baby.

Isobel tried to run with her baby towards the door. The grandmother blocked her way and I had to prise the child from her arms. 'Isobel, if you don't give this woman your baby, he will die. Probably today.'

We watched Isobel's baby attach to the young woman's swollen breast, which glowed in the half light like a lantern. He struggled to swallow at first but then his cheeks found the rhythm and I saw him relax. I put an arm around Isobel and steered her through the cottage to the door. She wailed but without any sound.

Our neighbours weren't people of wealth, so little was sold. By late afternoon, most of the villagers had gone and Grace had engaged two ladies, sisters who shared a pretty cottage by the church, to hire a man and a cart to pack up everything that remained and send it on to Traquair. I hoped that Charles would find buyers and send the money to me, wherever I might be.

There was still much to do and I walked through the garden with Anne trotting beside me, considering whether to stay one more night. I heard my name. One of our neighbours called to me from the terrace. He seemed distressed and I hurried towards him.

'My lady ...' he had been running and he struggled with the words, taking gasps of air between each phrase. 'Soldiers are on their way ... from Dumfries.' He bent over, holding his belly. 'They'll be here in two hours.'

'Thank you, thank you, my good friend,' I called over my shoulder as I ran to find the others.

I sent John and Isobel on the big horse to Traquair, pinning a note for Mary on Isobel's shift. I lied and said she was a hard worker and didn't mention how much she ate. I told Mary about the child and knew Isobel would be cared for. Isobel's baby would have to take his chance. As for John, he could make his own way home if he wished. I imagined Charles would persuade him to stay.

We left the house open, goods spread across the yard, trusting the sisters to save what they could. We were gone within an hour and by nightfall we were well on our way to Carlisle.

CHAPTER 25

O ur journey to London was untroubled, although we were always careful, and as we picked our way along a narrow track, somewhere in Leicestershire, I expressed aloud my puzzlement.

'Why do you think we attract no attention?'

'That's easy, my lady,' Alice grinned. 'They've been told to look out for the Countess of Nithsdale. They'll be watching out for someone grand, in a coach, with loads of servants. Just look at us.'

I saw what she meant and roared with laughter. Two middle-aged ladies, none too clean, travelling with their daughters, Anne and Alice, on ponies that would have fetched nothing at a horse fair. It was a perfect disguise.

We entered London in the early morning across the marshes of Moorfields. A deep mist hung across the fields, the orb of the sun visible as if viewed through fine muslin. Bulrushes rose from the invisible landscape and the snickering of goats the only sound of life. We fell silent, like the birds, and travelled in single file, trusting our ponies to find the well-travelled path to Moorgate, an entrance I had heard was less heavily guarded than the main London gates. But the guards were on alert and we were stopped and questioned. I made much of our guise of being country women on business and many more coins had to be exchanged before we were allowed through.

To attract less attention, we dismounted from our ponies and walked into the London streets, already throbbing with morning trade and people pushing through the crowd to their place of work. Anne folded her small body into my cloak and Alice linked arms with Grace. I saw that they were both terrified, neither having ventured further than Traquair House. Even for me, a frequent but privileged visitor, this felt like a different London and I was overwhelmed by the clamour of different tongues, the jostling of bodies and the smell of people who did not have the means to wash.

We found cheap lodgings with stables, two rooms with food provided by a couple who worked at the nearby Bethlehem Hospital; too busy to be curious and even better, absent for most of the day. The rooms were bare but clean and our new hosts rushed to provide us with bread and ale before they left for their day's work at the hospital. Leaving the others to doze under rough blankets, I pulled my cloak around me and risked the streets to find a private messenger. I sent word of our safe arrival to my brother, no longer wanting to involve our friends Mr and Mrs Mills, and begged him to meet me the following day at an inn close to our lodgings. That night I slept poorly, my blood humming in my ears as I listened to every footstep, every call from the street, fearing that the king's men had found us at last. Grace and I would be arrested, of course, but what of Alice and Anne, where could they go?

In the morning, our landlord brought word from my brother. If he was curious about the message with its unknown seal, his expression betrayed nothing. After reminding my companions not to leave our lodgings or answer the door, I travelled across the thoroughfare and down the opposite street with my hood over my face, expecting a hand on my shoulder at any moment. The inn was empty of customers and the innkeeper and his wife were busy sweeping dirty sawdust from the floor. I was directed to an upstairs room, suitable for a woman to meet a gentleman alone, and chose to sit in a corner by the window, since the light was poor. Splinters from the furniture caught at my clothes as I rested my arms on the chair. I waited for William, my breath fast and shallow, listening to the sounds from below.

I heard the heavy tread of footsteps rising up the external staircase and saw my brother enter the doorway, frowning as he searched for me in the dusty shadows.

My skin prickled with relief and I called out, 'Hello!'

William kissed my outstretched hand and sat heavily in a chair across from me. 'Thank goodness you're all safe. Everyone seems to know that you've been in Scotland and the king is furious. At court they say he regards you as the most troublesome woman in the country. I'm afraid they're searching for you again. You can still be prosecuted for your husband's treason.'

I tipped more of Charles' money onto the table between us. 'My dearest brother, can I beg two favours? Please try to secure our passage on the first possible boat to Ostend and don't reveal my identity.' I looked down at my clothing, 'We'll travel as an ordinary family.'

William glanced over my dirty cloak and gown. 'A most effective disguise if I may say so. I barely recognised you myself. The king wants you gone but not dead. He still hopes to be remembered as a modern king and executing women isn't what a modern king does. But you're not popular and there's been much unrest. Groups of lads calling themselves Jacobites and Whigs have been fighting in the streets. It's just an excuse for trouble but your capture could make things worse.'

He couldn't hide his pride at what came next. 'You perhaps haven't heard but my title has been restored and I seem to be accepted at court. I have the influence to make sure you escape safely. You'll be allowed to travel without hindrance if I let the right people know that you'll leave within days.'

I clapped my hands. 'That is good news and so much deserved. You have suffered a great deal. I'm proud that you've always tried to live peacefully for the sake of your family.'

William smiled and tipped his head in acknowledgement. 'I was arrested after your husband's escape and was so angry with you. It felt as if you'd repeated what our mother did to me. I thought I'd lose everything again; stuck for ever in a lifetime of gain, imprisonment and loss. But friends spoke out for me and I was quickly released.'

The innkeeper entered with ale and I waited until we had been served and coins exchanged before asking the question that most troubled me. 'I understand how my behaviour must have affected the lives of many ordinary people who trusted me but our Jacobite friends, what do they think of what I did?'

William's eyes became tender and he looked at me with an expression I remembered from my childhood. 'Win, you were always headstrong, impetuous and sure of yourself, so no one would have expected anything else. There will always be criticism but your bravery can never be in dispute.'

This wasn't what I wanted to hear but I recognised his honesty. If I was uncertain about the sense of my act, how could I expect other people to think differently? William saw my disappointment and ploughed on with his news. 'I'm convinced it won't be long before our estate is restored. I have my eye on the very cottage for Grace Evans.'

He watched my reaction, his face bright and seeking my approval. I thanked him but my words lacked conviction. I was not ready to part from Grace. 'I'm sure she'll be pleased,' I mumbled.

Other fears needed to be allayed before we parted. 'I trust that the Mills and Mrs Morgan have not come under suspicion?' I asked.

My brother stared into the empty grate between us and rubbed his hands as if there was warmth from a fire. 'None at all, so far. You planned it well and luck was on your side but we shouldn't prolong this meeting. I've probably been followed and if you are arrested, none of us will be safe. What was the other task?'

I gave him the legal papers retrieved from Terregles and asked him to deposit them with my lawyer. We both stood, awkward with a parting we knew would be final. Looking around, William reached into his cloak and produced a letter from my husband. Promising to send the tickets to our lodging he whispered farewell, holding my hands and pressing a small leather pouch of coins into my fist.

I stepped back and exclaimed, 'William you can't afford this.'

He laughed but his eyes glistened, 'I haven't forgotten your loyalty, Win. Visiting me every week in the Tower.' With a small bow, he was gone.

I hurried back to the lodging, only aware of the ragged trews, faded petticoats and worn shoes of passing pedestrians. Every time I dared look up from under my hood to make a safe crossing, I thought I saw Marian's vengeful face in the crowd.

The boredom and fear of waiting in lodgings made us too impatient with Anne, as she whined again and again about wanting to go home and, at last, I agreed that Alice could take her to see the ponies in the stable. In the simple parlour of our rooms, I was alone with Grace and she watched me read William's letter. I tossed it aside, impatient with his petulant rant about money and the boredom of living with the elderly remnants of the exiled Stuart court. Grace spoke casually, as if the question of my future had only just occurred to her.

'So are you planning to be with William when we reach France?'

I shook my head. 'No. I've made my decision. We're sailing to Ostend and from there, I plan to travel to Bruges, to Lucy's convent. I'll have the baby there, we'll be cared for and Anne can join the girls for lessons. I can't look too far into the future but I might remain within the convent. Grace, when we reach Ostend you can return to London. You're guilty of no crime – at least none that anyone knows about.'

Grace frowned. 'Is the pregnancy secure?'

I hesitated. 'I'm not sure. It's over four months now and the child isn't moving yet.'

'Then I'll accompany you to Bruges. When you're safe with the Abbess I'll come back.'

'Oh Grace,' I gasped in relief. 'But I promised to release you. My brother thinks that he will soon regain the estate and that means a home for you.'

She spread out her hands, resigned, 'And could I settle for a single moment in my solitary cottage if I was worrying about the most troublesome woman in England travelling to Bruges on her own? Of course I'll come.'

'But what about Alice? I've made mistakes, Grace, assuming too much and not thinking about what you might want. We mustn't repeat this with Alice. Perhaps she could return from Bruges with you.'

Grace looked wary and I hurried to make myself clear. 'I don't mean that you would be responsible for her but my brother might find her a post at Powis or she could return to Traquair. What I'm trying to say is, Alice must know that she has a choice.'

Grace frowned. 'Why can't she stay at the convent?'

'Of course she can. I'm sure my sister would be glad to employ her but she's only twenty-five. A convent is not the best place for a young woman. Think of what we were doing at her age!'

An enigmatic smile flickered across Grace's lips and her eyes narrowed. 'I remember what you were doing. As for myself, nothing more will be said.'

That evening, the papers for our passage from Gravesend arrived. We would leave in a farmer's cart the following morning and must be ready by dawn. I lay awake listening to the rhythm of night sounds from our shared beds and, sitting up, saw the shadow of our bundles tied and ready by the door. Parting the thin cloth at the windows, the streets were empty and the moon was waning. It was almost dawn. Kissing Anne's hot brow, I slipped out into the night.

This was my last night in London, my last in my country of birth and I wanted to feel the streets under my feet, smell the sewers and watch the people wake and light lamps in their windows, as they woke to an ordinary day. I had walked only a short way from our rooms when a hand reached out from a doorway and gripped my arm. From behind, I heard a rasping voice.

'I know who you are.'

'You know who I am?' I gasped, seeing the face of my assailant, an old woman with wisps of tangled grey hair hanging from the folds of a dirty shawl.

She tossed back her head and laughed at me, her wide mouth showing a few black teeth. Her grip tightened. 'I've found you. At last.'

Panic gripped my throat and stomach. Was I strong enough to push her away? A man stepped from the shadows and grasped the old woman from behind.

'It's fine, Mary. Let the lady go. She's not your daughter.'

I recognised my landlord and my legs trembled with relief. 'She's from the hospital, m'lady. Wanders off from time to time to find her daughter. She does no harm and we always catch her. Gave you a fright though,' he grinned.

'I was terrified. I can't thank you enough.'

He led Mary away by the hand, calling to me over his shoulder. 'Get off home now. Your transport will soon be outside the door. And I do know who you are. Godspeed on your journey, Lady Nithsdale.'

We left London before daylight and in the hours of travel, hidden underneath rough, woollen sacks and squeezed against crates that smelt of rotten vegetables, we were tossed and pummelled by the cart's movement, snatching blissful moments of sleep.

I worried most for Anne, how much discomfort and fear she had endured in her short life and tormented myself with thoughts that I had been irresponsible and selfish not to leave her at Traquair, where she had settled. The child slept for most of the journey, clasped to my breast, or chewed on crusts of bread, even tolerating having to relieve herself into a small pot. Our driver had made it clear that the miles between London and Gravesend were notorious for highwaymen, and he would not risk a stop.

At the harbour, we dragged our bundles towards coils of oily rope, where we sat to gulp down jars of ale, carried from London. I scanned the wharf, feeling the sea breeze on my skin and breathed in the smell of tar and fish. Grace caught my eye and smiled and we both turned to gaze at our small boat, the only one berthed, its four sails tightly furled. Freedom seemed tantalisingly close.

We joined a long queue of rumpled travellers, and my panic rose in tandem with the line's slow and tortuous progress. A cat ran across the harbour and Anne escaped from my grip to give chase, smacking into the leg of a soldier, one of a pair of king's men patrolling the quay. He stopped, grasped the child by the hand and led her back to me, staring into my face. I stared back, my chest tight, silently challenging him to arrest me at his peril. He gave a slight bow and nodded, before continuing his watch, as if he had seen nothing. I released my breath in a slow, drawn out gasp and wrapped my cloak around Anne.

My brother had fulfilled every word of his promise, but I couldn't relax. The sailor who checked our travel documents scrutinised every detail, his eyes scanning our faces, then dropping back down to the papers in his hand, again and again, as if there was something wrong. It was only when I saw his lips move, I realised he couldn't read and every impatient passenger in the line had endured this charade. Once on board, all travellers had to remain on deck while customs officers searched below. At last, they were whistled down the gangway, their backs stiff with pride. Only then, the ship's crew dropped our sails to flap and tug as they caught at the wind, while other men released our moorings, running up the gangway moments before we inched from the jetty.

The Kent coast retreated and I stood side by side with Grace, as the church spire of Gravesend became a needle on the horizon. Alice had taken Anne below deck to find our berths. We were alone.

'Did you notice we were spotted on the dockside?' I asked her.

'Of course,' she said. 'I thought it was all over. I had trouble holding onto the contents of my stomach, not that there was much to lose.'

'They weren't there to arrest us, just to see us out of the

country,' I replied. 'But I couldn't be sure, not until we were actually at sail. Now I can breathe.'

We stayed together, listening to the screaming gulls, until the coast became a grey smudge on the horizon. I placed my arm around her waist. 'Do you remember the last time we stood together on the deck of a ship, watching our homeland disappear? How young we were, how innocent.'

Grace laughed. 'And how excited! I can't pretend to understand the last few months, why we chose to leave behind our precious life in Scotland, but we're safe, and for that we must be grateful.'

I paused before trying to shape my unformed thoughts into words. 'As a child, I was tormented every day by fears that either my mother or my father would be executed. A fire burned inside me, one that would not allow my husband's life to be taken in that way. I hope we both have years ahead of us to reflect, in tranquillity, about our brave, impulsive, stupid actions. In time, we might reach a comfortable place of no regrets.'

Grace turned her eyes to settle on mine. 'My comfortable place will be in Wales. Where will yours be, Win? Once you are safe in the convent and the baby comes, will you make peace with your husband?'

'We saved his life,' I said, pulling her close. 'He must find his own way to make sense of our gift. Wherever my comfortable place turns out to be, my struggle will not be to live without him, but to live without you, my dearest friend.'

THE END

ACKNOWLEDGEMENTS

I am indebted to my original editor at Hookline Books, Yvonne Barlow, who showed great patience and stamina with the efforts of a debut author. Huge thanks must also go to Bloodhound Books for their support, flexibility, and expertise in publishing this second edition of *The Jacobite's Wife*. The members of Leicester Writers' Club have been consistently generous with their friendship and constructive comments. Thanks to my husband for his willingness to visit locations and talk about this story, and also to my children, for their interest. Finally, a special thank you to my late mother for giving me a lifelong passion for fiction.

ABOUT THE AUTHOR

Morag Edwards has spent over 30 years as an educational psychologist and uses her knowledge of child development to shape fictional characters in both historical and contemporary fiction. She has an MA in creative writing from the University of Manchester's Centre for New Writing and is an active member of Leicester Writers' Club. *The Jacobite's Wife* is Morag's debut novel and is the first in a planned trilogy. The second novel in the series, *Neither Love nor Money*, is now in preparation. Morag also writes contemporary romance-suspense and has recently self-published the novel, *Broken*. A second novel in this genre, *The Crash*, will soon be available.

A NOTE FROM THE PUBLISHER

Thank you for reading this book. If you enjoyed it please do consider leaving a review on Amazon to help others find it too.

We hate typos. All of our books have been rigorously edited and proofread, but sometimes mistakes do slip through. If you have spotted a typo, please do let us know and we can get it amended within hours.

info@bloodhoundbooks.com